Oh, Diary. Within a few weeks, I get not one but TWO big chances to become a famous actress. First, I turned down a permanent role on The Young and the Beautiful. *Now, I've turned down the lead in a movie!*

I can't believe I told Charles no. But I did the right thing. My relationship with Sam is more important than a role in a possibly bogus movie, even by a director with a famous family. Along with everything else, Charles is just too cute. Working with him would be an awful temptation. I can resist anything, except temptation. I HAD to turn down the part.

I hope I did the right thing. Normally I'd ask Elizabeth what she thinks. But Charles said it could jeopardize his financing if word got around about his movie this soon. He asked me not to tell anyone. . . .

JESSICA'S SECRET DIARY

VOLUME III

Written by
Kate William

Created by
FRANCINE PASCAL

BANTAM BOOKS
NEW YORK · TORONTO · LONDON · SYDNEY · AUCKLAND

To Hilary Berkowitz

RL 6, age 12 and up

JESSICA'S SECRET DIARY VOLUME III

A Bantam Book / July 1997

Sweet Valley High® is a registered trademark of Francine Pascal.
Conceived by Francine Pascal.
Produced by Daniel Weiss Associates, Inc.
33 West 17th Street
New York, NY 10011.
Cover photography by Michael Segal.

ISBN: 0-553-49216-0

Published simultaneously in the United States and Canada

Bantam Books are published by Bantam Books, a division of Bantam
Doubleday Dell Publishing Group, Inc. Its trademark, consisting of the
words "Bantam Books" and the portrayal of a rooster, is Registered in
U.S. Patent and Trademark Office and in other countries. Marca
Registrada. Bantam Books, 1540 Broadway, New York, New York 10036.

PRINTED IN THE UNITED STATES OF AMERICA

OPM   0 9 8 7 6 5 4 3 2 1

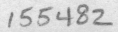

Prologue

Some guys really know how to wreck a date.

It was cool for southern California, so I felt totally justified when I shivered a little as Michael Lewis walked me to my front door Saturday night.

"Are you cold, Jessica?" Michael asked, wrapping a big, muscular arm around my shoulder. OK, so I wasn't frostbitten. In fact, I wasn't even chilly. But if a hunk like Michael wanted to keep me warm, well, what was the harm in pretending?

And I do mean *hunk*. Michael is six-foot-three, the same height as my brainiac twin sister's boring boyfriend, Todd Wilkins. Elizabeth and I have the same blond hair and blue-green eyes, but we have totally different taste in men. Todd's kind of lean all over, with the body of a typical basketball player. Unfortunately, he's got the personality of a typical dweeb.

I admit it. I like basketball players' bodies. And soccer players'. And tennis players'. But Michael is something special. Michael is *a football player.* In fact, he's a linebacker, with shoulders that go on forever, and gorgeous muscles everywhere. He's got light brown hair and dark brown eyes and a chin that juts out like a movie star's. All in all, I thought he was the best thing to happen to Sweet Valley High in months.

Michael transferred to my school when his family moved here from the East Coast. He's a senior, which means he's more sophisticated than the guys in the junior class. Yeah, I know. *I'm* a junior. But that's different. It's a proven fact that girls mature faster than boys. So a sixteen-year-old girl should date guys who are at least as old as Michael, who just turned eighteen. After all, my brother Steven is eighteen; he's even in college. But is he as mature as I am? *Not!*

Michael and I had a blast at the roller-skating rink. Then we went to Guido's for a pizza with everything but anchovies. Michael was a riot. He kept making jokes in his soft South Carolina drawl as he gave grief to the bonehead waiter. And he couldn't take his eyes off me—always a nice trait in a guy, especially a hunky guy.

I looked fantastic, if I do say so myself. My best friend Lila Fowler had contributed a ton of styling gel to help me arrange my hair in wild, sexy waves. I wore my new Purple Passion lip color, the exact same shade as the low-cut blouse that was tucked into my skintight black jeans.

2

To backtrack a little, let me say that Elizabeth and I hardly looked like sisters, let alone twins, as we prepared to go out that evening. Anyone at school will tell you the Wakefield twins are absolutely identical—and as close as sisters can be, even if we are harsh on each other sometimes. But nobody who knows us *ever* mixes us up.

That evening was typical. Elizabeth was pulling on a long, casual, broomstick-pleated gauze skirt with a simple blouse and a vest. Her hair was in a ponytail. She wouldn't even let me put some makeup on her face, to bring out her natural gorgeousness.

I, on the other hand, had gone to a lot of trouble with my appearance. So I was glad to see Michael appreciating me. Elizabeth hates being the center of attention. I adore it when guys worship me. Life's too short to fade into the background. Not that I would know from personal experience. Every person in that pizza parlor noticed Michael and me stroll in. I think about those envious looks now, and it's almost enough to make up for the way he acted later. Almost.

After Guido's, we drove to Miller's Point.

As every teenager in town knows, Miller's Point is the most romantic make-out spot in southern California. It's high up, with a view of the whole valley. At night, the lights twinkle up at you, and you can even see the ocean in the background, black and green and gray under the starlight.

This was my third or fourth date with Michael,

in between dates with other guys. Michael and I had kissed on our first date, of course. But this was different. This was our first trip to the Point.

Two things are crucial to a good make-out session on Miller's Point: a cool car and a hot guy.

Michael drives a Ford Explorer (which is what my Jeep Wrangler wants to be when it grows up). It's not a Porsche or a Jaguar—or a BMW, like Todd drives. But Explorers are cool, especially this one, which has a CD player and a moon roof. I discovered something important that night about the second element of a perfect make-out session: Michael is an awesome kisser. I already knew he was good. But he's more than good. He's—well, you know. Awesome.

Then Michael took me home. All in all, I thought it was a good date. A great date. And I looked forward to a romantic kiss on my front doorstep.

Well, as romantic a kiss as you can have when your parents are sitting in the living room, waiting to pounce on you for arriving home a measly twenty minutes after curfew—unlike your perfect identical twin, who was home early from a totally tame date with Todd, since her ambition in life is to have engraved on her tombstone, *She was always punctual.*

Michael turned me toward him, wrapped both arms around me, and leaned down to plant a deep, sensuous kiss on my lips. A minute later, I stepped back and gave him my sexiest smile.

"Jessica Wakefield, you are the most beautiful girl at school," he said in that deep, rich southern

4

voice that flowed over me like honey. "I haven't felt this way about anyone in a long, long time."

I smiled again. "I feel the same way," I told him. "I had a lot of fun tonight. Are we still on for the dance next Friday?"

That's when Michael ruined everything. He looked at me with a way-serious expression on his face. Serious expressions make me nervous. "Next Friday, and the Friday after that, and every Friday for the rest of the school year," he whispered, gazing into my eyes. "Saturdays too."

I laughed. I mean, he was joking, right? "I'll check with my secretary and get back to you on those dates."

Michael didn't laugh. "I mean it, Jessica," he insisted, caressing my back with his strong, warm hand. "When two people feel this way about each other, there's no reason to date anybody else, ever."

I was so flustered I couldn't even respond. My brother, Steven, would never believe that. He says I talk more than any human being alive. And I admit, I'm seldom at a loss for words. But as much as I liked Michael, I was floored by what he was suggesting. We'd known each other only a few weeks!

"Michael, that's flattering," I stammered after a minute. "But you can't mean—"

"Go steady with me, Jessica," he interrupted. "I love you! We don't need anybody else."

"Like, a standing date with you, every Friday and Saturday night?" I asked, trying hard to keep my mind off his hand, which was rubbing my back in slow, exquisite circles. "Like, indefinitely?"

"That's right," he said. "And lunches at school, and the Dairi Burger after football practice, and passing notes to each other behind Mr. Collins's back in English class—"

Already, I felt the ball and chain dragging on my ankle. "Hello!" I said. "This is way too much togetherness. You could be describing . . . *Elizabeth and Todd!*" I shivered, but this time I wasn't faking it.

"I know it's a big step, Jessica," he said. "But we're good together. You can't deny that."

"What if Paul Jeffries asks me to play tennis with him next weekend?" I asked him. "What if Danny Stauffer wants me to go to a movie?"

"Tell them no," Michael said, shrugging.

"I don't want to tell them no!" I exclaimed. "Don't you see? I'm not ready to be so . . . settled!"

"You told me you dated that guy Sam for a long time," Michael said gently.

I took a deep breath. It still hurt to think about Sam Woodruff. I had been so much in love with Sam. But he'd died in a car accident, only seventeen years old. I'd moved on since then. I had dated other guys—a few of them seriously. And I'd had my heart broken a couple more times.

"I loved Sam," I replied. "But he's gone. And I'm not ready for another serious relationship. Why wreck a good thing? Let's just go to the dance next week like we planned, and keep seeing each other when we want to!"

"I can't do that, Jessica," Michael said, his face sad.

"You've been doing it for more than two weeks!"

"I want a steady girlfriend in my life," he said. "I may play football, but I don't like being a free agent!"

"And I like playing the field!" I blurted out. I know it wasn't the most tactful thing to say. But he had me flustered.

Michael shook his head. "I can't live with that."

I sighed. "We don't have to decide this right now. We can talk about it more this week, maybe after the dance Friday."

"There's nothing to talk about," Michael said. "We obviously want different things. It would be easier if we just ended this now, with no hard feelings." But he was blinking fast, and I knew he was more upset than he wanted me to see.

"That's crazy!" I cried. "We like each other. We have a good time together. And because of that, we have to break up?"

"Try to understand, Jessica. I've just moved across the country. Everything else is new. I need a stable relationship."

Ugh. You know you're in trouble when they start using the *R* word.

"Let's think about this for a while," I tried again. "Let's talk some more. Maybe in a week or two—"

"Talking about it for a week or two isn't going to change your mind, is it?"

"No, it isn't," I admitted. "I need my freedom."

"Then you've got it," he said with a sad, lonely smile. He leaned forward and gave me a kiss on the forehead. Then he turned and trudged down the walkway.

I watched his big, sexy bod as he vanished into the murkiness away from the lights of the house, where his Explorer waited at the curb. I stood there, half expecting him to turn around, rush back up the walk, and take me in his arms. Instead, the engine revved up. I sighed deeply. Then I opened the front door and stepped into the house.

"I don't love Michael," I whispered to myself. It was the truth. I knew I'd done the right thing. But I felt a big, empty, hollow place inside of me.

The next day I was hanging out around the pool behind my house with my sister and a bunch of friends. It was one of those girls-only Sunday afternoons, when you swim a little and read a few fashion magazines and eat junk food and talk about boys.

"Barry and I are celebrating our anniversary at the dance this week," Amy Sutton bragged. She was sitting on the edge of the pool and looking like a girl in a shampoo commercial as she squeezed the water out of her long, sun-colored hair.

"Big deal," Lila said from her lounge chair. She lowered her copy of *Ingenue* magazine so we could all see her roll her big, brown, perfectly made-up eyes. "You and Barry celebrate your anniversary every month!"

"What's wrong with that?" Elizabeth asked, whirling around from the sliding glass door she was standing near. "Todd and I celebrate every month!"

I folded my arms. "Yes, but it's a well-known fact that you and Todd are duller than the chess team and the computer club put together."

"You think anybody with a committed relationship is dull," Elizabeth replied over her shoulder as she stepped into the house.

"Any teenager who's committed to one person ought to be committed!" I grumbled. "It makes me sick."

"What's wrong with a long-term relationship?" Amy asked.

"Long-term?" I scoffed. "It's not as though you've been dating Barry Rork and nobody else for all eternity!" I started counting on my fingers. "Let's see, there was Bruce Patman, Ken Matthews, Scott Trost—"

"You're projecting again, Jessica," Amy interrupted. "You do have a tendency to deal with your own shortcomings by pushing them off onto other people—"

"Please, Amy," begged Enid Rollins. Enid gestured with a nacho as she sat at the umbrella-shaded table to keep her fair skin from burning. "No Project Youth psychobabble! It's too nice a day to play Sigmund Freud."

Not surprisingly—since she is, after all, Elizabeth's friend—Enid is the World's Most Boring Teenager. I mean, how many sixteen-year-olds even know who Freud was—let alone *care?* But in this case, she had a point. Ever since Amy started working at the Project Youth hot line, she'd been spouting this stuff about insecurities and codependency and everybody's inner child. If she said one more word, my inner child would spit up all over Amy's bathing suit.

"Shortcomings?" I asked. "Since when is it a bad thing to be attractive to a lot of different guys?"

"Being attractive isn't the shortcoming," Lila said. "Being fickle is. Face it, Jess, you're not terribly discriminating."

"I am so!" I insisted. "I only go out with boys who are cute! They have to be taller than me, and they have to have great buns."

"And they have to let you date as many other guys as you want," Enid added.

I shrugged. "And your point is . . . ?"

"Well, I'm with Liz!" Maria Slater said from the pool. "I think it's sweet that Amy and Barry celebrate an anniversary every month."

"I think it's sickening," I said. I pretended to jab a finger down my throat.

"I hope Ted and I will want to celebrate every month after we've been seeing each other for a while," Maria continued as if I hadn't spoken. Maria, a former child actress, had lived in Sweet Valley as a little kid. She's tall and gorgeous, with ebony skin and short, curly hair in a style that looks a lot more New York City than Sweet Valley. She could have had any guy she wanted when she moved back to town from New York recently. So somebody please explain to me why she had just started dating Ted Jenson! I mean, he's not bad-looking. But he's one of those artsy types who does *dramatic poetry readings*. Ugh.

"Ted Jenson?" I asked. "Right. In the dictionary, there's a little picture of him next to the word *weird*. You, of all people, could do better, Maria."

"Jessica!" Elizabeth admonished me as she stepped back onto the patio with a tray of sodas. "Ted's a nice guy."

"You *have* to say that," I pointed out as I grabbed a diet root beer. "Maria's one of your closest friends."

"You're just jealous, Jess, because you aren't seeing anybody," Lila said in her I-am-superior tone of voice. "Pass me a sparkling water," she added, pointing to the tray of cans with one of her professionally manicured fingers. She sounded exactly like someone who's used to ordering around a houseful of servants. Unfortunately, that's exactly what she is. Money is wasted on people who are too snobby to deserve it.

"Right," I said, reluctantly passing her a can. "*You're* seeing Bo. But you never actually get to *see* him."

Lila had been dating a guy named Beauregard Crighton III for a while now, but he was totally G.U.—*geographically undesirable*. I mean, he lived in Washington, D.C.! Bo was a nice guy, and I had to admit, he was perfect for Lila, but he lived on the other side of the world!

"Bo and I are serious about each other—" Lila said.

"At least, for this week," Maria added.

Lila glowered at her for a second before continuing. Then she turned back to me. "At least Bo's flying into Sweet Valley, so *I* have a date to the dance next weekend," my so-called best friend announced to the world, *"unlike a certain blonde we all know."*

I jumped up from my poolside chair, wishing I'd dumped that can of mineral water over Lila's head. "Thanks a lot!" I exclaimed. "You weren't supposed to tell anyone!"

"Jessica!" Elizabeth said. "I thought you were going to the dance with Michael! What happened last night?"

I tossed my hair back and struck a sophisticated pose. "Michael is too juvenile for words," I said.

"In other words, he dumped you," Maria added.

"No way!" I objected. "I dumped him."

"That's not exactly how you told it to me on the phone last night," Lila pointed out.

"I did so dump him!" I said. "He wanted me to, like, never go out with anyone else but him! Can you imagine anything so lame? I told him it was out of the question."

"And that's when he dumped you?" Amy asked.

"No!" I protested. "That's when I dumped him. I said if he had to be so clingy, I could do without him."

Amy started in on the psychobabble again. "You've always had a problem with commitment—"

"Michael's the one with the problem," I

interrupted. "He's the one who's left without a date to the dance."

"Face it, Jess," Lila said, "you're just too superficial to ever really fall in love."

Coming from Lila, that was so ridiculous I nearly choked on my root beer. "*You're* calling *me* superficial?"

"You're the one who can't be serious about a handsome football player long enough to go to even one school dance," Lila said.

"So who will you go to the dance with now?" Enid asked me, her green eyes twinkling with amusement. She was finding my dateless state just a little too entertaining.

I glared at her. Enid was a fine person to act superior. I've dated more guys in one night than she goes out with in a month. But lately, Enid and her on-again, off-again boyfriend Hugh Grayson seemed to be on again. And I was totally sick of the way she'd been mooning around with that dreamy smile on her face. I mean, get real! The guy isn't even that cute! But when you're Enid Rollins, you have to make do with what you can get. Luckily, I have more options.

"I haven't decided who's taking me to the dance," I said, raising my eyebrows exactly the way Lila does when she's talking to someone who's beneath her notice.

"Do you have any offers?" Amy asked.

"Why is my love life suddenly everybody's business?" I demanded.

"I guess that's a no," Amy said smugly. I fought the urge to shove her back into the pool.

"You always make your love life everyone's business when it's going *well*," Lila reminded me. "For the last few weeks, all I've heard about is Michael's broad shoulders and Michael's perfect chin."

"And how good Michael will look, all dressed up for the dance," Amy said. She sighed dramatically, stretching out one leg to catch the sun. "And now you'll have to go alone."

"For Pete's sake, I only broke up with Michael last night!" I protested. "By the end of school tomorrow, somebody else will ask me to the dance. You know how easy it is to manipulate men! They're not the brightest people on earth."

"You have a point," Lila said.

"It's that defective chromosome," Maria added.

"I don't know, Jess," Elizabeth said, shaking her head sadly, as if she felt sorry for me. I *detest* having people feel sorry for me. "Just about everyone already has a date for this dance."

"Hello! This is *me* we're talking about—Jessica Wakefield," I reminded them all. "If the right guy has reason to think I'll say yes, he'll break his date. No sweat."

"Which 'right guy' are you setting your baby blues on this time?" Maria asked.

"I haven't made up my mind," I declared. "I haven't been out with Aaron Dallas in a while—"

"He's seeing Rosa Jameson," Amy pointed out.

"Maybe Peter DeHaven—"

"He's dating a girl from Lovett Academy," Lila informed me.

"Since when?" I demanded to know.

"Ever since Bruce Patman's party three weeks ago," Amy said. Her eyes had that triumphant look she always gets when she knows more gossip than the rest of us, which is most of the time.

"Big deal," I said. "It's not like there aren't a ton of other guys at school." I reeled off the names of a few acceptable specimens. "There's Charlie Markus, A. J. Morgan, Paul Isaacs—"

Amy counted on her fingers. "Lynne Jacobs, Alicia Benson, and forced to visit his grandparents for the weekend," she reeled off.

"Girl, do you stay up nights memorizing this stuff?" Maria asked Amy, impressed. "Or have you switched your volunteer work from the crisis hot line to the Psychic Hot Line?"

"I suppose Jay McGuire's still with Denise Hadley," I said, remembering how I'd tried to steal him away earlier in the year.

"Hook, line, and sinker," Amy said. "Disappointed?"

I rolled my eyes. "No! Any guy who'd choose Denise over me is not worth dating."

"Don't worry about it, Jess," Elizabeth said, no doubt trying to cheer me up. "There's nothing wrong with going to a dance by yourself, you know—"

Lila laughed. "Not if you're a fat little twerp like Lois Waller, or if you dress like Caroline

Pearce," she finished in her snobbiest voice.

"Actually, Lois Waller and Gene White are still going strong," Amy reminded us. "And Caroline Pearce is as gaga as ever about Jerry Fisher—"

I was mortified that my best friend—make that *former* best friend—would compare me to losers like Lois and Caroline. But I pretended it didn't bother me. "Ha, ha!" I said. "Don't any of you worry about me. I'll get a date to the dance Friday night. Wait and see."

"Maybe Steven's free that night," Lila said, arching her perfectly tweezed eyebrows.

I wanted to reach under those perfectly tweezed eyebrows and scratch out her beady little eyes. "Very funny," I said, trying to play it cool, even though she'd just implied the only date I could get was with my big brother.

"You just wait! I'll be at that dance with the most gorgeous guy any of you can possibly imagine. One look at him and you'll be convinced that playing the field is the only way to go!"

By Wednesday afternoon, I realized how hard it is to play the field when the rest of the players are going one-on-one. In my entire dating career, I'd never had a losing streak. Now I was striking out before I ever got up to bat.

After English, I dropped my copy of Jane Austen's *Emma* in the hallway in front of Steve Anderson. He bent down to pick it up for me, like

I knew he would. So I leaned forward so he could get the full benefit of my low-cut turquoise tank top. The creep barely noticed.

"You dropped this," he said, handing it to me without so much as gazing soulfully into my eyes.

You dropped this. How lame can you get? But Steve is great-looking, and I needed a date. As long as we were both on the way to Mr. Frankel's boring math class, I figured I'd plant in his mind the idea of asking me to the dance.

"Thanks, Steve," I said, flashing the smile no guy can resist.

He resisted. "No problem," he said. We were still walking together. But he opened his math book and was staring intently at the page we were supposed to have studied the night before.

"What's with this traumatic equation thing anyway?" I asked, rolling my eyes.

He looked up at me and blinked as if he'd forgotten I was beside him. "I think you mean *quadratic* equation."

I shrugged. "Whatever," I said. "All math is traumatic, if you ask me." I looked straight into his eyes. "I'm so glad I get to miss Mr. Frankel's class on Friday. My sorority is helping to decorate the gym for the dance that night."

"Huh?" he said, still glancing at that idiotic math book.

"You know, the dance on Friday?" I asked. "I guess you haven't had time to think about it."

17

"Oh," he said. "You're right, I haven't given it much thought—"

"Really?"

"Not since a couple weeks ago, when my girlfriend and I decided to go."

I bit my lip to keep from screaming. "Girlfriend?" I asked weakly.

"You know, Suzanne Devlin," he replied as he turned the page of his math book.

"Oh," I said. Great. Suzanne is tall and willowy, with coal-black hair and a wardrobe to die for. Come to think of it, I'd seen them together in the cafeteria a lot in the past few weeks. It just hadn't occurred to me that they were, well, you know. A couple. I considered whether it was worth trying to break them up. But the dance was only two days away. And let's face it. The guy was more interested in this traumatic quadratic thing than he was in me! *Loser.*

"Here's Mr. Frankel's room," Steve said, gesturing for me to walk in first. "Good luck on the quiz!"

I nearly dropped my books. "What quiz?" I screeched.

After school, I was walking through the parking lot toward the Jeep, where Elizabeth sat at the wheel, waiting for me. We used to have a little red Fiat that was a hand-me-down from Mom. But it was spending more time in the shop than on the road, so we finally put it out to pasture earlier this year and bought the Jeep.

18

In the parking lot I practically crashed into Jason Mann, who's a basketball player and a senior. As far as I knew, he wasn't dating anybody. And he was cute. So I struck up a conversation about the game that was coming up at Palisades High. Just as I started to shift the conversation to the topic of the dance, Andrea Slade appeared out of nowhere and linked her arm around Jason's.

"Ready to go to the Dairi Burger?" she asked him, her wild blond mane swinging around her shoulders. "Hi, Jess," she said to me, as if it were an afterthought. From the way they were staring into each other's eyes, I was surprised she'd noticed me at all.

They walked away, and I sighed. I decided to stick to football players.

"What's wrong with this town anyway?" I wailed to Elizabeth as I climbed into the passenger seat.

"Could you be more specific?" Elizabeth asked. But her eyes were twinkling with that superior, Jessica's-just-being-Jessica look.

"You know what I'm talking about!" I said grumpily. "All of a sudden, everybody's dating someone. Like, seriously dating. It's sick!"

"Like Jason Mann and Andrea Slade?"

"Why does Andrea need a steady boyfriend?" I demanded, staring out the window as the neighborhood began to roll past. A sophomore boy and girl I barely knew were walking home from school together, holding hands. I narrowed my eyes at them as the Jeep picked up speed.

"Why shouldn't Andrea have a boyfriend?" Elizabeth asked in her most reasonable voice. I hate reasonable voices.

"Her father's Jamie Peters—a rock star, for goodness sake! She's got money out the wazoo. Andrea could date a different big-time musician or actor every night of the week! What business does she have, taking a perfectly good basketball player out of circulation?"

"Still haven't found a date to the dance Friday?" Elizabeth asked. Now she sounded more sympathetic than amused. I wasn't sure if that was an improvement.

"Don't feel sorry for me!" I ordered. "That's the last thing I need."

"I could ask Todd if there are any guys on the team who don't have dates yet," Elizabeth offered.

I whirled on her. "I'm not a charity case!"

"I didn't say you were," Elizabeth replied calmly.

"Besides," I added, "I've checked out every boy on the basketball team. Jason was the last. Since when is every basketball player at school spoken for?" I demanded. "Not to mention football players, soccer players, and tennis players."

Elizabeth shrugged. "I don't know why you're making a federal case out of it. It happens sometimes. Right now, everyone happens to be involved with somebody else. A month from now, some of those couples will have split up."

"I can't wait a month! The dance is in two days!"

"Is it really that big a deal?" asked my twin. "Will the world end if you go to a dance by yourself? Plenty of guys will dance with you, even if they came with other people."

I glared at her. "I told you, I'm not a charity case. But I don't know why I'm talking to you about this. You and Todd have been together so long you're practically married."

"What's wrong with finding someone you love and having a serious relationship?"

"It's probably your boring, serious-relationship influence that's turned everybody else in town into boring, serious-relationship couples. It's like going to school with everybody's grandparents!"

"Thanks a lot," Elizabeth said, annoyed. "So what are you going to do about the dance?"

"I'll find somebody," I vowed. "There's got to be one boy in this whole dumb town who remembers how to have fun!"

But I'd flirted with at least twenty guys since Monday. And so far, I hadn't found a good prospect.

By Friday, nothing had changed. When the doorbell rang that evening at seven o'clock, I knew without a doubt that it wasn't for me. That was a first, for a Friday night. Elizabeth answered the door herself, dressed in peach silk and a fake pearl headband. I sat on the steps, just out of view, in my Sweet Valley University sweatshirt. And I listened while Todd told Elizabeth how beautiful she looked, which really turned my stomach. He stayed long enough to say hello to my mother, and then the happy little couple was gone.

I sighed loudly as I trudged into the living room and threw myself across the couch. "That's what happens when you date one guy for too long," I said glumly to my mother.

"What are you talking about?" she asked.

"Can you believe Liz?" I complained. "It's a disgrace to women everywhere. She was completely dressed and ready when the doorbell rang! Doesn't she know you're supposed to make a boy wait? She's training Todd to take her for granted."

Mom laughed. "I wouldn't worry about that," she said. "Todd is too much in love with your sister to take her for granted."

"Love stinks!" I said.

"Jessica Wakefield, you've fallen in love at least twice a month for the last five years," my mother reminded me. "Since when does love stink?"

"Lila says I'm too superficial to fall in love for real," I said.

My mother smiled, and her expression was the same as Elizabeth's it's-just-Jessica-being-Jessica look. "You're not superficial," she said. "You're just not ready to settle down. There's nothing wrong with that."

"There is, if it means spending every Friday and Saturday night alone, for the rest of my high school career!"

"It's only one dance," she reminded me.

"I know," I said. "But everyone else is there. And I'm the dork who's spending Friday night at home with my parents."

She shook her head. "Actually, Jessica, your father and I are going out."

For the first time, I noticed that my mother had changed out of her work clothes—she's an interior designer—and into a jade green wraparound dress. She looked terrific. Everyone says Mom could be a slightly older Wakefield twin. Well, a slightly older Elizabeth, since neither of them does glamorous things with her hair and makeup, the way I do. Mom is gold-blond, like us, and has the same blue-green eyes. Even though she's old—past forty—she still has a nice figure.

"Where are you and Dad going?" I asked.

"Your father called from work to say a client gave him tickets to a theater opening. As soon as he gets home, we're going to the play, and then out for a late dinner."

"Oh," I said.

"I could call the theater and see if we can get a third ticket—" she began.

"No way!" I interrupted, mortified. "I'm not going on a date with my parents!"

"I hate to think of you sitting here by yourself, bored."

"We've got a gallon of Triple Chocolate Surprise in the freezer," I said. "Maybe Prince

23

Albert and I will binge on ice cream all night."

"I have a better idea," she said. I followed her into the kitchen, where she spotted her briefcase lying on the table, open. She pulled out a bag from the video rental place. "I rented this movie for tonight, before I knew your dad and I were going out. I don't know anything about the plot, but it's an independently produced film that just won an award at one of the festivals."

I rolled my eyes as I took the bag from her. "Oh, one of those artsy movies Elizabeth likes," I said knowingly.

"I don't know about artsy," my mother said with a laugh. "But it's supposed to be excellent. Give it a try."

A half hour later I listened to the car start up outside as my parents drove away. I plopped myself down in front of the television and patted Prince Albert's neck. "OK, doggie," I told him. "Let's take a look at this brainiac movie. It couldn't be any more boring than you and me staring at each other all night."

I pulled the video out of the bag and shoved it into the VCR without even reading the title.

"With my luck, it'll be a love story," I continued aloud as the federal warning appeared on the screen. "It's bad enough, having people like Lila tell me I'm not capable of true love. But now, I'll have to spend the next few hours watching . . ."

My voice trailed off as the music started and the

opening shot materialized on the screen. It was an aerial view of a suburban neighborhood. The streets were perfectly straight, and the houses were laid out in neat rows and columns, like a checkerboard. The starting credits began to roll, and my mouth dropped open.

"Checkered Houses," I read aloud, almost in a whisper. *"A film by Charles Sampson!"*

Prince Albert barked, as if he knew something was up.

"Oh my gosh!" I breathed. At the end of the credits, just after *"Directed by Charles Sampson,"* came the dedication: *"To Jessica Wakefield, who believed in me."*

Memories flooded my mind, and my eyes filled with tears. "I can't watch this now!" I whispered. "I'm not ready!" I flicked off the power switch and dropped the remote control on the couch. Then I jumped up and ran to my bedroom.

Through my tears, I could see the purple walls and ceiling and the jumble of clothes and schoolbooks on the floor, the same as always. The familiar messiness was comforting, but it wasn't enough. The film director's dedication had brought everything back. Lila didn't know what she was talking about when she said I wasn't capable of true love. Nobody knew how truly in love I'd been with Sam Woodruff. Nobody knew how much I'd sacrificed for him.

But Sam was dead, and I was alone now.

I reached under my bed for the violet-covered notebooks that make up my special, secret diary. And I began to read. . . .

Part 1

Dear Diary,

I feel so bad for my brother, Steven, I could cry. Except that tears would mess up my mascara. What, you ask, is going on? Get ready for the big news: Cara Walker is moving to London! Suddenly, her mom has this promotion and a transfer to England. And just like that—poof!—Cara will be out of our lives in less than three weeks.

I can't believe she's going! Cara is one of my very best friends. And she's my brother's girlfriend, thanks to yours truly setting them up together a few months ago. What can I say? I was inspired! Now, Cara and Steven are really, truly in love. And they're going to be separated by a *whole ocean. And a continent. Cara is the first girl my brother has loved since Tricia Martin died. I don't know how he's going to handle losing another girlfriend.*

In a way, I wish it were me moving to England. London sounds a lot more exciting than boring old Sweet Valley. Maybe Cara will meet a handsome young nobleman, the son of a duke or an earl or something. . . . Nah. Cara's in love with Steven. And I guess I really wouldn't want to go— not if it meant leaving Sam.

I've got to think of a way to help Steven and Cara! I know that if I were about to lose Sam, I'd want my family to help me. Besides, I'm going to miss Cara so much! We talked about it this afternoon. . . .

Amy Sutton, Lila Fowler, and I sat with Cara in the apartment she and her mom had lived in since her parents' divorce. We were helping her pack some boxes to ship ahead to London.

"London is hideous!" Cara complained. "It's nothing like California! It rains all the time."

I opened my mouth to tell her maybe it wouldn't be so bad. But to tell you the truth, it sounded awful. With weather like that, Cara would lose her tan in less than a month!

"I'm going to hate it!" Cara sobbed before I could fit a word in. She wiped her eyes with the sleeve of her T-shirt. Amy and I were starting to cry too. Lila wanted to, I know. But she didn't. She was afraid someone might see that she's a human being underneath her three-hundred-dollar sweater. She can be such a brat. But I knew she'd miss Cara as much as Amy and I would.

Cara tried to smile, but it looked lame. "At least the apartment has a guest bedroom, so all of you can come and visit me," she said.

I squeezed her shoulder. "As soon as school gets out for the summer, I'll be there!" I promised.

That would be totally awesome! Imagine me shopping at all those posh European department stores and boutiques! (I was going to say "classy," but "posh" sounds so much more British, don't you think?) When I get home, I'll be the one telling Lila what all the fashionable women are wearing this season in Europe for a change!

Cara pulled a shriveled brown corsage from a box. Orchids.

"What dance was that from?" I asked. Cara said she didn't remember, but I knew better. Cara never forgot a dance in her life. And my brother is a sucker for orchids. Her eyes were getting all misty again, and I knew she'd was trying hard not to remember all the good times she had at dances.

Lila reached into a box. "An invitation to a party

at my house!" she exclaimed, pulling out a fancy invitation with lots of color graphics. The kind you can't do without an ultra-high-tech computer and a laser printer that costs about as much as a year of college.

"That was a great party!" Cara said with a sigh. "Remember? You had a live band. And Steven and I danced the whole night!"

"I really should have another party soon," Lila told Cara. "How about a party in your honor, a going-away party?"

I thought it was a terrific idea. I mean, any excuse for a party, right? But Cara shook her head. The rims of her eyes were as red as her Sweet Valley High T-shirt. "Thanks, Li, but I don't think I could take a scene like that. It's going to be hard enough to say good-bye to everyone."

Now my own eyes started dripping like faucets again. I jumped up and hugged Cara as hard as I could. "Oh, Cara, it's going to be so lonely in Sweet Valley without you! Don't move!"

Cara laughed, but she was crying too. "OK, Jess. If you say so, I won't go."

My notoriously brilliant mind began sifting through alternatives. There had to be a way for Cara to stay. There just *had* to be. "Seriously, isn't there *anything* you can do?" I asked.

"I wish!" Cara said, rubbing her forehead as though she thought a genie might pop out and grant her wish. "But the plans are already set.

Mom's contracted the movers and booked our flights. I'm going, whether I want to or not."

Lila suggested that Cara could move in with her father and her brother, Charlie, who live in Chicago. Of course, Lila would think of that. She'd lived with her father since her parents split up, which was practically her whole life. Cara's father isn't a millionaire like Lila's. But Cara could do worse.

"He probably assumes you're psyched about London," I reasoned. "I bet if you told him you aren't, he'd invite you to live with him and Charlie in Chicago."

Cara pointed out the obvious. "It's not like Chicago is right down the road," she said. "It's two thousand miles away! It wouldn't really be any better than London."

> She was right, Diary. It's not like Lila and I could drop by Chicago for an after-school makeover session! Unless Lila bought the Concorde or something. . . . No, that won't work. Even Mr. Fowler's credit cards have spending limits.
>
> Cara sounds as if she's given up. I guess I don't blame her. The situation sounds so not-fixable. When it comes down to it, teenagers are slaves to the parental units. Cara's mom says Cara has to move to England. So Cara is toast. She has to go. No appeal, no parole, no time out for good behavior. Life is unfair!

Still, I'm not giving up my friend—and the world's greatest matchmaking coup—without a fight. I'm going to think of a way for Cara to stay here with her friends.

Sunday afternoon

Dear Diary,

Am I a genius, or am I a genius? (Don't worry; that's a rhetorical question.) Jessica the Brilliant has struck again! No applause, please. Just throw jewelry and designer scarves. And money. I also take all major credit cards.

Cara and Steven won't have to say good-bye after all! I came up with a plan so wonderful and romantic that I can't believe none of us thought of it before. . . .

Inspiration struck on Sunday afternoon. It was raining, so Sam and I were indoors, watching *Love Story* on television. Well, *I* was watching the movie. *He* was griping about his dirt-bike race being rained out. And he was making fun of me. He says *Love Story* is a sappy movie. What do guys know about romance?

On the screen, Ali McGraw was dying. Ryan O'Neal—still young and cute back then—had tears in his eyes. I always had a thing for sensitive guys with curly hair.

For obvious reasons, Diary, the movie made me think about Steven and Tricia

31

Martin. Tricia was Steven's girlfriend, but she died of leukemia. Steven was devastated. And now he may lose another girlfriend. OK, so Cara isn't dying. But he might never see her again if she really moves to London! That would be almost as tragic.

I was wiping my eyes with a tissue. Sam was rolling his eyes and eating all my popcorn. And Ryan O'Neal was sitting at his wife's deathbed.

His wife! Suddenly, I had the answer to Cara's problem. It would be the perfect ending to Steven and Cara's real-life love story.

Luckily, my brother was home from college for the weekend. I raced up the stairs and skidded down the hall to his bedroom. "I've figured it all out!" I announced as I threw open the door. "You and Cara don't have to break up!"

Steven blinked as if he'd been asleep. I noticed he was reading a forty-pound textbook called *Tenets of Philosophy,* so technically, I guess he had been asleep. "We don't?" he asked.

"No!" I exclaimed, smiling triumphantly. "All you have to do is get married!"

"Get *what?*"

"Get married," I repeated. "It's the perfect solution! You and Cara are in love, right? You'd probably get married someday anyway. But if you get married *now,* Cara won't have to move to London with her mom. She'll stay in Sweet Valley with you. You'll be together forever!"

Steven slumped back in his chair like he'd been stunned with one of those hand-held phasers from the science fiction shows. After a minute, I began to wonder if he was unconscious, or in shock. Then he sat up straight. A grin spread across his face.

When Steven smiles, he is one of the most gorgeous hunks you have ever seen. Even if he is my brother. No, especially since he's my brother! I don't like to brag, but I come from the best-looking family in town. And who is better suited to marry my hunky older brother than one of my very best and prettiest friends? Did I mention that Cara is stunningly sexy, with long, dark hair and an awesome figure? She's also into all the coolest things: cheerleading, partying, and shopping.

If Cara moves away, who knows what kind of girl Steven will fall for next? My brother can be clueless when it comes to choosing girlfriends. Sometimes he goes all "but she's an interesting person" about those brainiac, do-gooder types. You know what I mean: Enid Rollins, the College Years. That's why I stepped in and made sure that he and Cara saw how perfect they were for each other. Now that they both know it, they've got to hang onto this relationship.

I know Steven's only eighteen and Cara's only sixteen. But he should take my advice and marry her now. It would solve all their problems.

Finally, my excellent suggestion sank in. Steven jumped to his feet with that huge smile on his face.

"Why didn't I think of that?" he shouted. "Jessica, you're a genius!"

Of course I am. But you already knew that, Diary, didn't you?

Sunday night

Dear Diary,

Cara said yes! This is all so romantic I could die. I wonder if Sam and I will get married someday. Of course, I need to become a famous actress first. But after my career is established, who knows? If we do get married eventually, helping my brother will be good practice for me. Guys are boneheads about things like weddings. I'm going to plan a wedding, Diary! I love secrets!

Now I just wish I could tell Elizabeth about it. And Sam. And Lila and Amy. What good is it, having one of your closest friends get engaged to your brother, if you aren't allowed to talk about it? Secrets are the pits.

Tuesday evening

Dear Diary,

The purebred Himalayan cat is out of the Gucci bag, as Lila would say. I know I promised Steven that I wouldn't tell Elizabeth or anyone else about the big elopement. Elizabeth is such a goody-goody that Steven was afraid she'd run straight to Mom and Dad to blab the news.

So Steven and I made up a cover story. Supposedly, he and Cara and some of his college friends are going on a ski trip the weekend before Cara moves. He told the family about it last night. OK, so I giggled like crazy. But I wasn't going to tell anyone the truth, even if I giggled myself into a coma. Really, my lips were sealed. Then, this afternoon, my twin pried that secret right out of me.

It was all Steven's fault for not being more careful about the rings. He practically forced me to tell Liz. . . .

Elizabeth accosted me as soon as I breezed into the house from cheerleading practice. "What's going on with Steven and Cara?" demanded the Romance Police.

I tried to look innocent. "What do you mean?"

"I mean that I just took a call from North's Jewelry Store, and apparently Steven has ordered wedding rings! What's going on?"

I tried to convince her that the store made a mistake. She wasn't buying it. So I gave up. I led her to the kitchen table and made her sit down before I announced it: "Steven and Cara are getting married!"

Elizabeth went as limp as overcooked pasta. "When?" she asked, almost in a whisper. "Where?"

"A week from Saturday. The ski trip is just a cover. They're really going to drive to Nevada—to elope! Isn't it exciting?"

Elizabeth wouldn't know excitement if it carried her off in an alien spaceship. "Exciting?" she asked, all horrified. "You've got to be kidding!"

"Of course it's exciting. Just think—Cara will be our sister-in-law. Isn't that wonderful?"

"No, it's not wonderful!" Elizabeth said. I don't know what I expected from someone who thinks *crossword puzzles* are fun.

I looked in those big, blue-green eyes, and I knew exactly what she was thinking. "Don't you dare tell Mom and Dad!" I warned.

Elizabeth took a deep breath and stared right back at me. I knew I'd won when she looked away first. "I . . . I won't," she agreed.

"Don't you dare!" I repeated. "Steven has a right to make his own decisions, Liz. They'd only try to interfere."

"But maybe somebody *should* interfere!" Elizabeth said. "It doesn't seem to me that Steven could have thought this through very thoroughly."

Jeepers, Diary. What is there to think through? They're in love, so they're getting married. What could be more simple than that? My sister's problem is that she thinks too much. Sometimes, you've got to turn off the analysis and just live!

Elizabeth started going on about how Steven and Cara are just students without any money.

"Don't be such a wet blanket," I told her. "They'll make it work somehow. Love conquers all, right?"

"Love doesn't buy groceries," Elizabeth replied, sounding about eighty years old. "Love doesn't get you through college."

"You're so depressing! Why can't you get just a little excited about the wedding and Steven's happiness?"

Elizabeth sighed. "I only wish I could," she said.

Well, Diary, it's now later Tuesday night. And Operation Elopement is going according to plan. With one small change. I kind of told Lila and Amy about the wedding. The four of us were at Guido's Pizza Palace tonight when I broke the news. . . .

Amy turned to Cara, almost too flustered to talk. For Amy, that's pretty darn flustered. The girl

37

can talk more than—well, more than *me!* "Does this mean—" Amy stammered. "Does this mean you're staying in Sweet Valley instead of moving to London with your mother?"

Cara nodded, a huge smile on her face.

"Oh, Cara! I'm so glad!"

Lila, as usual, got down to business. "Enough gushing," she ordered. "Let's hear the details. Did he ask you or did you ask him? And why don't you have an engagement ring?"

"He asked me," Cara said. "It was kind of spontaneous, so he didn't have time to buy a ring. And I don't want him to. We'll both wear wedding bands, and I think that's enough."

"You're not really engaged if you don't have a diamond," Lila said, as if it was the law. "No man's marrying *me* until I have a big, fat rock on my finger."

Cara said love was more important than jewelry. In the end, even Lila admitted that eloping was pretty romantic—even without a ring. "I've got to give you credit, Cara," Lila said. "I would never have thought you'd do such a wild thing!"

Cara suddenly looked scared. "It's not that wild, is it?"

"Are you kidding?" Lila said. "You'll be the only married woman in the Sweet Valley High junior class!"

"Will you stay in school?" Amy wondered.

"Of course I'll stay in school!" Cara cried. "And

so will Steven. Nothing's going to change. We'll just be . . . married. That's all."

"It'll be a blast!" I declared, already planning to spend a lot of time over at Steven and Cara's place. "Your own apartment! No parents around to give you a curfew and then ground you if you stay out late. And you can eat whatever you want. Pizza every night!"

A few minutes later, we got more serious. "This is really unbelievable," Amy said. "I mean, it's great! But I guess I'm glad Barry and I are still years and years away from talking about marriage."

"Same goes for me and Sam," I admitted.

"Thanks a lot, guys!" Cara said. "So being married is a fate worse than death?"

"That's not what we meant, and you know it!" Amy assured her. "I'm incredibly happy for you. I think it's fantastic that you've found the person you want to spend the rest of your life with. But the rest of your life is a long time, and I know I'm not ready to make a decision like that. That's all."

Cara frowned.

"The rest of your life?" Lila said. "Ugh!"

This was getting to be pretty heavy, Diary. I mean, the rest of your life? When you think about it that way, it sounds like a long, long time to spend with one person. Even if the person happens to be my brother, Steven, whom I admire more than anyone—

except Liz and me! But Cara would probably marry someone eventually. She's madly in love with Steven. And she'll never find anybody better than a Wakefield. So why not?

Thursday evening

Today, Lila, Amy, and I threw Cara the best wedding shower ever! We all had a fabulous time. Well, all but Cara. She just didn't seem psyched. All brides get jitters, right?

Well, I always say a party is the best cure for the blues! Especially a party with presents. Even with the size of Lila's bankroll, I knew Cara wouldn't get a lot of wedding gifts if the only people at her bridal shower were Lila, Amy, and me. So naturally I had to tell some other people. Who ever heard of a party with only four people?

I told just a few of the cheerleaders—Robin Wilson, Maria Santelli, Sandra Bacon, and Jeanie West. Oh, and I let Rosa Jameson in on it too. What's the use of secrets if you can't blab them?

Today's special cheerleading practice must have looked like a meeting of the Apathy Club. We ditched it to go to the shower, and of course we couldn't explain why! I bet Robin Wilson, my fellow co-captain of the squad, had a hissy fit, especially since the practice was for the boys' and girls' basketball games tonight.

I won't lose any sleep over it. We know the cheers cold. And Lila's mansion was a much more elegant place to spend the afternoon than a smelly old gym!

Fowler Crest looked more fantastic than usual. Lila decorated the living room with pink and white roses and big bouquets of silver balloons. She had the party catered by Palomar House—and told us sixty times that it's the most expensive restaurant in town. Whatever. But they sure know how to throw a calorie fest! There was this humongous pink cake too gorgeous to eat. And the little pastries and sandwiches were to die for.

We started to pig out. But we couldn't keep ourselves away from that stack of presents on the coffee table. At least, *I* couldn't.

"Let's open the presents!" I suggested, thrusting a package at Cara. "I can't wait any longer!"

When she opened the card from me, her eyes brimmed with tears. "It says, 'To my future sister-in-law, with love,'" she read.

"Don't cry!" I begged her, knowing I would lose it completely if she did. "We're supposed to be laughing!"

The present from me was a videotape of the movie *Barefoot in the Park*.

"It's about these newlyweds, played by Robert Redford and Jane Fonda," I explained. "They have some silly fights while they're getting used to living

41

together, but mostly they're just madly in love and . . ." My eyes were filling up again. "Well, I hope that's the way it will be with you and Steven."

Cara smiled. "Thanks, Jessica. I can't wait to watch it with Steven. Now if we only had a TV and a VCR!"

"Well, don't look at me," Lila put in. "I'm not *that* rich!"

Right. As if.

Lila picked up a box tied with a big silver bow, and she tossed it at Cara. "Here! Open this one next."

Cara unfolded Lila's present from that box, and all of our mouths dropped open. It was a sexy silk negligee, trimmed with lace, and it was way see-through. I actually saw Cara gulp. "A—a night-gown," she stuttered. "How pretty."

Lila raised her eyebrows wickedly. "For the wedding night."

"Ooh-la-la!" Amy hooted. Rosa whistled, and Jeanie and Sandra started singing one of those "ba-ba-boom" tunes that sound like a striptease. Cara's face turned pinker than the frosting on the cake.

Cara shoved the negligee back into the box and grabbed for the next present.

I don't blame Cara for being embarrassed, Diary. I mean, of course marriage means sex. We all know that. But one of my closest friends? With my brother? Wow. Weird city.

I'm not a prude like Liz. She and Todd

probably think they're being "naughty" when they hold hands. Sam and I go parking up at Miller's Point. We have a fantastic time. Sometimes a little too fantastic, if you know what I mean. Then we have to force ourselves to stop. We know we're too young for that kind of responsibility.

I'd never admit this to anyone but you, Diary, but as much as I like the kissing, the thought of actual sex is scary. (Intriguing, yes. But scary.) I'm not ready! I know I'm not.

I guess Cara's scared too. Until this week, she probably assumed she wasn't ready either. But now she's getting married. She had to sit there while everyone watched her open sexy "unmentionables" (as Winston Egbert calls them) like that sheer nightgown from Lila, and later, a black lace teddy from Amy.

I guess marriage is a lot more than a romantic wedding. It's living together—and sleeping together—in an apartment in San Farando, like the one Steven looked at today. Steven said the realtor called it "cozy." It's tiny, but it's the only thing he and Cara can afford. I'm sure they'll fix it up real nice.

Cara will get over her nervousness when the time comes. She's very mature for sixteen. And, as I said before, love conquers all.

Hey, it worked for Jane Fonda and Robert Redford.

Well, I gotta go change into my cheer-leading uniform for the basketball games at Ramsbury High tonight. Then I'm going with Sam, Liz, and Todd to the Dairi Burger so we can listen to Elizabeth gush over what a wonderful basketball player Todd "Whizzer" Wilkins is.

She's right. Todd is good. But I'd rather hear people talk about how wonderful my boyfriend is. Since Sam goes to Bridgewater High, that isn't likely to happen at the Dairi Burger, which is strictly an S.V.H. hangout. But they could take all that adoration they're spending on Todd and use it on somebody else who deserves it—perhaps a certain blond co-captain of the cheerleading squad. We'll do an awesome job of cheering tonight. But will everyone give us credit? Nooo. They're always too busy fawning over all the players, just for throwing a ball around. At least I can count on Sam to worship the ground I cheer on.

Thursday night, late
My sister and I just told Todd and Sam about the engagement. To be honest, it was Elizabeth who broke the news. And she says I'm the twin who can't keep a secret!

Sam guessed right away that the elope-ment was my idea. He knows me so well. . . .

44

Elizabeth made the announcement in the corner booth at the Dairi Burger. Todd nearly spit out a whole mouthful of root beer.

"Steven and Cara are doing *what?*" he exclaimed as his eyes bugged out.

Elizabeth motioned for us all to keep our voices down. The place was stuffed with the usual after-basketball crowd. And Caroline Pearce was sitting at the table across the aisle. When it comes to gossip, Caroline makes me look like an amateur. She can even outgossip Amy. If Caroline got wind of our conversation, Steven and Cara might as well rent an airplane and drop wedding invitations over the whole valley.

Sam turned to me. "You had something to do with this!" he guessed. "I knew something was up between you and Steven the other day, when we were watching *Love Story* and all of a sudden you kicked me out of the house."

Elizabeth gave me an evil-twin stare. "Don't tell me this whole thing was your idea! I should have known."

"I only suggested it to Steven!" I protested. "I'm not the one who popped the question to Cara. I don't know what you're all so upset about anyway! I think this is great news, and so did all of Cara's friends at the bridal shower today."

Elizabeth crossed her arms in front of her. "Cara's friends? Bridal shower?" she exclaimed. "I thought this was supposed to be a secret!"

45

"It wouldn't be any fun to elope if nobody knew about it," I reasoned, wishing she would get a clue.

Todd's fingers were drumming on the table nervously, as if they had minds of their own. "I assume your parents don't know," he said, sounding like a police officer. He was taking this even worse than Elizabeth.

"No," Elizabeth said. "Or Cara's mother either."

Sam grinned, and I could have hugged him for it. "What a wild scheme!" he exclaimed. Leave it to Sam to see excitement and romance where Todd and Elizabeth saw only gloom and doom.

"I always thought Steven had a good head on his shoulders," Todd said after a long pause. "I wouldn't have thought he'd make a mistake like this."

"He and Cara feel they don't have any choice," Elizabeth replied. "I agree it's a mistake, but it's understandable, don't you think?"

Todd shook his boring, pointy little head. "They'll regret tying themselves down so young."

"They're not tying themselves down!" I objected. "They're in love."

Then Todd found something to say that shut us all up: "But how do they know it's going to last?"

How do they know it's going to last?
This is scary stuff, Diary. How do any of us know? Even my own parents had some bad times in their marriage not long ago. For a while, Liz and Steven and I thought

46

we were about to become the products of a broken home. Luckily, Mom and Dad got their act together and patched things up.

I'd just die if anything happened to split up Sam and me! I wonder what we would do if I had to move to London. Would Sam want to get married so we could stay together? I'm almost afraid to ask.

Friday night

Steven told us at dinner tonight that he didn't get into the pre-law program he applied to at Sweet Valley University. At first, I felt awful for him. He's studied so hard all semester for it. On the other hand, he should still be happy. The wedding is only eight days away. Being in that high-pressure program would make it nearly impossible to hold down a job while he finishes college and law school. As a married man, he'll have enough responsibilities without extra-tough classes to worry about.

Did I just call my brother a man? What a concept. We're talking about a guy who loves to gross me out by sticking french fries up his nostrils!

I wonder if marriage will change him. I'll find out soon. The wedding night will be here before he knows it!

I'd better warn Cara about that french fry thing.

47

Monday, late

*Life in Sweet Valley hasn't been this ex-
citing in ages! Only five more days until
the Big Elopement!*

*I do have one complaint with life. Robin
Wilson ordered the new cheerleading uni-
forms Thursday, the day I missed practice.
She did it just to spite me. The outfits are,
like, so three years ago. The skirts are way
too long. Luckily, I'm gorgeous enough to
look sexy, even in a uniform that's too boring for words.*

*Speaking of sexy, Sam and I drove up to
Miller's Point tonight. Imagine, if you will,
a totally romantic evening. . . .*

The sky was full of stars. Sam was full of compliments. It wasn't idle flattery either. I truly did look
fantastic. I was wearing a short, flippy little dress I
borrowed from Amy—black, with rosebuds on it.
My hair was loose and wavy, the way Sam likes it.

An excellent Jamie Peters tune was on the
radio. Sam was kissing me on the lips, and I
thought nothing could feel so delicious. Then his
soft, warm kisses slipped down to my neck, and
that felt even more wonderful. I was getting hot
and tingly all over. My hands were on his back, and
I could feel the heat of his skin radiating through
his cotton shirt.

We paused for air, and I started thinking about

Cara and Steven and their wedding night. And suddenly, without knowing I was going to, I asked Sam the question that had been on my mind since Thursday night, when Liz and I told him about the elopement.

"What if it was me moving to London instead of Cara?" I asked, gazing straight into his eyes. "What if it was the only way we could stay together? Would you ask me to marry you?"

Sam gazed right back at me. I bit my lip as he reached up to brush a lock of hair from my forehead. His fingers sent little bolts of electricity into my skin. Then he smiled. "Absolutely," he said softly. "I wouldn't hesitate a minute."

"Really?" I asked, not daring to believe it.

"Would you say yes?" he asked. I realized he was holding his breath as he waited for my answer.

"Absolutely," I said, kissing him on the cheek.

"Todd's wrong about being tied down," Sam told me a minute later. His voice was as serious as I'd ever heard it. "I know we're young, but I couldn't stand to lose you, Jessica. I love you too much to let you go."

Oh, Diary. I knew I was in love with Sam. But now I'm truly, deeply, madly, head-over-heels, crazy in love with Sam. Who knows? Maybe we'll get married and live happily ever after. And maybe we'll do it soon! Wouldn't that be romantic?

Wednesday evening

I can't sleep. Steven and Cara are getting married in three little short days! It's hard to imagine my big brother being a husband. Until today, I never really thought about how much he's sacrificing to marry Cara. And now I know he's making a big mistake.

Why, you ask, am I suddenly cheering for the opposing team? You'll never guess, Diary. Something strange happened this afternoon. Something good. And bad. . . .

Steven and I were going to North's Jewelry Store to pick up the wedding bands. We reached his yellow Volkswagen bug, parked in front of the house. But Steven had forgotten his car keys, so I ran back into the house to get them.

With Prince Albert trotting at my heels, I raced up the stairs and into Steven's bedroom. I found the keys on the desk, just as he'd said I would. But then I found something else—something I hadn't counted on. It was an envelope lying on the floor. I glanced at the return address. The letter was from the university's undergraduate law program, the one that had rejected him.

Poor guy, I thought. I knew it must have been painful to be turned down when he'd wanted it so badly. I thought I knew what the letter said. Still, I absentmindedly slipped it from the envelope and unfolded the page. Prince Albert looked up at me reproachfully, as if he knew the letter wasn't addressed to me. But he's a dog, so I ignored him.

I found myself reading the opening words aloud: *"It is a pleasure to inform you that the committee has reviewed your transcripts and application materials and has accepted you into the Accelerated Program for Pre-Law Students."*

My jaw practically hit the floor.

"He got in!" I exclaimed to Prince Albert in an awed whisper. "He told us he didn't, but he did!"

The dog wagged his tail and panted appreciatively. A million thoughts tumbled through my mind. Then I remembered that Steven was sitting outside in the Volkswagen, waiting for me. I couldn't let on that I knew about his acceptance— not until I'd talked to my more logical twin and figured out what to do. So I stuffed the letter back into the envelope, dropped it on the floor, and nudged it with my toe until it was partly hidden under the desk. Then I ran outside to the car.

I talked the usual glib Jessica-talk to Steven on the trip to the jewelry store and back. But my mind wasn't on the conversation. The whole time, one question kept running through my brain: *Why did Steven lie to us about getting in?*

Later that day, Elizabeth supplied the answer.

"Don't you see?" she exclaimed when I told her about the letter. "Steven knows he can't join the law program *and* marry Cara, so he's making us think he was rejected. He's giving up his future for her."

"But he dreamed of getting into that program! It's all he's talked about for the past few months! Now he's just going to give it up?"

"It looks that way," Elizabeth said. She stared at me as if she could see into my brain. "Do you still think it's incredibly romantic that Steven and Cara are getting married?"

Suddenly, I didn't. "I never thought about what was going to happen after the wedding," I admitted, feeling a sense of dread rising inside me. "I just figured they'd live happily ever after."

Aw, Diary, I've screwed up everything. As much as I hate to admit it, Elizabeth was right all along. When I thought about Steven and Cara eloping, I pictured them driving off into the sunset with Just Married streamers billowing from their car. Or I imagined them as Jane Fonda and Robert Redford in a charming little apartment, having charming Hollywood adventures. I glossed over the parts about holding down jobs to pay the rent while finishing school.

What if Steven has to neglect school altogether so he can work at some lousy, dirty job, pumping gas? What if his grades drop and he can't get into law school? Cara will have to work too. She may have to quit the cheerleading squad to find the time. She won't have money to buy CDs and party dresses and new bikinis. And what happens when they have kids?

Lately, Cara is as jittery as a gallon of espresso. Steven keeps saying how happy he is about the wedding, but he doesn't look happy. He looks . . . determined. Do they realize their lives are ruined?

The whole thing is my fault. So I've made a decision. Steven is entering that accelerated pre-law program. Cara is moving to London with her mother. THEY ARE NOT GETTING MARRIED. *It's that simple. I was the one who made this engagement happen. I'll be the one who stops it!*

Two days later

My plan isn't working! I arranged for Cara to take a horrendous babysitting job for three obnoxious little brats, as trial-by-fire for the joys of parenthood.

If the Miller family was in one of those horror movies, the terrified babysitter would unlock the front door and beg the psychotic killer on the doorstep to come upstairs to the kiddies' room! But he'd take one look and run off, screaming, into the night.

The kids spent the evening screaming, scribbling on the parquet floor and giving each other haircuts. That should have

*turned anyone off to the idea of marriage
and kids. But Cara laughed it off when I
asked her about it at school yesterday.*

*I've tried everything else I can think of to
help her see the truth. But Cara is still planning to go through with the wedding. She'll
wear a tea-length cocktail dress she bought
for a sorority dance a couple months ago. It's
cream-colored silk, and it looks great on her.
But it's sad that she won't have a real wedding gown, with all the trimmings.*

*She showed me the dress tonight when
I stopped by her house to say good-bye.
And to try one last time to change her
mind about going to that wedding chapel
in Nevada tomorrow.*

I felt tears springing up in my eyes as I saw my
friend for what I was afraid would be the last time
as a happy, normal teenager. She was in her bedroom with the window open, and a cool breeze was
ruffling her dark brown hair.

"Next time I see you, you'll be a married
woman," I said.

Cara looked away, and I knew she was too emotional to answer right away.

"I can't stay long," I said. "Sam's waiting outside
in the car. We're on our way to a party at Ken's."

"Really?" Cara asked wistfully.

I gave her a pale blue hair ribbon to wear during

the ceremony, and I lent her the gold lavaliere necklace I always wear on a chain around my neck. Elizabeth has one exactly like it. "I thought you might want to wear this, now that you're going to be my sister."

We both cried.

Then I had to make a decision. I had debated with myself about whether I should tell her the one thing that might change her mind about marrying Steven. He obviously hadn't wanted her to know. But Cara deserved the truth. I couldn't let her walk down that aisle without hearing the facts. So I told her about the letter I'd found.

Cara was as stunned as I had been. "You mean, he was *accepted* by the law program after all?"

I nodded. "That's right. I guess he decided to turn down the offer and he didn't want any of us to know. He must have figured he couldn't focus exclusively on academics if he was married. That really proves it, doesn't it? He must really love you to give up something that important for you."

Saturday morning
Cara didn't call Steven last night to say she'd changed her mind, Diary. They're as committed to this elopement as ever. As I write this, I can see the back of Steven's yellow Volkswagen disappearing around the curve at the end of the street. They're really doing it. They're on their way to Nevada to get married.

*I've wrecked their futures! Why do I have
to stick my nose into everyone's business?*

> *That night*
> *This day will go down in history!
> Steven and Cara left for their alleged ski
> trip, as I wrote this morning. But at the
> last second, Liz and I couldn't let them do
> it. We ran to Mom and Dad and spilled the
> beans. And man, were they mad!*

Our parents were sipping coffee at the kitchen
table. I elbowed Elizabeth in the side. Everyone
says she's better at being diplomatic than I am.
"Um, we have something to tell you," she began.
"It's about Steven. Steven and Cara."

"Something about the ski trip?" Mom asked.

"They're not going on a ski trip," Elizabeth admitted. "They're driving to Nevada. To elope."

My mother choked on her coffee. *"To elope?"*

They both jumped to their feet. "We have to go
after them!" my father yelled, reaching toward the
phone.

"I know where they're heading," I said. "I
helped Steven find a chapel."

My mother whirled on me. "How long have you
known about this?" she demanded.

As usual, everybody assumes I'm the one to
blame. "Liz has known as long as I have!" I cried.
"Well, almost as long."

There was no answer at the Walkers' apartment, but my father finally reached Cara's mother at her office. The next few hours whizzed by. We jumped into my mother's station wagon, picked up Mrs. Walker at work, and headed east. We raced through the desert like wildfire, crossing the state line at warp speed. Finally, we reached the town of Red Canyon.

"The chapel's in the town hall!" I cried. "Hurry, Dad. We're late!"

"Where is the town hall?" demanded my father, leaning over the steering wheel as if pushing on it would make the car go faster.

"It's on Red Canyon Road!"

"I don't see any street signs," Mrs. Walker complained.

My mother pointed out the window. "There! I see it! Take a left, right here!"

"A left right?" I asked.

"A left!" she yelled. "Turn left!"

The station wagon squealed in protest as Dad wrapped it around the curve. But a minute later, we spotted Steven's VW parked by a squat, stucco building. We sprang from the car and ran into the town hall, one big mob of breathless people moving together like an amoeba. A sign pointed to the Wedding Chapel.

My father was in the lead as all five of us dashed through the doorway. "Stop the ceremony!" he commanded. His voice echoed all through the chapel.

At the other end of the aisle, Cara and Steven

57

stood with the justice of the peace. Cara's hair was in a French braid. She carried an armful of pink and white roses in front of her cream-colored dress. Steven wore a dark suit.

"What's going on?" he asked, his voice cracking. But it was Cara he was speaking to.

"Let me explain—" Cara began. She touched his arm, but Steven pulled away.

My brother's voice was so hoarse it was difficult to make out his words. "How could you do this to me?"

Cara opened her mouth and began to speak. But she never got the chance. Steven hurled two wedding bands across the room, pushed past us all, and ran from the chapel.

Cara couldn't stop thinking about Steven's willingness to sacrifice the education he'd wanted so badly. On the way home, she told us she just couldn't go through with the ceremony. When the justice of the peace asked if she took Steven to be her lawfully wedded husband, she'd said no. A second later, we burst into the room. But the wedding was already off.

Everyone is incredibly relieved. Except Steven, who feels totally betrayed. It makes me want to cry, just thinking about him. It's like Tricia Martin all over again. He's heartbroken.

Tuesday afternoon
Cara is gone. She's on an airplane heading

*toward London, the royal family, and Big
Ben. I miss her already!*

*At least she and Steven made up before
they left. I wish I could take the credit for that.
But it was Elizabeth's doing. Elizabeth drove
up the coast to Sweet Valley University first
thing this morning and visited Steven in his
dorm room. She told him Cara had learned the
truth about the letter he'd received. Elizabeth
painted the whole picture for me. . . .*

"But why didn't she tell me sooner?" Steven
asked Elizabeth. "Why did she wait until we were
standing in front of the justice of the peace?"

"I guess until the very last minute she couldn't
quite bring herself to give up her hope that you
might somehow stay together," Elizabeth told him.
"She still loves you. She didn't want to let you go."

For a moment, Steven's face was filled with
hope. Then his expression darkened again. "It's too
late," he moaned. "She's gone."

Elizabeth told him that he might be able to
catch her at the airport if he rushed. He sprang
forward like an Olympic sprinter. Within minutes,
Steven was battling rush-hour traffic.

By the time he reached the airport, Cara's plane was
boarding. He scanned the crowd of passengers at gate
A-5, desperately searching for Cara and her mother.

They're already on board, he thought, blinking
back tears. *I'm too late.*

Suddenly, he spotted a girl whose glossy brown hair cascaded down as she bent to pick up a carry-on suitcase. Cara caught sight of him, and joy transformed her face. The suitcase thudded to the floor. A minute later, Steven swept her up in his arms, and both of them were laughing and crying at the same time.

Before she boarded the plane, Cara gave him back the wedding rings. They promised to write each other. And they shared one last, lingering kiss. Then Cara was gone.

"Goodbye, Cara," Steven whispered as he listened to the plane's engines powering up. As sad as he was about losing her, I think he knew it was the right decision.

Diary, next time I talk about marrying Sam anytime soon, remind me that I'm insane. First of all, we're way too young. Besides, I'm not sure if Sam and I should get married, ever. All this talk about the future has got me thinking. I mean, Sam is a wonderful guy. But what's he really going to do with his life? Are there jobs out there for dirt-bike racers?

Because of Cara, Steven might have sacrificed his dream of becoming a lawyer. I'd hate to have to give up my goals because of Sam. And I'm not sure how well he fits into my plan to become the Next Big Thing in Hollywood.

Love is complicated.

> *Monday night*
> *I'm totally exhausted, Diary. But I can't*
> *sleep. Elizabeth is crying her eyes out. She's*
> *trying to muffle the sound with her pillow like*
> *she always does. But I can hear every little*
> *whimper. Poor Lizzie! I feel so bad for her!*
> *But I feel even worse for Toddy Boy. Because*
> *he's about to die—I'm going to kill him!*

Elizabeth was writing in her journal Monday night when I stormed into her bedroom. I tossed my bag and jacket onto the spotless off-white carpeting and plopped down on the bed beside her. I was mad. No, I was *incensed.* No, I was *seething with uncontrollable rage.* I wanted to punch somebody. Unfortunately, the thing that was making me lose it was a mechanically challenged car! And punching an ancient Fiat that's already gasping for its last dying breaths is as useless as scoping for hunks at a chess club tournament.

Besides, punching a car could be hazardous to my fingernails.

I had a right to be furious. This was the second time in less than a week that the Fiat had gone postal on me! I told her all about the car copping an attitude as soon as a light turned green.

"There I am," I concluded, "stalled at a green light, with all these cars behind me honking their horns!"

I flopped back against the pillows with an enormous sigh. The bedsprings creaked. But the comforter on my sister's bed didn't even wrinkle. A wrinkle wouldn't dare show its rumpled little face in my neat-freak sister's sterilized room.

"Thank goodness there was this cute boy in a Corvette who got me started again," I continued my story. Then I grimaced at the unfairness of life. "But you can't always count on that. Last time it was a middle-aged woman in a Ford."

"Well," Elizabeth replied.

That wasn't the reaction I'd anticipated. I mean, this was Elizabeth I was talking to. My other half. The Sympathetic Ear for dozens of frustrated teens. The Walking Doormat for other people's problems. Not to mention the co-owner and co-tormentee of the car in question.

And the best she could come up with was "Well"?

"Well?" I repeated. "Is that all you can say? *Well?*" I studied my sister's face expectantly. For the first time, I noticed her red eyes and raw cheeks. "Liz, is something wrong?" I asked, concerned. "You look like you've been crying. Has something happened between you and Todd?"

Diary, don't ask how I knew it was Todd. Twins just know.

Besides, it was a no-brainer. I'm the Emotional Twin, not her. Only a few things can turn my calm, rational sister into a basket case. A fight with Todd is definitely one of them.

62

It only took a minute to pry the truth out of her. "We've decided on a . . . a trial separation," Elizabeth said in a pitiful little voice.

For once in my life, I couldn't say a word. I'd teased Elizabeth for ages about her relationship with Todd being too boring to believe. Todd and my twin were the meat loaf and mashed potatoes of Sweet Valley High—they were bland and unexciting, but they always showed up together. Their predictable togetherness was reassuring, in a way. If Elizabeth and Todd could break up, the laws of the universe had been suspended! The possibilities freaked me out. Anything could happen. The sun could explode. The Law of Gravity could be repealed. Lila could wear flannel!

"It's completely mutual," Elizabeth assured me, speaking too fast. "We just feel that, you know, maybe we spend too much time together."

"A trial separation?" I asked. "Whose idea was this trial separation?" But I knew. I couldn't forget how totally unnerved Todd had been about Steven and Cara's near-marriage such a short time ago.

"It was mutual," Elizabeth insisted again, staring at the pen clutched too tightly in her fingers. "We both thought it would be a good idea."

I didn't believe her for an instant. "Oh, sure," I said, nodding slowly. A horrendous thought sliced through my mind. "He's not interested in somebody else, is he?"

I was ready to scratch his eyes out if he would

dare to diss a Wakefield twin that way.

"Of course not!" Elizabeth snapped. "I mean, we did talk about maybe, uh, eventually seeing other people, but there isn't anyone now." She shut her journal with a decisive motion and slipped it under her pillow. I'd have loved to get a look at what she'd been writing, but she'd been careful to angle it away from me. "We just feel we need a break from each other, that's all."

Todd dumped her! It's an outrage! But I'm a cheerleader. So my top priority at that moment was cheering Lizzie up. I hate to see her sad.

I know my sister. When she's depressed, she throws herself into school and into the school paper, The Oracle. *Liz tends to use work as a substitute for life. This time, I'm not going to let that happen. If Elizabeth becomes a drone, can you imagine what it would do to my reputation?*

So I acted bubbly and enthusiastic. And I was all, "This is the best thing that could happen. You can make new friends and do new things!" It's too early to see if she'll take my advice.

Thursday afternoon
I'm doing my best to make sure Liz doesn't crawl into her little shell and stay there. Enid

is helping too. My sister's best friend is chasing this guy, Hugh Grayson, who goes to Big Mesa High School. Enid and Hugh used to date, but they broke up. Elizabeth is helping her get back together with him. It seems point-less to me. I mean, Enid Rollins? Why bother? But it's keeping Elizabeth busy.

I hope she's too busy to agonize over Peggy Abbot. I have it on good authority— from Caroline Pearce, who's better than the Internet for providing information—that Todd's been going out with Peggy, a sopho-more bombshell who wears a very skimpy black bikini when she and Todd play volley-ball on the beach. In fact, it seems that they've been making eyes at each other since Cara's going-away party. So much for there not being another woman.

Lizzie's trying to be low-key about things. She refuses to believe Todd and Peggy are anything but casual friends. She hasn't even told Mom and Dad that she and Todd are toast. This morning I had to res-cue her from a maternal interrogation. . . .

Elizabeth and our mother were already eating breakfast when I bounded downstairs, late as usual. From the stairs I heard Mom saying, "We haven't seen Todd around for a little while."

I peeked in from the doorway just in time to

see Elizabeth's face turn rose-petal pink.

"Well, that's a little unusual, isn't it?" Mom honed in, her maternal radar blipping at a frequency only mothers can hear. She'd obviously figured out that my sister was hiding something from her. "He usually stops by or calls least once a day."

If Elizabeth was serious about wanting to keep the breakup a secret, she had a lot to learn about poker faces. "Oh, well, you know," she stammered, "we've both got so much to do. . . ."

As usual, it was *Jessica to the Rescue*. "Good morning!" I cried, breezing into the kitchen and throwing my books onto the table between them. I wrapped my arms around my mother's shoulders. "Mom," I coaxed, "I want you to do me one tiny little favor."

"Jessica, your sister and I were in the middle of a conversation."

But Elizabeth threw me a grateful half-smile.

"Two minutes, Mom," I promised. "Two incredibly insignificant minutes in your life. Please!"

"What do you want me to do?"

The way she glanced at me, you'd have thought my mother was wary of my request. I know, I have this reputation for talking people into things they don't want to get into. But it's a bad rap! My plans always work out OK, in the end. And this time, of course, I had no devious scheme in mind.

"Just listen to the Fiat," I urged, hoping to accomplish two goals at once.

*   *   *

OK, I had no scheme. But I did have an ulterior motive. If I can just get my folks to understand how terribly unsafe the Fiat is becoming—not to mention uncool—I know I can convince them to buy Liz and me a new set of wheels. Specifically, wheels that are attached to a brand-new Jeep. So far, my efforts have had no effect. But it's always worth another try.

"Jessica," my mother said firmly as she removed my hands from her shoulders, "your father told you—"

"Mom, all I'm asking is that you listen. Is that too much to ask? Just listen. And after you've listened, if you still think that it doesn't sound like there are rocks in the engine, then I won't say another word about it as long as I live."

"As long as you live?" my mother asked skeptically. She knows me too well.

"Well, at least for a day or two," I amended.

Friday afternoon
Phew! I've survived the Spanish Inquisition. Mom is no longer out of the loop on this one. In fact, the Mother of a Million Questions just grilled me for an hour about Elizabeth and Todd. I know Elizabeth likes to keep her problems to herself, but when my mother senses something

is wrong with one of her daughters, watch out! It's like a lioness protecting her young.

Anyway, I promised Mom that I'd help Elizabeth get over Todd. That's one promise I intend to keep. In fact, we start tonight! I'm going to convince her to come to the movies with Sam and me and some other cool people. I'll show my twin how to get a life. And then, it's watch out, Sweet Valley! Here comes Elizabeth Wakefield!

Tuesday
When it comes to getting a life, Elizabeth is clueless. Leave it to my twin to break up with her boring boyfriend—and then agree to go out with one of the weirdest boys at Sweet Valley High. . . .

Elizabeth had done well over the weekend. Since she was unattached, the two of us did more stuff together than usual. I'd forgotten how fun it is to be a matched set of blondes. Of course, I have a boyfriend. But there's no harm in having lots of cute guys stare at us twins at the mall and the beach! I think even Elizabeth was enjoying the attention, and she usually doesn't mind feeling invisible.

Then, out of all the cute guys who'd noticed her, the one she notices back is Kris Lynch!

Kris is OK-looking. He's a senior at school. He's tall, and he has sandy hair and nice eyes—a deep, dark blue. But he wears round, steel-rimmed glasses. And he's too skinny. I could deal with all of that if he were, like, a normal person. But Kris Lynch is one of those flaky artist types. He draws cartoons. And he hangs out with other flaky artist types—people who wear a lot of black, or else things like tie-dyed shirts and clunky "back-to-nature" sandals.

The other weird thing about Kris is that he's moody. In fact, he hardly ever seems to *talk*. I don't trust people who are that quiet. You never know what they're *not* saying, if you know what I mean.

Given all of that, Diary, my sister did the obvious thing that any insane person with no life would do. She agreed to be Kris's date to the dance this Saturday. Can you hear me rolling my eyes? Liz is making a huge mistake. She only accepted because Todd's taking Peggy to the same dance. She won't admit it, but she misses Todd like crazy.

I tried to convince Elizabeth to break her date with His Weirdness. Hello! Isn't it obvious that Elizabeth and Kris go together like apples and chili peppers? But I'm only her twin sister—the person who's closer to her than anyone in the entire world. And a certified expert on dating. So, does she care what little ole moi *thinks? No!*

Oh, the other thing that happened is that Elizabeth let Enid borrow the Fiat for a date with Hugh. And it broke down, wrecking Enid's pathetic little plans for the evening!

Elizabeth may be clueless about guys, but I think she's finally seen the light about cars and will help me in my campaign for new wheels. With the Responsible Twin's support, I know I can convince the Keepers of the Parental Pocketbook to shell out for a new Jeep Wrangler. It may take a while, but we'll wear them down in the end!

Cross your fingers, Diary!

Sunday morning

Dear Diary,

I had a great time at the dance last night. Sam and I were glued to each other the whole evening!

Elizabeth finally admitted while we were getting dressed that she didn't want to go out with Kris. I convinced her it was too late to back out. Damage control was the best option. Todd would be at the dance with Peggy Abbot—who laughs like a donkey but has a lower IQ. Besides, I reasoned, jealousy over seeing Elizabeth with another guy might work wonders on Toddy Boy.

In the end, Elizabeth decided to go. I told her not to sweat it. It was only one date

70

with Kris. They could have fun for a few hours, even if he wasn't the love of her life. After that, she never had to date him again.

Sam and I left before Kris arrived, but Elizabeth gave me a full report later. Here's what happened. . . .

Our parents gaped out the window as Kris pulled up in front of the house. He was driving *a rented limo!* And not just any limo. This was an enormous, glossy, pink Cadillac convertible! I wish I could've seen the expression on Dad's face when he caught sight of this overgrown bubble-gum-cigar-of-a-car.

"Hey, wait a minute!" my clueless father exclaimed. "That's not Todd! What happened to Todd?" Dad's a great lawyer. But when it comes to relationships, he needs to get with the program.

Kris brought flowers and candy. He wore a white suit that made him look like a movie star. OK, a skinny movie star. But a movie star, nonetheless. On the way to the school, he told Elizabeth that taking her to the dance in a pink Cadillac was a fantasy of his. I can't blame him. The car was way cool!

It had no hot tub, but my sister knew she was in hot water. This evening was special to Kris. But before it ever started, Elizabeth was dying for it to be over.

For most of the night, I was busy gazing into Sam's shining gray eyes. But now and then, I glanced around and noticed that there were other people in the room. Elizabeth noticed only two other people—Todd and Peggy.

I couldn't believe the way she was acting! Elizabeth danced in Kris's arms. But over his shoulder, her eyes were locked on Todd as he held Peggy. Elizabeth stood at the food table with Kris. But she ignored him, straining her ears to hear what Todd was murmuring to that pretty, twitty sophomore.

At home after the dance, I admitted to Elizabeth that Kris wasn't a total loser. He had style! I mean, Sam's idea of sweeping a girl off her feet is dedicating a dirt-bike race to her.

So I confronted her about the way she'd treated him. "I saw you, Elizabeth Wakefield, following Todd and Peggy around all night with your eyes!"

Elizabeth groaned. "I couldn't help it, Jess," she confessed. "It was awful. Absolutely awful! Kris really is nice, but the problem is that he isn't Todd!"

How pathetic, I thought. I consoled her by pointing out that at least she'd gotten a ride in the pink Cadillac. "And now you'll never see him again," I concluded.

My sister blushed the same color as that Cadillac. "Well, actually, I did say I'd go to a movie with him next week."

"You *what?*"

"He asked me on the way home," she explained, avoiding my stare. "We were sitting in the car, and the radio was on, and there were all these stars twinkling above us. . . ."

"And then what?" I asked. "He put a gun to your head and said you had to go out with him again?"

Elizabeth smiled weakly. "I think it was just that I was so surprised he wanted to see me again after the way I'd treated him all night that I said yes before I could figure out how to say no."

I could not believe we were having this conversation! I mean, we'd had it lots of times. But the roles were always reversed. "If you don't like him, Liz," I said, playing the role of the responsible, mature twin, "why lead him on?"

Elizabeth blinked. "Are *you* lecturing *me* about leading people on? You, of all people?"

She had no right to criticize me when I was trying to help. But I held my temper. "Liz," I explained in a controlled voice, "it's different when I do it. Everyone expects me to act like that. I'm a flirt! But they don't expect it from you. It's like being lied to by George Washington!"

For a moment, I was afraid she would cry. "Please don't make me feel worse than I already do," she begged. "I just couldn't help myself."

"Well, it's not too late. You still have time to change your mind."

Sunday evening
Twice in one day! I guess all the writing

Elizabeth has been doing in her diary is rubbing off on me. She's at it ALL THE TIME! But I really do have big news. . . .

I had gone to the beach with Lila and Amy on Sunday afternoon. And at one point, I suddenly found myself alone on our beach blanket. Amy had joined a volleyball game with her boyfriend Barry and some other kids. And Lila was buying sodas at the concession stand—supposedly. Her real goal was to saunter by Peter DeHaven, John Pfeifer, and Bruce Patman while wearing the newest of her six thousand bikinis.

I should mention, Diary, that Lila isn't serious about these guys. She dates Peter now and then. She hates Bruce's blue-blooded guts. And she's never even mentioned John, who's sports editor of The Oracle, *and who's dating Jennifer Mitchell, besides. But all three are tennis players, and Lila has a thing about tennis players.*

More importantly, she'd identified them as the cutest group of guys on the beach. Lila is a pragmatist. If you're outside, you might as well enjoy the scenery, even if you don't plan to pick any flowers. Not a bad philosophy.

The sun was hot—almost as hot as my lime-green one-piece suit, which was low-cut on the top and high-cut on the bottom. The back of my thighs began to feel that prickly sizzle that means *"We're tanned enough for now, thank you."* So I folded the copy of *Ingenue* I'd been reading, and I rolled onto my back. Squinting, I groped for Lila's dark sunglasses and slipped them over my eyes. Soon, the warmth of the sun and the swish of the water had almost lulled me to sleep.

A shadow fell across my face and I opened my eyes. A tall boy was standing over me. Even through Lila's sunglasses his form was silhouetted dark against the dazzling white sun, so I couldn't see who it was at first.

"You're in my sunbeam!" I complained.

"You're not Liz!" the boy replied, shifting position.

I sat up. "Sorry to disappoint you," I said, annoyed. I hate being mistaken for my twin.

Kris Lynch sat down beside me. "No, I'm sorry," he said. "I've never had trouble telling the two of you apart before—I mean, when I saw you around school. But the dark glasses . . ."

"It's OK," I said, remembering the Cadillac and the flowers. This guy wasn't all bad. "No problem."

"Is Liz here?" he asked. I'd never noticed before that he wore a tiny silver hoop earring in his left ear.

"Nope. Just me and you and a hundred other sun-worshipers," I said, though he was too pale to be a regular.

"Jessica, would you answer a question for me?" he asked, hesitantly. "I mean, if it isn't too much trouble?"

I shrugged. "Ask away."

"Has Elizabeth said anything about our date last night?" he asked in a pleading kind of voice. His eyes were navy blue, and they were so intense that they seemed out of place on such a sunny, lighthearted kind of day.

I avoided answering directly. I couldn't tell the poor guy outright that Elizabeth was leading him on. "Like what?" I asked.

He took a deep breath. "Jessica, for a long time, I've had this feeling about Elizabeth. I've watched her all year, but she was always with Todd Wilkins. I didn't think a girl who'd date a basketball star would give me a second look."

"She and Todd have been very close," I agreed.

"But they've broken up," he said, his eyes getting even more intense. "And last night I realized that my instincts about her were right."

I bit my lip, wondering exactly what it was about Kris that was making my skin crawl. Maybe it was the way his shyness had morphed into a creepy clinginess about Elizabeth. "Instincts?" I asked warily. "What instincts?"

"Your sister and I are meant to be together," he declared. "It's karma! I know she must feel it too! What did she say about me last night?"

"She, uh, said you were nice," I answered

76

truthfully. She *had* said something like that, I remembered. It had come right before the part about how he wasn't Todd. "But Kris, there's something you need to realize about Elizabeth—"

"Tell me, Jessica," he urged, those dark eyes focused on my face as if he was trying to read my mind. "I want to know everything!"

"My sister dated Todd a long time," I said carefully. "She's kind of on the rebound right now."

"Are you saying I shouldn't go out with her?" Kris demanded. "I can't accept that, Jessica. I know this was meant to be!"

"All I'm saying is that you need to move slowly. Give Elizabeth time to get over Todd."

"You don't understand!" he cried. "Elizabeth and I have this connection. It's a spiritual thing. We have to be together!"

"Yeah, right," I said. I decided my original assessment of Kris had been on target. He was one weird dude.

Lila came back right then, and one look of disdain from the Ice Queen was all it took for Kris to stride away over the hot sand.

Now I'm torn about whether to describe to Liz the conversation on the beach. I want to tell her how strange Kris seems—like he's totally obsessed with her. But she practically jumped down my throat when I suggested last night that she shouldn't lead him on.

77

And then she almost cried. *I don't need her to get hysterical on me! Or to yell at me to mind my own business. Or to accuse me of being prejudiced against artsy guys. Besides, Elizabeth will do exactly what she wants about Kris, no matter what I say to her.*

She's a smart person. It won't take her long to figure out all by herself that Kris is not a person she wants to spend time with.

Thursday night

Elizabeth hasn't figured it out yet. In fact, she's been spending loads of time with Kris.

She says they're only friends. I asked her if anyone had bothered to tell Kris that. Because the guy has a serious crush on her. Even Enid tried to tell her that everyone at school has the wrong idea about them. Elizabeth can't imagine why anyone would think she and Kris are a couple. On Saturday they're going to Maria Santelli's party together. But my clueless sister still insists they're just pals.

I have a very bad feeling about this.

Saturday night, late

Elizabeth has misplaced her journal. But I've got mine. It's a good thing too. There's lots to tell.

I wish I'd told her about what happened

*at the beach. Maybe it wouldn't have made
a difference. I don't know. I had decided to,
but it totally slipped my mind. Maybe if
she'd known how obsessed he was, she
would have been more careful tonight. . . .
Nah. She probably would have said I exag-
gerated the whole conversation.*

*Guys can be such pigs! Especially Kris.
You'll never believe the crazy stuff he
pulled with my sister tonight after they left
Maria's party. . . .*

It only took being bludgeoned over the head with
the truth. But finally, Elizabeth noticed that the
whole school had paired her up with Kris as Sweet
Valley High's newest and most improbable couple.
And finally, she decided she had to tell Kris it wasn't
so. For some reason, she thought Maria's party
would be a good place for this little heart-to-heart.

*So there she was, trying to find herself
and Kris a spot in the Santelli house that
wasn't already packed with teenagers and
potato chips and loud music.*

*"Come on!" Elizabeth called over a
screechy guitar solo. She grabbed Kris's
hand and pulled him through the door of
Mr. Santelli's study. Mayor Santelli's study,
actually. It's a good thing the mayor of
Sweet Valley didn't see what was going on*

in his study that night. Unfortunately, Elizabeth did see, and later she told me exactly what went down. . . .

Full of resolve and determination, Elizabeth opened the door and stepped into the room, with Kris a few steps behind her. She froze. On the sofa, sitting close together in one corner, were Todd and Peggy. Todd's arm was draped over the back of the couch. And he was leaning in close as if to kiss her.

Elizabeth could hardly breathe. She couldn't hear their words, but she knew instinctively what she had interrupted. Todd was telling Peggy he loved her. She was sure of it. She swallowed hard and tried to look nonchalant. "Oops!" she said brightly. "Wrong room!"

She ducked out the door so quickly that she stepped on Kris's foot. Later that night, I bet she wished she'd broken it.

"Hey," Kris murmured gently, pulling her over to the staircase. "Don't get so upset. We don't need a room. We can be alone right here."

Before Elizabeth knew what was happening, Kris's arms were wrapped around her. Then he kissed her. And Elizabeth found herself responding to him. Todd might not find her attractive anymore, she decided with reckless abandon. But at least somebody did.

Yes, it was dumb. But Elizabeth was too upset about Todd to be thinking straight.

80

So there was my sister, Miss Goody-Two-Shoes of the Century, locked in a passionate embrace with a guy who wasn't Todd. And in full view of most of our friends!

Just wait, Diary. It gets worse. . . .

Kris actually pulled Elizabeth down onto the stairs with him. They were kissing like they were trying to swallow each other's lips. And half the junior class had front-row seats. Finally, Elizabeth came to her senses. She told me later that it was like alarm bells chiming like crazy in her head. Not only was she making a public spectacle of herself, but she was using this boy to get back at Todd!

"Stop it!" she ordered, pushing Kris away. "Stop it! I want to get out of here."

To my sister's relief, they left the party immediately. But when they climbed into Kris's car, she realized he'd misunderstood her intentions.

"Why don't we drive up to Miller's Point?" he asked in a husky voice.

Elizabeth couldn't believe what she was hearing. "I don't want to go to Miller's Point, Kris! I want to go home!"

When she added, "And I don't want to go out with you anymore," Kris thought she was teasing him.

"Oh sure," he said. "You drag me out of the party to make out, and then you decide that you don't want to see me anymore."

"No! I didn't want to make out with you. I wanted to tell you that I wasn't going to see you anymore."

Elizabeth realized instantly that it was a lousy way to break the news to him. She opened her mouth to explain that seeing Todd had made her crazy. But Kris didn't give her a chance. "What are you talking about?" he demanded. Suddenly he was shouting, shaking his fist in the air. I mean, the guy went off like a letter bomb. He was screaming, accusing her of leading him on and trying to make a fool of him.

Elizabeth tried again to explain herself, but Kris was too far gone to listen to reason. Besides, he was starting to scare her.

"Pull over!" Elizabeth finally ordered, trying to keep her voice from shaking. "Pull over right now!" She was still a few blocks from home, but there was no way she'd stay in the car with him acting that way.

To her surprise, he pulled over. Elizabeth unclasped her seat belt, grabbed her handbag, and opened the door. That's when Kris grabbed her arm. "You're just teasing me, aren't you?" he asked. "That's it, isn't it? You're just teasing me. You couldn't have kissed me like that if you didn't like me. You weren't pretending. That was for real!"

And then the jerk tried to kiss her again!

"Let me go!" Elizabeth shouted, pushing him away. Now she was really frightened.

"No! I don't believe you! You want to go out with me. I know you do!"

"Stop it!" Elizabeth screamed. "I mean it, Kris, leave me alone!" She grabbed hold of the door handle again, as he jerked her hand. As they struggled, her bag fell, spilling its contents all over the floor mat. "Now look what you've done," she whispered, fighting back tears.

Kris apologized, as though he finally realized he'd gone too far. But by the time Elizabeth scooped up her things and jumped from his car, Kris was yelling at her again.

Todd may have been boring as a boyfriend, but at least he's not a crazed freak. I wish Elizabeth would work things out with Todd. She won't be happy until she does.

Wednesday night
Somebody is spreading nasty rumors about Elizabeth. She's been Ms. Square for her entire life. But now everyone's talking about what a wild child she is.

For a little while, things had been look-ing up. Starting Monday morning, Liz's luck did a one-eighty. First, Kris apolo-gized for morphing into Mr. Hyde. And just a few minutes later, the missing diary turned up at the bottom of Liz's locker.

That afternoon, Elizabeth and Todd actually made up! Todd said Liz totally misunderstood what she saw in Mr. Santelli's study. Todd hadn't been professing his undying love to Peggy of the Donkey Laugh. He'd been confessing that he couldn't see Peggy anymore because he was still in love with my twin! So Todd and Liz declared the trial separation to be officially over. And Elizabeth was ecstatic. For a little while....

After school on Monday, I got my first hint that something freaky was going on. Caroline Pearce bummed a ride off me, since she lives just three houses down from us. And I could practically see her gossip antennae wiggling as she trolled for information.

"So where's Elizabeth?" Caroline asked as she climbed into the Fiat. "Does she have a hot date with the enigmatic Kris Lynch this afternoon?"

I slammed my door shut. "No," I answered coldly. "She had something to do for *The Oracle*. And anyway, Liz and Kris aren't seeing each other anymore." I told her that on purpose, figuring putting information on the Caroline Network was as good as calling the Associated Press.

Caroline raised a meticulously shaped eyebrow. "That's not the way I heard it," she said.

"I just told you that she's not seeing him anymore, and I think *I* should know!"

Caroline tossed her bright red hair over her shoulder. "Well, presumably *he* knows whether they're seeing each other or not," she said, her voice as smooth as her ivory skin. "And I have it from some very reliable sources that the reason Kris and Elizabeth left the party in such a hurry the other night was because they couldn't wait to get up to Miller's Point!"

That was such a hoot that I didn't know whether to be shocked or amused. I told her she'd lost her mind. But then her story got even more sordid.

"I'm not only saying that she went there with him," said Caroline smugly. "I'm saying that she had a pretty wild time!"

I assured her over and over again that her sources were wrong, but I didn't think she believed me. As I walked into my own house after dropping her off, I told myself not to worry. Caroline was a drip. No reasonable person who knew Elizabeth would actually believe such garbage. Then the phone rang.

"Why didn't you tell me?" squealed Lila's voice. She was so excited that she'd lost her usual facade of utter coolness. "I don't believe I had to hear it from someone else!"

"Tell you what?"

"Oh, don't play games with me," Lila ordered. "It's all over school about Elizabeth and Kris Lynch and their night of passion at Miller's Point."

That night, I told Elizabeth what Caroline and Lila had said. She laughed it off. But at school Tuesday, everyone was talking about this wild night of passion.

By Tuesday night, Elizabeth wasn't laughing anymore. Enid and Todd, the two people closer to her than anyone but me, seemed to believe the stupid stories. Todd stood Liz up for their big reunion date at the Box Tree Cafe. And Enid hung up on her without saying why.

I walked into Elizabeth's room late Tuesday night. She'd fallen asleep with the lights on, her journal open beside her on the bed. There were tear stains on her face, and her dress was lying in a heap on the floor. In my room, clothes on the floor are part of the decor. In Elizabeth's room, they're a sign of something seriously wrong.

I covered my sister with the blanket, and I picked up the journal to lay it on the bedside table. I wasn't trying to snoop, but the last line she'd written caught my eye and sent a dagger through my heart: *"What hurts most is that Todd and Enid, two of the people I love most in the world, have turned against me. Why? I've never knowingly done anything to hurt either of them."*

My sister is lonely and confused and hurt. It's bad enough when the rest of the school acts as if she's a criminal. But Enid and Todd? No way! I've got to do something to help her. I can't stand to see Elizabeth like this.

I'm going to clear my sister's name and expose the slimeballs who've wrecked her reputation. By the time I'm through, Enid and Todd will be begging Liz to forgive them. Nobody treats a Wakefield twin that way and gets away with it!

Friday night, late
Jessica the Great strikes again! I knew Kris Lynch was a jerk. And he proved me right. If you were thinking all along that Kris Pond Scum Lynch was spreading the rumors, you were absolutely right. The skinny, slimy little weasel actually stole Elizabeth's diary! The night of Maria's party, when Kris yelled at my sister and her bag spilled in his car, the diary fell out. That worthless creep read my sister's diary, and then slipped it into her locker when he apologized at school the next morning, so she'd think it was there all along.

He told Enid that Elizabeth had blabbed to him all of Enid's most private secrets. And he did the same thing with Todd—and told Todd that Elizabeth was only pretending to love him again, to pay him back for dating Peggy.

87

Todd and Enid should have known better than to take Kris's word for any of it without talking to Liz. They must have been temporarily brain dead.

Luckily, I figured out the whole tangled mess, confronted Enid, Todd, and Kris about it, and led them by the noses until Kris repented, and they all agreed on a way to clear Elizabeth's name. It was a brilliant piece of detective work—and deal-making, if I do say so myself.

Then I brought them all to The Oracle office this afternoon to talk to my sister. . . .

Elizabeth was expecting only me when she walked down the hall toward the newspaper office on Friday. When she saw who was with me, the color drained from her face as if someone had pulled a plug. She began to turn away, but I grabbed her hand.

"Wait a minute, Liz! I think you're going to want to hear this."

Elizabeth stared at me as if I had turned traitor too.

Kris stepped forward. "Jessica's right, Elizabeth," he said gently. "I've come here to apologize to you for what I've done. Not only did I start all those rumors about you, but I lied to Enid and Todd."

Todd couldn't meet my sister's gaze. "And we believed him," he admitted in the most dejected voice imaginable. "Even though we know what sort of person you are, we believed everything Kris told us."

Enid began to cry. "I'm so ashamed of myself," she sobbed. "How could I have treated you like that?"

Elizabeth kept opening and closing her mouth like she was trying to talk but couldn't remember how. But she squeezed my hand, and her touch said it all.

Kris handed her a piece of paper. At the top was a cartoon he'd drawn. It showed Elizabeth sitting in a chair with Kris kneeling on the floor. The caption read "Begging Forgiveness" and beneath it was a full apology for everything.

"I want you to run this in the paper," he told her. "I don't expect you ever to forgive me, but I want at least to set the record straight."

So everything worked out for the best, Diary. Everyone has forgiven everyone else. Elizabeth thinks I'm the greatest sister in the world (she's right, of course), not just for saving her reputation and setting things right, but for being the only person who stuck by her. Todd and Liz are back to their normal, boring selves—totally in love with each other.

Now I can start enjoying my own love life again. I'm sneaking out in fifteen minutes to meet Sam at Miller's Point.

And we all lived happily ever after!

Thursday night
Elizabeth is the worst twin sister in the

*world! We have an actual chance to be-
come rich and famous. And to help pay for
the Jeep Wrangler I absolutely must have.
We could be famous television stars!
What's more, we could be famous stars on
The Young and the Beautiful, which is only
my very favorite soap opera in the world,
starring the most gorgeous guy on daytime
television, Brandon Hunter.*

*It's my big chance! But Elizabeth wants
to blow it. . . .*

At dinner Thursday night, Elizabeth stared at
her plate while I tried to drum up some support
from the folks.

"I saw an advertisement in *Hollywood Digest*,"
I told our parents. "The producers of *The Young
and the Beautiful* are looking for identical twins to
appear on the show for a week. I thought it would
be a good idea for Elizabeth and me to try out."

"What do you think, Liz?" Dad asked.

Elizabeth got that stubborn look on her face.
"This is more Jessica's idea than mine," she said.
"She's the one who wants to be an actress. I'm not
really that thrilled about soap operas. Besides, I'm
pretty busy right now."

Busy? Ha! I thought. *It's not like she has a life
or anything. What could possibly be more exciting
than being a television star?* Of course, I couldn't
tell her that. I had to use psychology. Elizabeth

wouldn't be swayed by dreams of stardom and Hollywood parties. Elizabeth would understand only the most boring, sensible arguments. *I can do that,* I decided.

"C'mon, Liz," I cajoled. "A week! That's all I'm asking. A week's work that might make us a lot of money. Look. We need a new car. The Fiat is on its last legs. It breaks down about every five minutes. And what about that word processor you've been wanting?"

I kept trying, and Elizabeth kept hedging.

"It sounds as if you two need to discuss this further," our father said after a few minutes of listening to us argue. "I don't really see a problem in the girls trying out or performing on a show like that for a week. Do you, Alice?"

"I'm sure it would be fine, and Los Angeles isn't too far away—" Mom started.

"See, Liz!" I pointed out. "It's OK with Mom and Dad!"

"I told you that it was against my principles," Elizabeth said for the hundredth time. "I think soap operas are all fluff and no substance, and I wouldn't be caught dead on one! Mom, Dad? Don't you see my point?"

The parental units were too chicken to take sides. They insisted that they were totally neutral. Oh well, at least they're not siding with Elizabeth, as they usually do.

My stuck-up twin told me that soap operas don't have any "moral or intellectual value." She needs to lighten up. What about entertainment value? What about escapist value? What about gorgeous-hunk value?

I'm going to change her mind . . . one way or another.

Saturday afternoon
At Amy's party last night, Lila and I started on an amazing scheme to get Elizabeth to audition for that soap opera with me. . . .

Our brilliant idea began Friday night at Amy's house, just after Elizabeth and Todd left. I'd been trying all evening—with the help of most of our friends—to convince Elizabeth to try out for *The Young and the Beautiful*. It wasn't working.

I flopped down in the wing-back chair next to Amy's living room window, and we tried hard to think. After a lot of discussion and a few false starts, Lila grabbed my arm. "I've got it!" she cried. "You have to quit bugging her. Just drop the whole subject."

"What?" I shouted. "I've got to keep the pressure on, to wear her down!"

"That's just what you have to stop doing. Liz is holding up against your pressures. What you need to do is play it cool, act as if you've given up. Then do something really sneaky, and make it look like it came from someone else."

Now she had my attention. "What do you have in mind?"

Lila flipped her long, light brown hair over her shoulder and pulled her chair closer to mine. Then she reminded me again of why she's my best friend.

"What does Liz like to do more than anything else?" she asked.

"Write and study," I answered automatically. I couldn't help rolling my eyes as I said it, and neither could Lila.

"That's right. She really likes to research stuff and find out about things in depth. What if you sent her a letter from a fake research company and it asked her to come to a market research discussion group for identical twins?"

Now, I was catching on. "She couldn't resist that," I said, feeling the adrenaline of a brilliant conspiracy starting to flow through my veins. "She'd probably want to write an article about it for her newspaper!"

"Exactly. Then you take her to the audition instead of the research group!" Lila concluded triumphantly.

The idea, Diary, is that Elizabeth hates to make a scene. Once she sees she's been duped, she'll probably just go through with the audition, figuring we'll never get picked, anyhow.

So this morning, Lila and I mailed off a letter about the focus group, printed out on fancy paper, courtesy of the computer in Mr. Fowler's study. Now I have to keep my mouth shut and my fingers crossed. In other words, I'll practice my acting skills! In the meantime, I'll work on Elizabeth about the Jeep instead.

Friday night

The audition was this afternoon. We drove to Los Angeles, supposedly for the market research project. Elizabeth didn't suspect a thing until we pulled into the lot of a television studio. She scrunched her eyebrows then, like she was getting wary. But I suggested maybe the focus group discussion was being videotaped, and that seemed to satisfy her for a few minutes. Then we walked in, and it was Twin City inside. . . .

The letter from "California Research Associates" had mentioned "a cross-section of participants with a diversity of opinion." (Am I good, or what?) But the waiting room was filled with at least twenty sets of pretty, blond twin girls, all around sixteen years old.

A woman walked into the room wearing the

wildest hairstyle I'd ever seen. It was twisted into a unicorn horn on the front of her head, all wrapped in technicolor ribbons. She was wearing skintight leather pants, and her shoes had sequins. It was totally cool, just the way a television casting director should dress. At least, I thought so. Elizabeth looked as though she thought the woman should be committed.

"All right, girls," the Unicorn Woman announced. "I'll call your names, one set at a time, and you can read for the selection committee in the other room. When you're finished, just go on home and we'll call you with the news."

Elizabeth's face turned purple. Suddenly, she knew exactly where she was and why. She nudged me, hard, and tried to pull me aside for a private "discussion" while the Unicorn Woman was giving us all more instructions. I ignored my twin's protests. So Elizabeth tried again and again, until her whisper grew too loud for anyone to ignore.

"Now, Jess!" Elizabeth screeched.

"Later," I whispered.

"There won't *be* any later," Elizabeth cried. "You've brought me here against my will, and I will no longer submit to your devious, underhanded tactics!"

The Unicorn Woman stopped speaking. Now, everyone in the room was watching us.

"Shh! Liz!" I cautioned her. "You're making a scene!"

"I don't care if the whole world hears me!" she shouted. My calm, rational twin was losing it, big time. "You had no right to trick me into coming to Los Angeles. And if you think for one minute I'm going to stay here and pretend to be thrilled about auditioning, then you had better think again!"

She spun on her heel and headed for the door, and I could see my career in soaps spiraling down the drain.

"Please, Liz! Don't do this to me! Don't do this to *us!* We're a team. You can't leave me here alone, stranded!"

"Oh, I'm sure you'll be able to scam your way out of it," Elizabeth said. "Maybe you'll even be rescued by one of your famous daytime heroes. As for me, I'm leaving. I'll wait for you in the car, and if you don't show up, I'm going home!"

Then my sister marched out the door, leaving me standing in the middle of the room, hoping I wouldn't burst into tears in front of everyone. The other girls began making snide remarks about us, as I started mumbling a lame apology.

Then, the most amazing thing happened.

"Brava!" exclaimed Unicorn Woman, clapping her hands. "Outstanding performance! I couldn't have asked for a better Tiffany and Heather argument, even with a script."

"But our names are Jessica and Elizabeth," I said, not catching on.

"Wakefield, right?" the woman said, consulting her

clipboard. "Well, congratulations. Tiffany and Heather are the twins you'll be playing in the show—that is, if you're still interested in a week on *The Young and the Beautiful*. That *was* your audition, wasn't it?"

WE GOT THE PARTS! Can you believe it, Diary? Liz and I have been chosen to guest star on The Young and the Beautiful! *Natasha Talbot (the Unicorn Woman) cast me as Heather, the demure twin, and Elizabeth as Tiffany, the fiery twin. Isn't that a riot? It's because Elizabeth had the more fiery "role" in our "audition."*

Elizabeth is still furious and insists that she won't do the show. But it's in the bag. We don't start filming until next week, but we're supposed to go to a cast luncheon to-morrow. Holy Hunkaroony, Batman! In twelve short little hours, I'm going to meet Brandon Hunter, live and in person! What will I wear?

But don't worry, Diary. When I'm a rich, famous actress, I promise I'll remember you and all the little people I knew before my big break. Well, some of the little people. But only the ones who were nice to me.

Sunday night
I think I'm in love! With Brandon Hunter. Sam is great, but let's be honest. What

can he really do for my career? Nada! He's not even excited about my big break. Friday night he just kept going on about how I was more interested in being a star than in watching him race his little dirt bikes. Well, yes. Is there some reason why I shouldn't be? In the end, he suggested that I forget about guest-starring on The Young and the Beautiful. *And then he dropped me off without even a goodnight kiss!*

That proves it, Diary. Now I'm going to throw all my energy into making Brandon fall madly in love with me so he can help my career. I started this weekend, with a fabulous trip to Los Angeles. Luckily, Lila's father had to be there on business. So Li, Amy, and I had an all-expenses-paid room at the Belmont for the night. The Belmont! And my parents actually thought Mr. Fowler was going to be around to keep an eye on us. Ha! Like, get real.

We drove into the city on Saturday morning for the cast luncheon, where I pretended Elizabeth was home with the flu. And Brandon and I hit it off right away. . . .

I was at the cast luncheon, standing at the buffet table.

Then I turned around and almost dropped my plate. Brandon Hunter, the sexiest, hunkiest star on daytime television, was standing beside me. He looked even taller in person than he did on the screen. His dark, curly hair was crying out for my fingers to ruffle through it. And his eyes were the same warm brown as hot chocolate.

"Hi!" I said, trying to sound as if I met famous TV stars all the time. I stuck out my hand to shake his. "I'm Jessica Wakefield."

"My new *amour*," Brandon said. And then he leaned over to kiss my outstretched hand. I couldn't wait to tell Lila and Amy.

> *It's true about being his new "amour," Diary! I've read the script, so I know that I'm the twin who ends up with Jeremy— that's Brandon's character—on-screen. This weekend gave me the feeling that I might end up with Brandon offscreen as well! We ate lunch together, and he told me oodles of stories about himself and his work. Brandon has led the most fascinating life. He's only twenty-two years old, but already, he's climbed Mount Whitney, gone hang gliding, and broken wild horses! It sure beats dirt-bike racing.*
>
> *Lunch was over and I was getting ready to leave, when Brandon leaned over and whispered in my ear . . .*

"I hope you're not going to run off and disappear

like Cinderella," he said. "Are you busy tonight?"

I shivered in anticipation. "No," I lied. I had plans with Lila and Amy, but I knew they would understand.

"I've been invited to a party at Bill Lacey's mansion tonight. You know Bill Lacey, don't you? He sings."

He sings? Bill Lacey is only the lead singer for Shining Steel, the hottest rock band in the country.

Brandon invited me to be his date at the party. And he took me to the studio's wardrobe department so I could pick out something to wear—a red-sequined top and silk pants, with glittery earrings that reached practically to my shoulders.

Brandon sent a limousine to pick me up at my hotel. As I stepped out of the limo in front of the Lacey mansion, I felt like Cinderella on her way to the ball. Except that the place looked more like it was from *Gone With the Wind.* I was at the bottom of a huge, graceful flight of stairs that led up to an entryway with elegant columns and crystal chandeliers. I was just about to feel intimidated, when my handsome prince stepped out from under the twinkling lights and rushed down the stairs to greet me.

"I've been waiting for you," Brandon said, taking my hand.

All my life, I added silently.

A minute later, I was engulfed in the most glamorous party I'd ever imagined. For one thing, the mansion was fabulous. It made Lila's place look like a doll's house. My mom's an interior designer, so I know a little about furniture. And there wasn't a single chair in Bill Lacey's house that cost less than the Jeep I've got my eye on.

The party was full of famous people. Television stars, movie directors, musicians, and celebrity authors were all there in the most beautiful clothes I'd ever seen, chatting it up, ignoring the priceless works of art on the walls, and taking fancy foods from trays carried by bustling waiters. Reporters kept appearing everywhere and photographers' camera flashes kept popping. I felt as if I were swirling around in the center of a very expensive kaleidoscope.

A tall man wearing a custom-tailored leather outfit strode up to us and amiably slapped Brandon on the back.

"Jessica, I'd like you to meet our host, Bill Lacey," Brandon said, as if meeting a famous rock star was about as ordinary as meeting a schoolteacher.

"It's a pleasure, Jessica," said the lead singer for Shining Steel. To Brandon, he added, "I have to hand it to you, old chum. You always bring the prettiest women."

Then he told me to call him Bill. *Bill!*

While we were talking, a photographer popped up and snapped our picture. The rest of the evening went by in a glittering whirl of color and sound and celebrities. Brandon kept having to run off to talk with one business contact or another, but I didn't mind. I met Steve Limbo, the bass player for Bill's band. And so many other famous people that it was getting hard to keep track. But I tried to remember it all, so I could give Lila and Amy the full report.

As we watched the sneak preview of the new video Shining Steel would release soon, Brandon leaned in close to me. I could feel his warm breath against my ear as he said the most amazing thing: "Say, Jess, I've been such a poor date that I'd like to make it up to you. Would you care to go with me to a movie preview tomorrow afternoon?"

The movie preview was just as exciting, Diary. I got to wear another stunning outfit from the wardrobe department. This one was worth three thousand dollars—eat your heart out, Lila! Then Brandon drove me home from the city and met Mom and Dad. He was charming, of course. They approve!

The only pimple on the complexion of my weekend is Elizabeth. She still hasn't agreed to actually be in the soap opera, though of course I haven't said that to Brandon! She can't ruin this for me, Diary! I'll just die if I can't guest-star on The Young and the Beautiful!

Wednesday night

Elizabeth and I got a new Jeep! It is so way cool! Dad took Elizabeth and Todd shopping for it tonight. I felt dissed when I learned they went without me. But then I saw our very own Jeep Wrangler, black with chrome trim! I love it! And it's perfect for driving to L.A. every day next week to tape the show.

Life would be awesome right now if it weren't for the fact that my sister and my boyfriend have been abducted by space aliens and replaced with brainless automatons. Elizabeth still says she won't be on a soap opera. She doesn't like the way they portray women and relationships. She thinks the people in them are silly, superficial stereotypes. I can recite every stupid argument, but that doesn't mean I have a clue as to what she's talking about. It's entertainment, not brain surgery! If nothing else, you'd think she'd agree to do it just because she owes me a favor, after that whole Kris Lynch episode.

Well, I found a surefire way to change her mind. I've written a letter from Elizabeth to an editor at the Los Angeles Times, proposing a series of articles about our week as soap stars. She'll be mad when she finds out. But she'll thank me if it actually works. She's *always wanted to publish in the* Times. *Am I a good twin, or what?*

As for Sam, he's acting all possessive. And possessed. He says I'm the one who's being selfish. All I'm asking is for him to share me with Hollywood for a week or two.

Thursday night
Elizabeth said yes! Hollywood, here we come!

Monday
Life is wonderful! We filmed our first episode today. I'm a natural in front of the camera. And Elizabeth isn't bad either. . . .

"OK, twins," announced director William Green from the control booth, "this is your first scene. Now, you know the story. Liz—now known as Tiffany—is a real schemer. She knows that Brandon, as Jeremy Howard, is leaning his affections toward Jess, now known as Heather. We'll call everyone by their stage names from now on. So in this scene, Tiffany is going to pretend to be Heather to try to trick Jeremy into noticing her. Got it?"

"Got it!" Elizabeth and I said together.

"Unh-unh, hang on!" Brandon called. He shuffled through his script. "Why didn't someone tell me we were doing this scene first? I'm ready for the restaurant scene, not this one."

"Take five, everybody," William said. "Brandon, get those lines down!"

"It's not my fault that the whole taping schedule gets changed around for a couple of schoolkids."

I felt guilty about that. It must be hard for Brandon, having everything turned upside down on the set, just so Elizabeth and I can tape our scenes early and get back to Sweet Valley for a few hours of school in the afternoons. Elizabeth thought Brandon was being unprofessional, but she never gave him a chance. She decided to dislike Brandon from the start, because she thought I was neglecting Sam for him.

Brandon had trouble with some of his lines, but I guess everybody has a bad day. He also had trouble telling Elizabeth and me apart. I don't blame him, since I'm playing the meek, quiet twin. In Hollywood, we call that "casting against type." The costume people are putting a necklace on me so that Brandon always knows which twin is which.

Elizabeth and I were talking about him in the Jeep on the way home to Sweet Valley. . . .

"Brandon and I are going to dinner at Spago in Los Angeles!" I said as I steered our new baby through traffic. "Isn't that exciting? All the stars eat there!"

"Have you even given a thought to Sam during all of this?" Elizabeth asked. Just because she was born a measly four minutes before me, she thinks she has the right to play big sister. "A guy can only take so much, you know."

"He should have thought of that before he walked out on me the other day at the Dairi Burger!" I said hotly. *Nobody walks out on a date with me.*

"He walked out on you?" Elizabeth exclaimed, her eyebrows high on her forehead. "You didn't tell me that! You said he was just having a little trouble because you were so busy."

"Well, it was a little more than that," I admitted. "He told me that he didn't think he'd ever understand me. See, I had to turn down a date with him to get my homework done. Some sacrifices have to be made, you know."

"You're not sacrificing your dates with Brandon," Elizabeth replied. "Maybe that's why Sam is so upset."

"My dates with Brandon are more like business," I said as I steered onto the ramp to the freeway. "But I have to tell you, I could easily fall for Brandon Hunter!"

Elizabeth lost it. "You have to be kidding!" she cried. "Sam is so much more . . . so much better than . . ."

"Yeah, but why should I hang around with someone who can't handle my fame?" I asked. It was certainly a reasonable question. "Sam hasn't been the least bit supportive of me. Brandon, on the other hand, understands the spotlight, and the demands that an acting career makes on a person's social life."

Elizabeth was opening and closing her mouth as though she couldn't believe what she was hearing.

I threw my head back and felt the warm wind streaming through my hair as I accelerated into the fast lane. "Let's not fight," I said, raising my voice to be heard above the wind. "Just think. This afternoon we get to watch ourselves on *The Young and the Beautiful* for the very first time! Let's invite everyone over for our premiere to celebrate!"

Diary, I think Brandon is really starting to fall in love with me! Even before today's show aired, our photograph was in all the tabloids. Everyone says we're the hottest new Hollywood couple, on and off the screen. Of course, it's all hype, so far. But it's turning my supposedly loyal, supportive boyfriend into a lunatic. I wish Sam would try to understand how much acting—not to mention fame and fortune—means to me.

Wednesday night, late
I thought Sam and I were finally going to get our relationship back on track this

*afternoon when he showed up at my door
after today's home screening of* The Young
and the Beautiful. *All our friends had come
for the show—except Sam. Everyone was
eating popcorn and listening to my "in-
sider" stories about the stars on the show.
Then the doorbell rang. . . .*

"Yes?" I said, pulling the door open wide. "May
I help you?"

Standing in front of me was a guy dressed as
Batman, in full black-and-gold costume, including
the mask. He handed me a big bouquet of flowers
and a note.

"Dear Jessica," I read aloud, *"I miss you and
want to speak with you as soon as possible. Will
you please send a return message to let me know if
I still mean anything to you? Love, Sam."*

Tears stung in my eyes as I realized that
Elizabeth had been right. I had neglected Sam. I
wasn't mad at him anymore. I just wanted him to
understand how much my acting career meant to
me. And now he'd gone to all this trouble just to talk
to me—probably to apologize. It was so sweet!

Elizabeth and everyone else were gathering behind me to see what was going on. I showed them
that the note was from Sam. And I told the mes-
senger that I was free that night.

Suddenly, Batman's stoic face broke into a wide,
familiar grin. He let out a whoop and tore off his

mask. And then Sam grabbed me and bent me backward for a long, passionate kiss.

In other words, the magic was back. Sam and I decided to ditch everyone and take advantage of the romantic momentum we'd just built up. So we raced outside and jumped into the Jeep. Sam pulled off his Batman outfit, and underneath it he was wearing shorts and a fluorescent green tank top that looked terrific with his tan.

"Let's go to the beach!" I yelled, inspired by his outfit.

"Anywhere is fine with me, as long as we can talk," Sam agreed. So I drove to Route 1, where there's this secluded little beach that nobody goes to much, so we could be alone. I checked for reporters as I parked the Jeep. They'd been following me around so much in the past few days that it was becoming second nature. And I didn't want Brandon to see a picture of Sam and me in Thursday's tabloids.

As we walked on the sand, I started telling him a funny story about a tight costume I'd been wearing on the set that morning. Sam interrupted me. "Jessica, why haven't you returned my phone calls lately? What's going on with you and this Hunter guy? I don't really like what I'm reading in the papers."

I slipped off my sandals and dipped my toes in the foamy surf. "There's nothing to worry about," I assured him.

"I'm not blind. I've seen the way that guy is looking at you in those photographs. And the way you're looking at him. I know that you've been going out with him almost every night. I'd like to know who you think your boyfriend is."

"I'm not going out with him tonight," I said, trying to ignore the accusing tone in his voice. "Tonight I'm out with you, walking along a romantic beach, waiting for the sunset." I kissed him slowly. "Does that answer your question?"

"No!" Sam cried, pulling away. "You kiss me as if nothing has changed, but everything has changed. I don't like playing second fiddle to a second-rate actor. And besides, everyone thinks you're having an affair with him!"

"An affair?" I scoffed, not liking the way that sounded at all. "That's simply not true. All our dates have been very innocent."

"Maybe on your part, Jess," Sam said. "But the gossip columnists are having a field day. I read an article just today about Jessica Wakefield's tips for holding on to an older man. There were a bunch of quotes from you that didn't sound very innocent to me!"

Whoa, I thought. I hadn't seen that article. I wasn't sure if I should be flattered or horrified. "Well, they were made up," I told him. "I haven't told any reporters stuff like that. It's just harmless publicity."

"A little publicity is one thing. I can handle a

little publicity. But I don't like being made to look like a fool!"

"No one is making you look like a fool," I assured him.

I tried everything I could think of, Diary, to make him feel better. I tried making jokes. And I tried sitting quietly with him, holding his hand and watching the sunset. But the sunset gave me a great idea for a background for some publicity shots the director had suggested. And when I told that to Sam, he got really quiet and angry. . . .

"I'm tired of the glitz and the glamor, Jessica. You've gone off on some crazy tangents in the past, but this one is the craziest! I don't even know you anymore!"

That ticked me off. Maybe he had a right to be a little jealous. But I didn't deserve this kind of scorn for something that was so important to me. I wasn't going to put up with another minute of it.

"You want to talk? Let's talk!" I said, my voice rising. "If you ask me, you're the one who's overreacting!"

"I may be, but I'm not going to follow you around like a puppy dog, waiting for you to toss a few tidbits my way. I think you need to make a choice, Jessica. It's either Brandon Hunter or me!"

I was totally furious. I'm my own boss. I don't take ultimatums from anyone, not even a boyfriend.

"Well?" Sam prompted. "Who is it going to be?"

"Fine!" I shouted. "You made the choice for me with your demands and accusations. I have more important things to do than soothe the overinflated ego of a high-school boy!"

And I stomped off to the Jeep, Diary, leaving Sam stranded on the beach. Do I care? No! High-school boys are so immature. I've got my future laid out in front of me. If Sam doesn't want to try to fit into it, that's his choice!

Thursday, after midnight
I've been such a fool! Brandon Hunter doesn't care about me at all. He's just been using me to further his career. True, I've been doing the same thing to him. But somehow it feels different when I'm doing the using. . . .

I was really excited about Thursday's shoot. First, Elizabeth and I did our very first—and only—scene with just the two of us on-screen. It was a big, rousing argument—something we have loads of experience with. And it went beautifully, if I do say so myself.

Then Natasha told me our characters might be extended; we could be on the show indefinitely. I was psyched. I couldn't wait to tell Brandon. I skipped to his dressing room door, and just as I was about to burst in, I heard my name mentioned inside.

"Yep, this publicity stunt was the best one you've dreamed up yet," said a voice I recognized as Marve Akins, one of the producers.

I put my ear against the door so I could hear better.

"As soon as I saw her, I knew she would fall for it," Brandon said, chuckling. "She's such a naive and quiet little thing, just like her character."

I clenched my fists.

"She really believes that you fell for her," Marve continued. "And so did all the papers. Our ratings have soared this week. . . ."

He went on about ratings and publicity photographs, but I was so enraged that I could hardly stand to listen. And it only got worse.

"I'll be glad when this week is over and she heads back to high school," Brandon said. "I need a little more sophistication in my life. I think I'll start pursuing Sandi Starr. Now there's a woman who would be good for my career!"

Marve let out a low whistle. "The daughter of the studio's owner? You sure know how to stack the deck."

I didn't wait around to hear any more. I ran down the hall with tears in my eyes.

Tonight Brandon and I had a date for an awards banquet. I took another trip to the wardrobe department and borrowed a floor-length purple gown in chiffon and lace. Brandon wore a five-thousand-dollar tuxedo. Oh, we looked terrific, Diary, the very picture of the perfect young Hollywood couple. I smiled for the cameras. But I was seething inside.

For the first time, I watched Brandon objectively. I noticed how he told the same unbelievable stories over and over again, and how much sweeter he acted toward me when there was a camera nearby. In short, I noticed that every word out of his mouth was fake.

Elizabeth was right all along. I hate when that happens.

And I actually broke up with Sam over this jerk!

When I got home that night, I told Elizabeth everything. She was totally sympathetic, especially when I told her I planned to talk to Sam the next afternoon and apologize for everything.

Working together, Elizabeth and I even came up with a plan for getting back at Brandon, that arrogant creep! Friday during shooting, we would do every-thing possible to screw him up. We'd keep him off balance—but not enough so that anyone else would figure out why. He would flub his lines and have to do a million takes. And it was our last day on the show, so there wasn't a thing he could do about it!

It's not hard to throw Brandon off, Diary. Now that I know what he's all about, I see that he's not very bright. Certainly no match for the Wakefield twins when we're out for revenge.

We'll trade off on that necklace I'm sup-posed to wear all the time. Brandon will never know which twin he's talking to! Elizabeth has made friends with all the backstage people. If she asks him to, the special effects guy will make it snow during one scene when Brandon is looking out the window—in southern California! We've got loads of other tricks up our sleeves.

Brandon is in for Double Trouble!

Friday evening

Dear Diary,

It worked better than we could have dreamed! We did everything I mentioned last night to mess around with Brandon's overinflated head, and a lot more. And he never knew what hit him!

"This is the big party scene, the climax for the week," William said on Friday morning from his usual place in the control booth. "Take your chalk marks, everyone. Is everybody in position? Remember, this is where Jeremy makes his choice, and he and Heather begin their happily ever after."

"Fat chance of that," I muttered to Elizabeth. "Brandon had the nerve to kiss me good luck this morning! It took every ounce of willpower I had to keep from punching him in the nose."

"Don't get mad now—" Elizabeth began.

"I know—get even! Is Harold ready with the snow? I've already asked Elaine from props to dress up in an outfit like mine to give Brandon a little double vision."

I think William and some of the other cast and crew figured out what we were up to before the end of the day's shooting. But nobody called us on it. Heck, they're all fed up with Brandon's prima donna attitude. I bet they loved every minute! So we went home, happy with the work we did on The Young and the Beautiful—*but also relieved that it was over.*

Yep, that's right. Even me, Diary. The schedule has been killing me! Leaving at five every morning to get to Los Angeles in time for our early shooting schedule, rushing home to get in the last few classes of the day, and then trying to fit in homework in between awards banquets and movie screenings with Brandon. . . . Well, it's been a great experience—some of it anyway. But I'm not ready to be a soap opera star just yet. It takes too much time. Not to mention what it took from my relationship with Sam!

Anyhow, Elizabeth and I had just gotten home from our last day of shooting. And the phone rang. It was William, calling us back to the studio. Brandon didn't like the way he looked in the final scene—"our" scene. So we had to drive back to the studio to redo it. There wasn't time to tape it again, so we'd be doing the scene live.

Then, Dear Diary, I had a brainstorm. I thought of the perfect, devious way to get back at Brandon once and for all. At the same time, it was a way to tell Sam how much I loved him. So I dialed Sam's number and left a message on his machine, begging him to watch that day's episode. Then Elizabeth and I climbed into the Jeep to head back to the studio.

You could feel the excitement in the air when we arrived on the set. A live show! With a live audience! But only Elizabeth and I knew just how lively it was going to be. . . .

"Action!" called William.

Elizabeth had the first line. "I've been waiting for you," she purred into Brandon's ear. "Isn't it a beautiful day? Why don't you walk with me to the window?"

Brandon seemed wary, but Elizabeth played it straight, doing everything exactly like the script said to do. This time, no snow was falling outside the window. And when I entered from the left a few minutes later, my necklace was in place.

"Heather!" Brandon greeted me. He seemed relaxed now, certain that we wouldn't dare repeat that morning's performance on a live broadcast. "Tiffany and I were just talking about you. I'm so glad you were able to come."

The scene progressed as it was supposed to, without a missed cue or a flubbed line. When Elizabeth/Tiffany tried a new tactic to steal Brandon/Jeremy from me, I swooned onto the sofa, and Brandon ran to fetch me a glass of water.

Here it comes! I thought. Even my toes were tingling in anticipation.

Finally, we reached the climactic exchange. And I was ready.

"I don't care for Tiffany. I care for you!" Brandon declared. I was sitting on the sofa, and he knelt on the floor in front of me. "I love you, Heather. I've never felt like this before. Please tell me you'll be mine forever."

According to the original script, I was now

118

supposed to throw myself into Brandon's arms and kiss him passionately. The new-and-improved script, the Wakefield Version, was different.

I rose from the couch and looked down at Brandon. "No, Jeremy," I announced loudly, as his mouth dropped open. "I don't love you! The truth is, I'm in love with somebody else."

"But—"

I hurried on with my speech, while the cast and crew watched, incredulous. "I'm in love with Sam, the boy I left behind. I could never love you the way I love him. He's caring and wonderful and kind. And you're nothing but a big jerk!"

Then, with a flick of my wrist, I tossed the contents of the glass of water into his face.

Naturally, Brandon had a fit as soon as the cameras stopped rolling. William was ready to kill me. But he reconsidered when he heard how Brandon used me all week. Obviously, he can't stand Brandon. I think he enjoyed seeing him humiliated on live TV.

In fact, William called tonight and asked if Elizabeth and I would be interested in appearing on the show regularly! I was tempted, but I turned him down. Everybody said I made the right decision—except Bruce Patman, who's on a kick lately about how dull Sweet Valley High has become. He thinks having two

*television stars in the junior class might
liven things up. Bruce is the only person I
know who's as arrogant as Brandon
Hunter, so I won't lose any sleep over dis-
appointing him.*

*By far the best thing that happened
today is that Sam and I decided we're more
in love than ever. There was a party for Liz
and me at our house when we got home
from the studio. I talked to him out by the
pool. . . .*

"I'm sorry," I said for the third time. "I went
overboard—"

"As usual!" Sam interrupted. But he was smiling, and he had an arm around me as we walked
along the edge of the swimming pool.

"It's just that I want to be a movie star so
badly I can taste it!" I said. "A soap opera just
doesn't make sense for now. The schedule is too
grueling. There's no way I can be an actress on
daytime television and still have time for school.
And you," I added with a grin. I pecked him on
the cheek.

"So you're holding off on your dreams of becoming an actress?" Sam asked, his forehead wrinkled up as if he didn't quite believe me.

"I don't know," I said honestly. "I'm definitely
holding off on anything that takes up my whole life
the way *The Young and the Beautiful* did."

"What if another opportunity came along?" he asked. "One that fit into your school schedule a little better?"

I shrugged. "Like, an acting job I could do during the summer?" I asked.

"Yeah, something like that. Would you take it, even if it meant less time for me?"

"It would depend on the opportunity," I answered, trying to be as honest as I could. "Sam, what if I did have a chance like that? Would you stand in my way?"

"I'd love to see you achieve your dreams. But right now, you aren't mature enough to handle Hollywood!"

"I handled it OK last week!" I insisted.

Sam sighed. "No, you didn't," he said. "Don't be mad at me. But I don't like the person you turn into when you're around all that money and all those fake people. It changes your whole personality!"

I opened my mouth to argue. But then I saw myself fawning all over Brandon while he endlessly described his hang-gliding trips in Tibet or his four-hundred-thousand-dollar Arabian stallion. I heard myself telling Sam I had more important things to do than "soothe the overinflated ego of a high-school boy." And I knew he was right. The girl who'd done and said those things just wasn't me.

"You're right," I admitted. "It *killed* my whole personality!"

Sam blinked, and I knew he was surprised to hear me agree with him. "Does this mean you really are going to put your dream on hold for now?" Sam asked.

I nodded sadly. "Yes," I said in a small voice. "I don't want to. But you're right. My priorities have been screwed up. I'll have plenty of time to become a famous actress after I finish high school."

"Does that mean what I think it means?" Sam asked, biting his lip.

"It means you're back to number one on my priority list!"

> And then, Diary, I grabbed him in the biggest, tightest, warmest hug I could manage. I was happy. I mean that. I really was happy that things were back to normal between us. I'm still happy. I love Sam more than I've ever loved anyone.
>
> But do I love him more than my own goals and dreams? I can't say that, Diary. I can't! Why should I have to choose? Elizabeth can have her writing and Todd, both. Amy dates Barry and still volunteers at the hot line. Of course, Enid has no life besides Hugh. But hey, she's Enid.
>
> The romance novels say true love is more important than anything. I used to believe that. Now I'm not so sure.
>
> And whether I'm mature enough to handle fame is beside the point.

I guess I made the right choice, for now. But I still keep coming back to one fact: If it weren't for Sam, I could already be on my way to becoming a big star.

Saturday afternoon
Something strange happened a little while ago, Diary. I was taking a long bike ride up the coast, toward Moon Beach. The weather was awesome, I was wearing spandex, and it was my first full day of freedom since Elizabeth's and my roles on the soap ended. All of a sudden, this incredibly gorgeous man in a vintage Mustang convertible pulled up beside me. . . .

I noticed the car first. That's unusual for me, when there's a good-looking guy within range of my radar. But I was pedaling my bike along the edge of the road, and suddenly there was this gleaming white hood of a Mustang alongside me. I turned to look at the driver, and I nearly fell off my bike. He was about twenty-five, with reddish brown hair. I couldn't tell how tall he was, but he was wearing a short-sleeved polo shirt. And I couldn't help noticing his broad, perfect shoulders and incredible biceps.

"Excuse me," he said, slowing the car.

I knew I should get away. Men who call to teenage girls from moving cars are the kinds of

Men Our Mothers Warn Us About. But this one was so darn good-looking.

"You're Jessica Wakefield, aren't you?" he asked.

I stopped the bike and stood straddling it. How did this man know my name? "Yes," I said tentatively. "And you are—"

He smiled. "Sorry," he said, reaching into his pocket and pulling out a business card. "I guess I look like a suspicious character, accosting a girl on the side of the road. I promise, I'm harmless! My name's Charles Sampson."

He handed me the business card, and I kept half an eye on him as I raised it. "Charles Sampson, film director," I read aloud. This man was more than a hunk with a classic car. He was a movie director!

"I saw you on *The Young and the Beautiful*, and I think you've got something special," he told me.

"What do you mean?"

"I want to make you famous," he said.

This was intriguing, in a girl-gets-discovered-at-the-drugstore way. But it was just too weird. I held the business card back out to him. "I, um, I don't think so."

"Please, don't answer me now," he said. "Keep the card and think about it. Call me if you want to learn more."

OK, Diary. I took the guy's card. There's no harm in that, is there? I'll never actually call him. Legitimate film directors don't stop cyclists in the street to cast them in movies. Do they? Besides, Sam wouldn't like it if I called this guy back. After what we've been through lately, I don't want to do anything that's going to wreck our relationship.

Here, Diary, it's yours. I'm tucking Charles Sampson's business card in between your pages, right here, as proof that I didn't imagine the whole scene. But here is where it's going to stay.

Part 2

Sunday, two weeks later

Dear Diary,

Sorry I haven't written in so long. I've been busy reacquainting myself with Sam. Sigh. . . . We're as much in love as ever. But Sam left yesterday for Colorado. He was chosen for a special program for high-school students interested in environmental science. He'll be gone for weeks!

I'm already bored stiff without Sam here. Especially since I have no money to spend on my favorite boyfriendless activity—shopping! But all the soap opera money went to pay for the Jeep. And my parents won't give me another advance on my allowance until I pay off the last one.

Saying good-bye to Sam was hard. . . .

I met Sam at Secca Lake for a picnic on Saturday. The weather was perfect, and the lake is one of our favorite romantic spots. But he was catching a plane to Colorado in a few hours, so I was totally bummed.

"Maybe I can stow away in your suitcase," I suggested, gesturing with a brownie.

Sam shook his head. "I'm bringing my duffel bags," he explained. "You'd never fit." He leaned forward and took a bite from the brownie I still held in my hand.

"I guess you're right," I agreed. "Besides, then I'd be stuck at a university program for nerds who like environmental science!" I grinned, but inside I was already lonely. I ate the rest of the brownie, but it didn't help.

"Nerds?" he asked, pretending to be offended.

"Cute nerds," I amended, ruffling his curly blond hair.

"Well, in that case," he began. He pulled me close to him and kissed me. His lips were soft and warm and tasted chocolaty, but mine probably did too. I kissed him back for a long, long time.

"It's a shame that we have to be apart for so long, after we finally got back together," he said after we'd caught our breath. "I'll miss you too, Jessica. I love you!" I gazed into his sexy eyes, and I was about to kiss him again. But he continued before I had the chance. "You know how much this program means to me," he said. "It might help me decide if I want to major in environmental science in college."

"I know," I said hopelessly. Sam was a senior and a year older than me, but college seemed like a long way off. Still, after my recent attempts to jump-start my own career, I was in no position to give him a hard time about it. "I want you to go, Sam," I lied. "I really do. And I hope you have a great time. It's just that I'll miss you so much!"

Sam smiled. "It's not as though you'll be pining away in your room alone the whole month," he said. "You've got more friends than Mr. Rogers! I'm sure you'll find something to do with yourself while I'm away. You always do."

I shrugged. "I guess so," I admitted. "But it won't be the same here without you."

"Just don't go out with any other guys while I'm gone," Sam said. "I don't want to see you and some Hollywood stud on the cover of any supermarket tabloids!" He spoke lightly, but then he bit his lip. I knew he couldn't quite get Brandon Hunter out of his mind.

I wrapped my arm around his shoulders. "You have nothing to worry about," I told him, tears in my eyes. "I'm in love with you, and nobody else. I promise I won't even *look* at another guy while you're away!"

Sam raised his eyebrows, and I knew exactly what he was thinking.

"OK, OK. I might *look!*" I amended. "But I won't mean it."

So Sam is gone, Diary. And I'm so bored that I'm actually contemplating doing some homework. What is the world coming to?

Monday night
I did it. I called Charles Sampson, that movie guy who gave me his card. I couldn't help myself, Diary. Things have been so dull around here! I had to do something to liven them up. Besides, I was curious. But I'm not getting involved in any show biz schemes. Really, I promise! I'm just going to meet him for coffee the day after tomorrow. That's all.

Wednesday evening
My hands are shaking. But that's because I drank about ten cups of coffee this afternoon. It's not because I met Charles Sampson today.
After cheerleading practice, I drove to L'Autre Chose, which is this totally chic coffee bar near Valley Mall. I told myself he wouldn't even show. But there was that awesome vintage Mustang parked out front, gleaming white. I parked my own

129

gleaming black Jeep. Then I sat at the wheel a minute longer, obsessing.

I was nervous. I mean, get a clue! What kind of man stops a teenage girl on her bike to say he wants to make her a star? I was ready for Charles Sampson to turn out to be a pervert. I figured I was safe, meeting him in a public place. If he was a weirdo, I could just leave. Or scream. If nothing else, I'd get a free snack at a fancy coffee bar. It's not like I could afford it myself, with my current state of broke-ness.

But deep down, I didn't think Charles was a weirdo. Maniacs don't drive classic Mustangs. And they don't have nicely printed business cards. Do they?

"Well," I said aloud to myself, "I'm never going to know unless I get out of the Jeep and go inside to meet the guy." So that, Dear Diary, is exactly what I did. . . .

"Thanks for coming, Jessica," Charles Sampson said as I slid into the booth across from him. "I know this must seem like a funny way to do business. But I want you to star in a movie I'm making."

"I've never gotten a job offer while riding my bike before," I admitted, my mind racing as my mouth stalled for time to think. "Most of the guys I meet on my bike rides are only trying to sell me stocks and bonds."

He laughed. "Sorry about that," he said. "I knew you lived in Sweet Valley, but I hadn't gotten an address for you yet. When I spotted you on your bike that day, I figured it was fate."

Is this guy for real? I thought. He wanted to make me a star, and he claimed our first meeting was fate. It was right out of a bad movie.

"I guess that sounds fishy," he said, noticing my skeptical expression. "But I really am a director, and I need a girl about your age or a little older for the lead role in my first independent film. When I saw you on *The Young and the Beautiful*, I knew you were perfect for the part."

I sipped my mocha latte. "You know, Charles, I've heard a lot of pickup lines. And this one's about as unoriginal as they get."

He bit his lip. "I know what it sounds like. But I'm telling you the truth. Maybe this will help. My younger sister's name is Grace Sampson. No doubt you've heard of her."

"The Grace Sampson who was in that blockbuster spy thriller last summer?" I asked. "I don't suppose you have any proof that she's your sister."

"Sort of," he said. "Look at me, Jessica."

I stared at him thoughtfully, and it took only a moment for it to dawn on me. The straight reddish-brown hair, the wide mouth, the dark brown eyes. . . . As much as I hated to admit it,

131

Charles looked just like a hunky male version of the up-and-coming actress.

"If Grace Sampson is your little sister, then that means Patrick Sampson is your father," I noted. "Patrick Sampson, the director."

Charles nodded. "Guilty as charged."

"OK, let's say you're telling the truth. Let's say you really are a director. And you really do need a girl to star in your film. Why me? There are lots of actresses with more experience."

"Frankly, I don't have the budget of one of my sister's mass market flicks," he said. "I can't afford Winona Ryder. Besides, I don't want her! I saw you on that soap opera, and I knew you were exactly right for this role."

"My twin sister was on the soap opera too," I pointed out. "We're so identical most people can't tell us apart. Why me and not her?"

He shook his head. "I wish I could explain it, but I can't. I went over and over the videotapes of your performances—and Elizabeth's. You're both promising actresses. But *you* are more than that, Jessica. You have a spark I don't see often. They used to call it 'star quality.'"

I was beginning to like this guy.

"Would this get you in trouble with your sister?" he asked. "Are you hesitating because you're afraid she'll resent it if I single you out this way? I could talk to her—"

"No, it isn't that," I assured him. "Elizabeth has

zero interest in acting. I had to drag her to the soundstage, kicking and screaming, to get her on that soap for a week."

"Then do it!" he urged. "This could be an incredible opportunity—your first film, and it's the lead! The script is beautifully written. I could be biased, but I think it's Oscar material."

"When do you start filming?" I asked, more tempted than I wanted to admit.

He shook his head. "I don't know yet. I'm still looking for financing. Does that mean you're interested?"

"No!" I said quickly. "I can't. I mean, I'm only in high school. I have too many other commitments. . . ." *And Sam would have a cow—even if he didn't know that Charles Sampson is the cutest guy ever to drive a Ford.*

"I won't take no for an answer," Charles cautioned. "At least not yet."

"Not yet?"

"My financing could take weeks or even months to come through," Charles explained. "Until it does, I'm in no hurry to cast this part. You've got my number. Please think about my offer, and call me if you want to know more."

Oh, Diary. Within a few weeks, I get not one but TWO big chances to become a famous actress. First, I turned down a permanent role on The Young *and the*

Beautiful. *Now, I've turned down the lead in a movie!*

I can't believe I told Charles no. But I did the right thing. My relationship with Sam is more important than a role in a possibly bogus movie, even by a director with a famous family. Along with everything else, Charles is just too cute. Working with him would be an awful temptation. I can resist anything, except temptation. I HAD to turn down the part.

I hope I did the right thing. Normally I'd ask Elizabeth what she thinks. But Charles said it could jeopardize his financing if word got around about his movie this soon. He asked me not to tell anyone.

Thursday afternoon

Dear Diary,

I need a major distraction until Sam gets back. So I'm joining Bruce Patman's new club! It'll also keep my mind off the fact that I just threw away another once-in-a-lifetime chance for stardom. I made up my mind today during a cafeteria argument with Bruce and his sexist-pig friends. . . .

Bruce and his friends stood near our lunch table, bragging about their new club. "I bet they play with G.I. Joes in Bruce's backyard," I scoffed, grabbing a french fry from Lila's tray.

"Bruce gets to be the general, and the other guys have to be grunts," Rosa Jameson said with a salute. "Yes, sir! No, sir! Yes, your mighty general-ship, sir!"

Bruce is even worse than Lila when it comes to wanting to order everybody around. He thinks he has a right to just because he's filthy rich. "So, Bruce," I said. "When are you going to let girls join?"

Amy backed me up. "No fair making it boys only. What about equal rights and all of that?"

"Girls just don't have what it takes," Bruce explained in his most condescending tone. "It's just a fact of nature."

"What exactly does it take?" I snapped back. "A big mouth?" Everyone except Bruce laughed. "Come on, Bruce! They even let women join the army, you know."

"I think Sam should hurry up and get back to Sweet Valley so he can keep Jessica in line," Bruce told his friends. This time, he was the one who got a laugh, but only from some of the guys.

I was so angry I couldn't speak for a minute. Luckily, Rosa did. "You are the biggest sexist pig in this school, Bruce Patman!" she accused. "No, scratch that. You're the biggest sexist pig in *California.*"

"I bet I can do whatever it is a person has to do to join your stupid club," I declared.

135

Then Bruce went too far. A big, nasty grin spread across his stupid, handsome face. "I know, you just want to spend more time with me to rekindle those old flames of passion."

It's true that Bruce is gorgeous. It's even true that I had a crush on him once, back when I was temporarily insane. But our thankfully short relationship wasn't exactly one-sided. I couldn't believe he had the nerve to bring it up now. My face was probably turning three shades of purple. It's a good thing it's my favorite color.

"Whoa!" Aaron Dallas called. "Stand back—she's gonna blow!"

As I swallowed my anger, Lila looked back and forth between Bruce and me. She was on my side, but I knew she enjoyed the fireworks. "You're not going to let him get away with that, are you, Jess?"

"Get away with what?" I answered in my sweetest voice. "I don't consider Bruce's lies or his dumb, sexist comments much of a threat. They're the mark of a small mind."

Ken Matthews howled with laughter and slapped Bruce on the back. Not nearly hard enough, in my opinion.

"Ouch!" Ken told him. "That one was a killer, Bruce. She got you good."

Bruce turned his back on my friends and me. "Anyway, as I was saying," he said to the rest of the boys, "it's a club only guys have the guts to handle."

This argument has been going on all week, Diary. Bruce and his dopey friends keep saying women aren't as brave as men, that we fold under pressure, and that a helpless little woman can't find her own elbow without the help of a big, strong man. Have you ever heard anything so completely ridiculous?

All I know about Club X is that being a member involves taking risks, probably the kinds of lame, macho things guys do to prove their manhood to each other. This morning, for instance, someone set off all the fire alarms at school. I have to admit, it was cool! Bruce and his gang aren't saying, but I know they were the ones behind it.

I'm not a feminist. I have no problem with being a sex symbol. If you've got it, flaunt it, right? But it burns me up when somebody like Bruce tells me I can't do something—especially when there's so much evidence staring him in the face that proves women can do the same things as men.

Look at astronauts like Sally Ride and Shannon Lucid. Look at scientists like Marie Curie and that woman who studied the gorillas. (She should've come here for her research—Bruce would be a perfect subject!) Look at athletes like Jackie Joyner-Kersey. Right here at Sweet Valley

High, we have Claire Middleton as second-string quarterback for our varsity football team. Even Ken, who's first-string, admits she's as good as he is. And Shelley Novak plays basketball as well as any boy.

I don't want you to think I'm a feminist like my twin. I believe women can be senators and surgeons, but I also think it's OK for us to be beauty queens and cheerleaders. I don't think that makes me a feminist . . . but maybe it does. Women should have the right to be whatever they want to be. Or at least I should have the right!

Anyhow, Diary, a bunch of the other girls backed me up through most of our discussions. But only until I wore Bruce down. He finally told me to come to my first Club X meeting, which is at his house tonight. I know he only invited me because he wants to prove that I can't do whatever he can. Ha! I intend to go to that meeting tonight and teach him a lesson he'll never forget. Lila and Amy are coming too. We'll show him!

I am strong. I am invincible. I am woman!

Very, very late Thursday
Did I mention that I'm strong and invincible? Jessica Wakefield Rules! Life

around here is going to be exciting for the next few weeks. Tonight was awesome! It was radical! It was exhilarating!

I'm sworn to secrecy about what went on at the Club X meeting. But you're different, Diary. You're the only one who can hear the whole scoop. . . .

I wasn't surprised when Lila and Amy chickened out at the last minute and didn't come to the meeting Thursday night. Like Bruce, they're all talk. They're happy to spout off their opinions, but when it comes to putting themselves and their reputations on the line, they bail. That was OK. I did fine all by myself.

When I arrived at the Patman mansion, the other Club X members—Ronnie Edwards and Tad Johnson—were already there. Bruce explained the rules. We weren't allowed to tell anyone what Club X does. Membership was for life; nobody could quit Club X. We were all supposed to watch for ways to stir things up—like setting off the school fire alarms that morning.

Then there was The Wheel. Bruce had this roulette wheel with all our names on it. We'd spin the wheel, and the person it stopped on had to perform a dare that the other members named. If one of us chickened out or failed at our task, we'd have our name added to another space on the wheel. So there'd be a better chance of getting picked the next time.

Bruce let me spin the wheel first. And wouldn't you know it? It stopped on my name.

I was a little worried, but I acted cool, like I couldn't wait for the fun to begin. Ronnie and Tad seemed impressed by my attitude, but Bruce looked disappointed, like he wanted me to freak. He turned his chair around and straddled it before he explained my dare.

It's not fair! I thought. *Why does somebody so good-looking have to be such a rat?*

"What you have to do is relatively simple," His Lordship told me. "Just drive down to the bottom of the hill. It's about a mile."

I knew that sounded too easy to be true, given the source. "What's the catch?"

"Without headlights," Ronnie said, his eyes gleaming with anticipation. "It should be pretty dark by now."

In my head I saw the disapproving face of my conscience, Elizabeth. She'd have had a hyperconniption fit if she knew what I was about to do. Even Sam, who raced dirt bikes, would never take a risk like this, just to prove himself to some arrogant jerk. Both their voices yelled *"Don't do it!"* in my head. It was a steep, twisting road; it would be dangerous driving it blind. And there was the risk of scratching or denting my brand new baby Jeep.

At the same time, I felt this incredible rush of adrenaline, almost like I get when Sam and I are necking at Miller's Point.

That was it. I was hooked.

*I did it, Diary! I drove all the way
down that hill. At first, my heart was beating so loudly I could hardly hear the hum
of the engine. A cat jumped out in front of
me toward the bottom of the hill, but I
braked around it, and it scurried into the
bushes.*

I pulled onto the gravel shoulder at the bottom
of the hill. A pair of headlights flared on, illuminat-
ing the rest of a familiar black Porsche with the li-
cense plate 1BRUCE1. I smiled victoriously as
Bruce jumped out of his car.

"You did it, Wakefield," he said. His voice was
controlled, and I couldn't read his expression in
the glare of the Porsche's lights.

"Surprised?" I asked as Ronnie's Camaro and
Tad's VW Rabbit pulled up behind me. They had
been stationed along my route to make sure I
wasn't cheating.

"You never surprise me, Jessica," Bruce said
with a grim laugh.

Ronnie and Tad were more enthusiastic. "Way
to go, Jessica!" Ronnie exclaimed. Tad gave me a
high five.

Bruce pulled something out of his car and
handed it to me. "Welcome to Club X," he said.

It was a black leather jacket with a big, white X
embroidered on the back, the same as the three of
them were wearing. I was official.

I'm still on an adrenaline high! I can't wait for my next dare. Even more interesting is the thought of Bruce's next dare. I proved to him tonight that I can rise to the challenge. Let's see if he can! We meet again tomorrow night.

Tuesday night
Club X is a blast. Friday night, we climbed a fence to get to a public swimming pool that was closed and totally dark. Ronnie's dare was to dive off the high diving board, even though it was so dark you couldn't see the water. But Bruce started in on me, claiming I didn't have the guts to do it. So I followed Ronnie up the ladder to the diving board, and I dove right into that dark pool.

I was ecstatic! Bruce was furious.

So is Elizabeth. I've told her a little about the dares we've taken (I know, it's supposed to be a secret, but she's my twin sister, so it's practically like telling myself). She keeps begging me to quit the club. She's such a baby.

This weekend she asked me not to do anything she wouldn't do. Ha! I told her I almost always do things she wouldn't do. And she always does things I wouldn't be caught dead doing. Lately she's into this geeky project that Chrome Dome Cooper, the principal, recruited her for. Elizabeth, Todd, Enid, and a few other nerds are acting as guides for a delegation of teachers from foreign countries. Doesn't she see enough teachers during her classes?

Club X is much more interesting. Ronnie glued a bunch of kids' lockers shut. Tad shut off the electricity in S.V.H. I even smoked a cigarette in Chrome Dome's office this morning! To be honest, it was disgusting. I was seriously considering quitting Bruce's silly little club, despite his rule about it being a lifetime membership. Still, not getting caught was a thrill.

Teachers are staring suspiciously every time they see a kid in a Club X jacket. Soon, they'll see more. Michael Harris, Charlie Cashman, and Jim Sturbridge are thinking of joining.

My name came up on the wheel tonight, again. I'm beginning to suspect that Bruce is rigging it against me. I was horrified when I heard my dare: He said I had to steal a car and drive it to the Dairi Burger. This was different from breaking into a swimming pool. We're talking Grand Theft, Auto! People go to prison for that.

So I showed Bruce. I hot-wired his Porsche! Man, was he mad!

Oh, Diary! My hands are shaking so hard I can barely write. I completed another Club X dare. How could I let Bruce talk me into something so dangerous? How could I be so stupid? I nearly got killed. . . .

I felt queasy as I walked slowly toward the train trestle at the edge of town. A diving board is one thing, but I've always had a problem with real heights. Walking across a trestle bridge under any circumstances wouldn't be my idea of fun. But with the extra risk of a possible freight train roaring along at any minute, well, I was terrified.

The ground dropped steeply into a gorge with a trickle of stream at the bottom. The train tracks ran to the edge of the ravine, and then shot out across a hundred-foot-long metal-and-wood bridge, only exactly as wide as the train tracks.

"Yo, Jessica!" called Ronnie. I looked down the tracks. There was the rest of Club X, waiting for me on the far side of the bridge.

I nodded to the guys, trying to look nonchalant. Then I took a deep breath and stepped onto the tracks. A hot, oily smell rose from the gravel beneath the rails.

"Come on!" Bruce yelled, his voice faint on the wind. He had sworn to me that there were no trains scheduled. But what if he'd lied? Or what if there was an unscheduled run?

"What am I doing here?" I muttered to myself as I took slow, careful steps from tie to tie. A hot draft blew up from below. "Am I completely crazy?"

"Are you coming?" Bruce yelled.

I looked across at his smug face, and I knew I couldn't back down. "Yes, I am completely crazy," I whispered.

I nearly had a heart attack when a loud cry screeched out from beneath me. It was only a bird. A crow had flown beneath the bridge. I took a deep breath and continued, walking a little faster now. I was already halfway across. I could do this.

Then the rails began to hum. My heart thudded to my stomach. The bridge began to vibrate. A train was coming!

Without looking back, I began to hurry, my eyes riveted on a pine tree at the far end.

"Jessica!" Michael shouted. "Hurry up!"

"A train's coming!" Ronnie yelled.

No *duh*. The bridge was shaking harder. I was twenty feet from the end. Then my foot slipped and I lunged forward. I fell on one knee, and I found myself staring down the rails at Bruce's face. It was ashen.

"Get up!" Jim yelled. "Get up!"

The train trestle lurched. The train was on the bridge. I pulled myself up and ran, leaping three ties at a time. My heart was hammering louder than the train whistle. The boys' mouths were moving in their terrified faces, but I couldn't hear what they were screaming. For a few seconds, I knew with certainty that I was going to die.

Then the bank of the ravine swooped up to meet me. I threw myself to the ground, five feet below, as the train clattered by.

The guys in the club—except Bruce— now think I'm Wonder Woman. What I really am is insane. I've made a decision, Diary. I'm quitting Club X. But first, I'm getting even with Bruce.

Friday night
Goodbye, Club X. I'm finally through with Bruce and his macho club. I guess I taught him a lesson. But in the process, I got myself grounded.

Bruce did rig the roulette wheel against me! I found the magnet he'd slipped under my name, and I secretly moved it to his name. So he got the last dare: He had to ruin yesterday's assembly for the foreign teachers by playing loud rock music over the P.A. system.

I tried to stop the prank when I learned Elizabeth, not Mr. Cooper, would be speaking onstage. I didn't want my sister to be embarrassed in front of the whole school! But Mr. Collins saw me trying to leave the

146

assembly early and assumed I was creating trouble instead of stopping it. So Bruce played his music, Elizabeth was humiliated, and all of Club X got after-school detention for two weeks.

Even worse, Mom and Dad grounded me for a week. I can't go out at all except to school. Cheerleading is history. I can't even use the telephone! Bummer. At least Sam came home tonight. I begged Elizabeth to pretend to be me, so I could meet him long enough to tell him why I wouldn't be able to see him all week. . . .

Just before eight o'clock on Friday night, I arrived at the Dairi Burger, dressed like Elizabeth.

"Sam!" I called, spotting him in the back.

For an instant, he looked confused. "Jess—Liz?"

I looked up into his adorable face, and I could hardly keep from kissing him right there in front of everyone. I hadn't realized how much I'd missed him. But I was supposed to be Elizabeth. "Come outside," I said loudly. "I have a message for you from Jessica."

My heart was pounding as I turned to face him in the darkest part of the parking lot. And a thrill ran through my entire body—a much more enticing thrill than anything I'd felt while performing dares with Club X. I had to admit to myself that part of that thrill was from impersonating my sister so well that nobody but Sam knew it was me. But most of it was from being close enough to feel the heat from his body.

"So what's the message from Jessica?" Sam asked softly, leaning close to me.

"This!" I announced, just before flinging my arms around him and kissing him on the lips. His arms wrapped around me, and he held me tight.

> When Sam and I kissed, I remembered how much I love him. There isn't a better, cuter, more exciting guy in the whole world!
>
> As I drove home afterward, I got to thinking how easy it was to convince a room full of people—and even my parents—that I was Elizabeth. Gosh, Diary, I am a good actress! Club X distracted me for a few weeks, but now I can't help thinking about Charles Sampson's movie. I wish I could be in it!

> Monday evening, weeks later
> Ooops. It's been ages since I've written. Sorry. I guess I was busy. Sam and I have spent tons of time together. The Dairi Burger, the lake, the Beach Disco. . . . I've even gone to an occasional dirt-bike race, though I still think it's a rough, filthy sport.

*Why couldn't Sam be into tennis or rac-
quetball or in-line skating?*

*Elizabeth is freaking out about a story
she's working on for* The Oracle. *Actually,
the original idea came from me, as so many
wonderful ideas do. . . .*

Amy had told me about a caller at the Project
Youth hot line who said a teacher sexually harassed
her. Amy wasn't allowed to talk about hot line calls,
but she was so upset about this one that she had to
tell me. She kept all the details secret, except for
the fact that the girl went to a different school, not
ours. I felt awful for this poor girl! So I told
Elizabeth. And my journalist sister decided it was a
good topic for an article in *The Oracle*.

We hadn't had any incidents reported at Sweet
Valley High. Well, a few months earlier, Suzanne
Devlin had accused Mr. Collins of making a pass at
her. He came close to losing everything—not only
his job, but even custody of his little boy. Luckily, it
finally came out that Suzanne made up the whole
story. What a brat!

Anyhow, Elizabeth's article wouldn't have anything to do with the Suzanne Devlin incident. She
wanted to write about what sexual harassment is,
how to recognize it, and what to do about it. She
had the story all planned out, and she was hot on
the research trail.

But at lunchtime on Monday, it was clear that

something had happened with her beloved article. I don't think I'd ever seen my sister as angry as she was in the school cafeteria that day! For a change, it wasn't me who she was mad at.

Lila and I sat in the lunchroom, watching with idle curiosity while Denise Hadley and the supposed love of her life, Jay McGuire, had an enormous argument on the other side of the room. I had no idea what it was about, but I always like to keep tabs on who's dating whom. Of course, I loved Sam. But you never know when you might need a good-looking date to something or other.

Suddenly I noticed that Penny Ayala and my sister, at the table right next to mine, were talking in low voices, with their heads close together. I smelled a secret. So I scooted my chair over and leaned my chin on my elbow. "Is this a private conversation?"

Lila rolled her eyes at the thought that two workaholics like Elizabeth and Penny, who's editor in chief of *The Oracle,* could have anything interesting to hide. *Yeah, right.* "They're plotting your overthrow as Miss Teen Sweet Valley," Lila warned. "Look out!"

We pressured them for a few more minutes. They might not have spilled the garbanzos, except that Enid got into the game. She was sitting on the other side of Elizabeth and Penny, with Todd, Maria Santelli, and Winston Egbert.

"OK, now we're all curious," Enid prodded.

"What are you two getting so worked up about?

"Probably something like whether or not to change the typeface in the newspaper," Lila speculated through a yawn.

Finally, Elizabeth and Penny told us the scoop. As I'd suspected, it was about Elizabeth's story on sexual harassment of students by teachers. Mr. Collins had been wary about the article because of what had happened to him. But he'd agreed that she could go ahead with it. Then Mr. Cooper found out. And he nixed the story completely. *Do not pass Go. Do not collect two hundred dollars.* He said *The Oracle* absolutely couldn't run the article. He wouldn't allow it. He called it inflammatory, and he worried that it would upset parents.

"Newspapers aren't about making people feel good!" Penny declared, sounding just like Elizabeth when she gets on her First Amendment soapbox. "Newspapers are about information that's important. The question right now isn't whether or not Liz has a good idea for a story, though she does. The question is, will we be told what we can and cannot print in our own paper?"

"Hey, that's right!" I agreed. I admit that I don't have strong feelings about freedom of the press. But I do have strong feelings about being told what I can and cannot do. So I knew exactly why Elizabeth and Penny were so ticked. "Either it's a student newspaper or it isn't a student newspaper. Chrome Dome is telling you to shut up, and if there's one thing I can't stand, it's being told to shut up!"

We all discussed it for a few minutes, and finally, I suggested the only logical course of action. "Look," I said. "There's a simple solution to this mess."

"What?" asked Elizabeth.

I shrugged. "Just go ahead with the story."

For one thing, Chrome Dome shouldn't have the right to tell students what we can print in our newspaper. But there was another principle at stake here: the excitement factor. School has been deadly dull since Chrome Dome disbanded Club X and outlawed our jackets at school.

There's nothing like a little controversy to liven things up!

Friday night
I've done it again. Another of my brilliant ideas is about to be put into action! It all goes back to my last entry, about helping my sister stand by her moral principles.

I just love going against authority! And this time I have my parents' approval. Luckily, they were into the whole radical, civil-disobedience scene in college. Mom, especially, even did love beads, tie-dye and

fringes, and sit-ins! So I don't have to
worry about being grounded again. . . .

Elizabeth finished her story, and it sounded
great. She called it "When We Are Afraid to
Speak." In it, she told me, she compared censor-
ship of articles on topics like harassment to the
pressure society puts on women and girls to "shut
up and put up" with horny guys taking advantage. I
hadn't read it yet, but I was proud of her for going
out on a limb.

Unfortunately, Mr. Cooper intercepted a copy
of *The Oracle* before it was printed, and he was
outraged that they'd ignored his orders. Again, he
refused to let Elizabeth and Penny run the story.

Elizabeth was totally bummed at dinner Friday
evening. I was just sitting there at the table, eating
salad and thinking about my cheers for that night's
basketball game at Big Mesa. And suddenly I
thought up yet another in my recent series of
beautiful, wonderful, genius-level ideas.

"If he starts censoring us now, who's to say he
won't do it again?" Elizabeth protested, telling our
parents about Mr. Cooper's decision. "That's no
way to run a newspaper!"

I speared a tomato with my fork. "Then put out
your own newspaper," I suggested.

It took a minute for that to sink in with
Elizabeth. But gradually it seemed to work its way
into her brain. "I could do that," she said finally,

her forehead wrinkling up in an unattractive, brainiac way. "I could get the story out another way."

"I think it's a totally cool idea!" I said. "A revolutionary, counterculture, underground kind of thing. It's hot."

My mother laughed. "First it's cool, then it's hot," she said. I guess my parents are OK, but they are *so* twenty years ago.

Elizabeth still wasn't sure she wanted to do anything so drastic.

"Mr. Cooper won't appreciate your going behind his back," Dad pointed out, about as welcome as a wet blanket.

They jabbered about it some more, and Elizabeth almost convinced herself to wait until the next school board meeting and bring up the issue there. My hopes for some lively chaos and controversy were dimming by the second.

"No way!" I cried. "Strike while the iron's hot. That's what I always say."

It was exactly the right thing to tell my twin. A minute later, Elizabeth was resolved to go ahead with her—*my*—plan. I offered to help her photocopy the article on Dad's machine at work, and to pass out copies at school.

"And I'll even come visit you in prison!" I promised with a grin. "I'll bake a cake and hide a file in it, OK? Then you can bust out and run away to South America."

Elizabeth laughed. "You'll do anything if there's some kind of risk or danger involved!"

"Oh, sure. You know me," I said lightly. "Show me a bridge and a bungee cord. . . ."

". . . or a bridge and a speeding train," I thought wryly to myself, remembering Bruce's ashen face at the end of the railroad trellis.

Anyhow, Diary, we start the revolution tomorrow. By Monday, everyone at school will be talking about our underground newspaper! This is almost as exciting as starring in a movie, don't you think? Well, almost. . . .

Monday afternoon
There's good news and bad news. The good news is that Elizabeth's article made a huge splash at school. Everyone, and I mean everyone, is talking about it. The bad news is that Elizabeth is getting all the credit!

We all gathered at the Dairi Burger after school, and people were psyched about Elizabeth's article.

Even Lila had nice things to say. And her idea of freedom of the press is that newspaper owners should be free to charge high subscription prices.

"This is an awesome article, Liz," Lila said, holding out a copy of our underground paper. "Of course, *I* know how to handle myself in any situation. But most girls are clueless about stuff like this."

"Unfortunately, it happens a lot more often than anyone likes to admit," Amy said in her Project Youth tone of voice. "So many girls have been socialized to have low self-esteem, which prevents them from telling anyone—"

John Pfeiffer shook his head. "Don't overstate the problem, Amy," he said. "I mean, it's not like there are girls being harassed at school every day—"

"But John, you helped me distribute the article," Elizabeth said, perplexed. "Don't you agree with what I've said in it?" John, the sports editor, along with some of the other *Oracle* staff members, had helped Elizabeth and me pass out copies that morning.

"Of course I agree," John said quickly. "Any girl who is harassed needs help and understanding. Now she'll know how to get it, thanks to you, Elizabeth."

Thanks to Elizabeth? I thought. *All she did was write the article. What about the person responsible for getting it out to everyone?*

I figured my usually loyal and modest sister would speak out and tell everyone whose idea the underground paper had been. But Enid started praising her for her "bold, courageous move," if you can believe a sixteen-year-old saying something so drippy. And Elizabeth just sat there, basking in it.

"Actually, guys," I began, "the whole idea was—"

"I heard you got called down to Cooper's office," Maria Santelli said to Elizabeth and Penny.

Rosa whistled. "I bet old Chrome Dome wasn't a happy camper."

"To tell you the truth," Winston said, draping one arm around Maria's shoulders while the other raised a milkshake in salute, "we were expecting to go in afterward to recover your bullet-riddled bodies after the firing squad finished with you."

Elizabeth laughed. "That thought crossed my mind too."

"At first, Mr. Cooper was so mad I thought he'd blow a gasket!" Penny said. "But we talked about things for a few minutes. And once he understood how important this was to us, he calmed down."

"By the time we left his office, he was raving about our 'willingness to take the heat for our convictions,'" Elizabeth said.

Great, I thought. Nobody had praised *my* willingness to be a revolutionary. If it had been *me* in Mr. Cooper's office, he'd have convened Winston's firing squad, for sure. He always thought Elizabeth and Penny could do no wrong. I was thoroughly sick of everyone paying so much attention to Elizabeth. After all, none of this would have

157

happened if I hadn't come up with the idea in the first place!

I found myself thinking about Charles Sampson. I wondered if he'd found another girl to play the lead in his movie. I suddenly realized I had a sure way of grabbing my share of the spotlight from Elizabeth at the Dairi Burger that night. All I had to do was casually mention that I'd been asked to star in an independent film. But I'd promised Charles I'd keep quiet about it. Besides, I reminded myself, I wasn't going to be in his film.

Sam must have realized I was feeling dissed. He squeezed my hand, smiled sympathetically, and pecked me on the cheek. I looked at his curly hair and cute face, and I remembered why I'd turned down Charles's offer.

But I still hated to see everyone treating me like the Invisible Twin.

> *By the time I left the Dairi Burger tonight—early—I was bummed to the max, Diary. I'm so sick of people praising my perfect twin. I helped her with this. A lot! But does anyone remember that? Oh no. They conveniently forget that Elizabeth had to be given a little push before she made her "bold, courageous move."*
>
> *I'm sick of everyone saying how successful and accomplished Elizabeth is. What am I? Chopped liver?*

Tuesday afternoon

Finally, Diary, a juicy piece of gossip hits Sweet Valley High! Just when you think everyone's stuck in a boring rut, something scandalous happens! I just love that about life.

My first inkling that something was up came last night, when Lila called to tell me what had happened at the Dairi Burger after I'd left. She said Denise Hadley and Jay McGuire came in together, hanging all over each other! Remember, Diary, I mentioned not long ago that they'd broken up in the school cafeteria recently? Well, they're back together. But it's more complicated than that!

Denise was best friends with Ginny Belasca, who worked at the hot line with Amy. Denise and Ginny are an unlikely duo, if you ask me. Denise is gorgeous, with long, red hair, big brown eyes, and a knock-out figure. She's outgoing, poised, and elegant. Ginny, on the other hand, is a shy little mouse with dull brown hair, average looks, and a boring wardrobe.

Ginny got some hot-line calls from a guy named Mike Perrine, who had a problem with his mother's new fiancé. Ginny's advice must have actually helped him. And they practically fell in love over the phone! They planned to meet, though it's against Project Youth's rules. But Ginny chickened out and sent Denise, so Mike wouldn't be disappointed when he saw she wasn't gorgeous.

Denise liked Mike a lot. She even broke up with Jay over him. But Mike thought the girl he knew as Ginny was more in tune with him over the phone line than she was in person. To make matters worse, Ginny went along with Denise one day to meet Mike and satisfy her curiosity. Except she had to pretend she was Denise, of course, since Denise was already pretending to be Ginny. And the real Ginny realized she liked Mike even more in person than she had on the phone.

It's all rather messy, Diary. But in the end, Denise told Mike the truth. She and Jay got back together. And the newest couple in town is Ginny Belasca and Mike Perrine!

Pretty wild! It reminds me of the time I met a guy over a teen "gab" line and arranged to meet him, only he was afraid he wasn't cute enough and sent his gorgeous-but-dumb friend instead. In the end, they both ended up going gaga over Amy Sutton. I know, there's no accounting for taste. But since then, I have to see the merchandise before I'll make a purchase. Ha! Or even a rental.

Don't get me wrong, Diary. Sam is

*still the man for me. What a babe!
Unfortunately, we've got a date tonight
and I don't have anything at all to wear.
Lila wanted me to go shopping with her,
but I'm broke like you wouldn't believe.
And my folks laugh in my face every
time I hint about another tiny little advance on my allowance. I guess I'll have
to borrow an outfit from Elizabeth's
room. What she doesn't know won't hurt
her!*

*As for the Ginny story, who'd have
thunk it? Why would any guy prefer dull,
mousy Ginny to beautiful, flashy Denise?
The world is filled with mystery!*

Wednesday night
*You know, Ginny is lucky in a way. I
mean, she knows Mike loves her for herself—not for her looks, since she doesn't
have any to speak of. Sometimes I wonder
if Sam would date me if I wasn't beautiful.
I mean, he always tells me how pretty I
am. He never compliments me on my intel-
ligence, my sense of humor, or any of my
other excellent qualities. I wonder if he
even notices them.*

*We're going to the Beach Disco Friday
night. Maybe I'll try to talk to him about it
afterward.*

Friday night
I'm so mad I feel like sneaking into Sam's garage and taking apart his precious, greasy little bike, piece by piece. Sometimes I wonder why I put up with him and his disgusting hobby!

I was all dressed up in a sexy black jumpsuit I bummed off of Amy, with a shiny silver belt Elizabeth let me borrow. Actually, she didn't exactly *let* me. But she would have if she'd been around when I needed it. And that's almost the same thing.

Nobody else but Prince Albert was home when Sam rang the doorbell. So I had to violate my usual make-'em-wait rule and rush to answer it myself. I skipped downstairs in my to-die-for borrowed outfit, slipping huge rhinestone earrings through my ears as I tried not to trip over the dog. I stood for a moment behind the door, patting my hair to make sure it was tousled in exactly the right way to look spontaneous and sexy at the same time. The doorbell rang again, and I could feel Sam's impatience through the door.

"OK, I murmured to myself, "if he's that anxious to see me—"

I pulled open the door, draping myself artfully along the edge of it, to give him the full effect of my tight black jumpsuit. "Hi, Sam!" I began in a husky voice. "I'm almost ready—"

I stopped in mid-sentence. He was standing there on my front step, impatiently shifting his weight from one foot to the other. And he was dressed in ripped, grease-stained jeans and a racing shirt.

"Sam!" I protested when I'd halfway recovered my voice.

He scanned me up and down and whistled. "You look great, but I've got to cancel tonight," he said, glancing at his watch. "I'm sorry, Jess, but this is an opportunity I can't pass up!"

I crossed my arms. "Better than an opportunity to go dancing with me?"

"Of course not!" he said too quickly. "But we'll do it next week, I promise. It's just that Minks Janks is in town!"

"Unless Minks is a famous mink-coat dealer, I don't see the attraction," I told him.

Sam rolled his eyes. "Minks Janks is only one of the best dirt-bike racers in the entire country!"

"Of course. How silly of me to forget," I said. "Minks just won the Nobel Prize for Bike Racing, right?"

"Don't be mad, Jessica!" he said. "I want to run over to the track and get some pointers from a real pro. I swear I'll make it up to you!"

"Let me get this straight," I said, not believing my ears. "You're standing me up so you can have fun getting greasy with some big, hairy guy whose name sounds like a weasel?"

Sam laughed. "Minks isn't a big, hairy guy. She's a thin, pretty girl."

This did not make me any happier. "Tell me you're joking!"

"No, I'm not. But it's not like that, Jessica! It's—"

I slammed the door in his face.

That's it, Diary! I'm tired of worrying about Sam's needs and Sam's wants all the time. He's allowed to go tripping off to Colorado for weeks to look into a career in environmental science. But he freaks out when I spend one week as a TV star. He can break a date with me to go see this biker chick. But I'm toast if I go to a party with a famous actor, even if he did turn out to be a creep.

It's not fair, Diary! And I'm not playing along with it any longer. From now on, I'm going to start looking out for Number One.

Saturday afternoon

I did it. I called that cute movie director, Charles Sampson. We're having breakfast together tomorrow. And if Sam doesn't shape up, Charles and I may discuss more than business!

Sunday, the crack of dawn

I feel horrendous. I haven't slept all night. Sam came over last night with a dozen roses and a huge apology. He said the whole time Minks was giving him and the rest of the guys tips on racing, all he could think about was my sad face when he broke our date. Naturally, I forgave him. And we had a great time making up.

There's just one problem. I still have plans to meet Charles today. And I accidentally on purpose forgot to mention those plans to Sam.

Sunday evening

Dear Diary,

I'm sooo confused! My meeting with Charles blew my mind!

Café Mirabeau is up the coast, at least thirty miles out of town. So I figured it was a safe place to meet Charles for brunch without anyone from school seeing us. Besides, it's one of the ritziest places around. If there's one thing I've learned from Lila, it's to always go first-class—if someone else is paying.

"I've raised more than half the money I need for the film," Charles told me after we'd ordered. "I'm looking for a partner to help me get the rest."

"Do you think you'll get it?" I asked. But in all honesty, it was hard to concentrate on financing when I wanted to sink into his deep brown eyes and run my fingers through his thick, straight hair.

165

"I think I will," he said. "I try not to rely on my family connections. But I can't change the fact that people are more open to my ideas when they hear who my father and sister are."

"I know what you mean," I said, rolling my eyes. "My sister is famous around town for being Ms. Perfect. I can talk until I'm blue in the face about some great idea I've had. But nobody pays the least bit of attention until they know that Elizabeth's involved too."

"Even without the Sampson name, I really believe this film, *Checkered Houses*, would fly," Charles continued. "The script is intelligent, thought-provoking, and utterly real! The critics will love it! But I'm convinced it has commercial appeal, as well."

"When can I read it?"

"It's going through a rewrite at the moment, but I'll bring you a copy next time we meet. You'll love it, Jessica. I promise!"

"So who do I play?" I asked. "I mean, if I were to decide to go ahead with the film."

"The character's name is Blythe Carson. She's a girl on the brink of womanhood, wholesome, but sexy—"

At the word *sexy*, an alarm started jangling in my head. "Wait a minute," I cried. "Time out! This isn't one of those porno things, is it?"

Charles laughed. "Definitely not!" he assured me. "This is a serious role, the kind of challenging,

166

interesting part that young actresses don't often get to play. Blythe is torn between a conventional suburban existence and a life of urban adventure and excitement."

I nodded. "Hmmm. I can relate to that."

"I can see you in this role, Jessica. You're the only actress I want!"

I imagined myself at the Academy Awards ceremony, accepting my first Oscar. I would wear a long, black dress, very bare on top, with silver spangles all over it, and my hair swept up in a dramatic arc.

"Miss?" a voice asked. I blinked. A waitress was trying to set a plate of French toast in front of me. I shifted my position to give her space.

"So what happens to Blythe?" I asked after the waitress had gone.

"She finds love with an older man," Charles continued. "But he's dishonest, and Blythe gets herself involved in some things she can't handle. Kind of a modern-day Bonnie and Clyde situation. In the end, she realizes the glamor of the fast life is a facade."

"So she ends up in jail?" I asked, not sure if I liked that.

"No, not at all," Charles said quickly. "She's disillusioned, but she learns to move on and create a new life for herself. I'm sorry, Jessica. I can't do justice to the story this way. It all sounds so cliché, until you read the script and it comes alive!"

If nothing else, I could see that Charles Sampson was committed to this screenplay, heart and soul. "No, I think you're describing it well," I said. "The part sounds, uh, like something I could consider."

I kept my voice low-key, but I was desperate to play Blythe Carson. I wanted to be in this film more than anything in the world.

"Of course, I wouldn't expect a commitment until you've read the script," Charles assured me.

"Of course," I agreed. In truth, it hadn't occurred to me that reading the script was important. But I saw right away that it made sense. Then I remembered that even a Pulitzer-quality script might as well line a birdcage if Charles couldn't find the money to film it. "What about the financing? Is there anything I can do to help you get it?"

That last question was out of my mouth before I'd even thought about it. I mean, seriously, what could a high-school student do to help raise the thousands of dollars it takes to make a movie? I couldn't even raise enough to buy the new CD player I'd been coveting. And my entire personal fortune amounted to exactly seventeen dollars—less, if you counted the money I owed my parents and Elizabeth.

"As a matter of fact, there is a way you can help," Charles said. "Once I have this new version of the script finished, I might want you to join me in pitching it to some venture capitalists. It's helpful if I can show them a whole 'package'—director, script, and star."

"Some star!" I said. "I know I'd be great in this role, Charles, but I'm not exactly a household name."

"If I'd wanted a household name, I'd have asked my younger sister." Charles shrugged. "And I suppose she could play the role. But Grace isn't who I imagine when I visualize Blythe Carson. *You* are."

He was staring at me intently from under that long, sexy, red-brown hair. And then he reached across the table and placed his hand on mine. "I need you, Jessica."

I nodded slowly, mesmerized by the electric currents traveling from his hand to mine. "I'll help however I can."

Wow, Diary. Even if this guy wasn't gorgeous, with great shoulders and dark, intense eyes, I'd be blown away by his sales pitch. HE WANTS ME TO STAR IN A MOVIE! Is this really happening? My feet weren't even touching the pavement as I walked across the parking lot to the Jeep after brunch.

All the way home, I could think of nothing but Blythe Carson. An innocent, suburban girl seduced by the lure of the city. Alone at the end, disillusioned but wiser. I can play Blythe! I know I can do this role better than anybody!

Then I got home and walked into my room. And there was Sam's dozen roses from last night. Sam. Aw, Diary. What am I supposed to do about Sam? The last time I got an acting job, we nearly broke up. What am I going to do? I don't want to blow my big chance. But I have to tell Sam the truth. Don't I?

Wednesday night, late
Sam and I had a moonlight picnic at Secca Lake tonight. It was totally romantic! But then I broached the subject of Charles's movie—well, sort of. That part of the evening didn't go exactly as I'd hoped. . . .

I unwrapped dessert—oatmeal chocolate-chip cookies that Elizabeth had made that evening. OK, they were probably meant for Todd or Enid or some other boring person. But I didn't think anyone would notice if I swiped a few. I handed one to Sam and gave him time to notice how great they were.

"I made these myself," I announced. I figured it couldn't hurt to have him thinking of me as The Perfect Girlfriend before I popped the question I was already carefully phrasing in my head.

By the light of a few candles we'd scattered

around the picnic blanket, I watched Sam's eyes widen. After all, he'd already taken several bites of the cookie, and he wasn't even dead yet. What's more, it was good! Sam was well aware of my reputation as a disaster in the kitchen. The whole town knew about the time I poisoned my entire family with a seafood dish.

"These are delicious," he said through a mouthful of cookie. He swallowed. "Your culinary skills are improving."

"Thanks, Sam," I said, pecking him on the cheek. "You know, I wanted to talk to you about some of my other skills."

His eyebrows rose suggestively, and he slipped a hand around my waist. "That's one of my very favorite subjects," he murmured, just before he leaned in to caress my lips with his. "I always thought you were extremely skillful," he added when he came up for air.

I ran my hand down his arm, strong and warm beneath the cotton of his long-sleeve T-shirt. "That was nice, but it wasn't what I meant."

"Oh? Then what did you mean?" he asked, kissing me on the neck. "Cheerleading skills? Shopping skills?"

I swallowed my annoyance at being seen, once again, as a brainless clothes horse. And I pulled away from his kisses, though they were melting me into jelly. They were too distracting. "I was talking about my acting skills."

"I see!" Sam replied. "Let's try them out right now. You act like you can't keep your hands off me, and I'll—"

"Sam, this is serious!" I protested weakly.

"OK, Jess. What's up?" I had his attention now, but one of his hands was still running up and down my spine, sending shivers throughout my body.

"I keep thinking about the talks we had after my career as a soap star," I began, trying to ignore the shivers. "And I know I was right not to continue on *The Young and the Beautiful*—"

Sam rolled his eyes. "That's for sure! It wasn't a very realistic dream. I was glad you finally came to your senses."

"Sam!" I objected, pulling away from his hand. "That's a rotten thing to say!"

"Why? You admitted that you went overboard!"

"Overboard, maybe. But not completely out to sea!"

"Are you saying you want to be on another television show?" he asked.

"No!" I said. "You were right. A television series is an intensive, long-term commitment. I don't have time for that in my life."

"Good," Sam said. "I'm glad you're over that phase."

"Phase?"

"Come on, Jess. Being an actress is a great dream. But it's not like a serious ambition. You know the odds against success in Hollywood!"

"About the same as the odds against being asked to become a regular on my favorite soap opera," I reminded him.

"But you turned that down," he said. "And even if you still want to be an actress, you just said you don't have the time right now!"

"I'm worried that my acting skills will deteriorate if I don't use them. We haven't done a school play in ages. What would you think if I kind of kept my eyes open for a professional production to audition for?"

Sam's eyes narrowed. "A play?"

I shrugged. "Maybe a play. Maybe a movie. I know, it would be a lot of work for a month or so. But then it would all be over. No long-term commitment!"

"What about *our* long-term commitment?"

"You went to Colorado for almost a month!" I reminded him.

"That was a serious career program!"

"Why is your career more serious than mine?"

"That's not what I meant, Jessica, and you know it!"

"I thought I did, but now I'm not so sure," I said, biting my lip. "Sam, are you telling me you don't want me involved in professional show business?"

"That's exactly what I'm saying!" Sam insisted. "And it's what we agreed to!"

"Not really," I said. "What if a great opportunity

173

comes up? Say I run into a film director—oh, I don't know—maybe while I'm out riding my bike some weekend. Say he says he watched me on *The Young and the Beautiful,* and he wants me to star in his next movie. Would you want me to turn it down?"

"Absolutely!" Sam cried. "Luckily, nobody ever gets offered a part in a movie that way."

"But if I did—"

"Jessica, I'm absolutely serious about this," Sam warned me, his face grim. "If you get hooked up with another Hollywood acting gig, then you'd better find another boyfriend. I have *no* desire to go through that again!"

Needless to say, Diary, I decided it was not a good time to tell Sam about Charles Sampson and Checkered Houses. *Maybe it will never be a good time. I don't know what to do!*

Friday night
Liz and I will soon be millionaires! We're going into business for ourselves. And believe me, Diary, with this idea, we can't lose!

A bunch of us were hanging around in my backyard after school Thursday, sitting by the pool. But after an hour, Lila rose slowly to her feet and folded her sunglasses into the pocket of her blouse.

"You're not leaving so early, are you?" Amy asked her.

Lila's mouth twisted in distaste. "Stuff to do," she commented. "Nothing I'm thrilled about doing, that's for sure."

"Homework?" Amy asked.

"No way. I wouldn't let homework keep me from socializing!"

Typical, I thought. But it wasn't a bad approach to life.

"No," Lila said, rolling her eyes. "I have to write a letter to this dippy cousin of mine in New York. I've been putting it off for weeks. We don't have a thing in common, and we're barely on speaking terms. But our parents insist that we correspond for the sake of the family."

"How dull," Amy agreed. "That's almost as bad as the letter I've been putting off writing."

A butterfly of an idea fluttered softly in my mind. "What's yours about?" I asked Amy.

"My great-aunt knitted me a ridiculous orange-and-green sweater for my birthday, and I have to write her a thank-you letter."

Elizabeth gave her a look like, *What's the big deal?* Amy just rolled her eyes and continued.

"The trouble is, it's hard to be sincere about something that makes me look like the Great Pumpkin," Amy explained. "I wish I could talk someone into writing the letter for me. I'd even pay them!"

"Me too," Lila said. "Writing to Cousin Pete is a huge waste of my time. I'd gladly pay someone else to write the letters."

Don't you see, Diary? I decided to start a letter-writing business! I know what you're thinking. You're thinking, "But Jessica hates writing letters just as much as Lila and Amy!" True, but Jessica has something Lila and Amy and other potential customers don't have. A twin sister who's a regular writing machine!

"I thought if Lila and Amy were willing to pay, then there must be dozens of others out there who hate writing letters too!" I explained to Elizabeth after we were alone. "Anyway, I thought we could advertise and offer to write the letters for those people for a fee—and we would make them happy, save them time, and make a quick profit in the process."

Elizabeth smiled—definitely not her usual reaction upon hearing about one of my brilliant ideas. I wasn't sure if that was a good sign. But then she said the magic words: *"It sounds like a great idea."*

We decided that Elizabeth would write the letters, with help from me. I would be in charge of mailing them, sorting through them, picking things up at the post office box, keeping track of the business things, and other boring details like that.

We both knew that Elizabeth is usually better than me at administrative tasks. She's Ms. Well-Organized, while I'm best at blowing people away with my creative ideas. But this was different. There was money involved! Maybe a lot of it. Even Elizabeth could see right away how committed I was to our new business. And I knew I wouldn't let her down.

> *I really do need the money, Diary. I sort of put a new CD player for the Jeep on layaway at Stereo City, with no concept of how I'll make the payments. Besides that, I want to earn money to help Charles with his movie! I know, it'll be ages before I can make enough to make a real difference in a film budget. But you have to start somewhere, right? I know he'll appreciate any help I can give him.*

> *Elizabeth usually has money saved up. But not right now. She just bought that new computer she wanted, and we're both supposed to cover gas and maintenance costs on the Jeep. So she's poorer than usual— right when she wants to buy Todd a nifty warm-up jacket she saw in a catalog.*

> *Maybe I should do that too, Diary. No,*

I'm not buying Todd a new jacket! I feel so bad about keeping the movie a secret from Sam. Maybe if I give him something way nice, I'll stop feeling so horribly guilty. He's been talking about needing new bike-riding gloves.

Saturday

I'm thinking about painting my bedroom, Diary. I'm tired of brown walls. When I painted it this way at the beginning of the year, I liked the idea of living inside a giant Hershey Bar. But I need more color in my life. No, the clothes all over the floor aren't enough! Besides, I'm sick of Steven saying my room looks like a cross between a bargain-basement sale and a mud-wrestling pit!

I need color. Blazing, blaring color. What about painting the whole room in a bright, lipstick red? Wouldn't that be awesome?

Sunday, obnoxiously early

I'm normally sound asleep at this hour. But I met with Charles again last night. He gave me the script for Checkered Houses, and he's right. It's awesome! The dialogue is so realistic that I feel as though I've known Blythe all my life. I started reading

178

the script last night, and I totally couldn't put it down! I read it all the way through.

Diary, I am Blythe! I know I am. It's like this part was written just for me. I know I can play her better than anyone else, no matter how badly Sam wants me to stay away from show business.

I really have to tell Sam about this. Preferably BEFORE he catches my Oscar acceptance speech! I promise I'll tell him, Diary. Soon.

Tuesday afternoon

I feel sick, Diary. My stomach is turning back flips, and my head is buzzing.

I stopped by the Dairi Burger on the way home from meeting with Charles again. And Sam was there . . . with Minks! And I don't mean the furry kind, though she is a weasel. She's a pretty, blond, petite weasel. And she was wearing an extremely tight T-shirt.

I confronted Sam, of course. It's bad enough that my boyfriend is going out with a biker chick. But he actually had the nerve to take her to the place where all my friends hang out! What will people think when they see him with another woman— even if they really were discussing pistons or something? Will everyone laugh at me

179

at school tomorrow? Or even worse, will they feel SORRY for me?

I was about to get good and mad at Sam. I was ready to explode at him in front of everyone. At least if I could stay angry rather than burst into tears, people wouldn't be talking tomorrow about poor, jilted Jessica. But Sam assured me there was nothing going on, and even he invited me to sit down with them. He said he tried to call me to join them, but I wasn't home and my family didn't know where I was.

Where I was, of course, was with Charles. So I realized I didn't even have the right to be mad at Sam. I swallowed my pride and sat down with them for a while. And I have to admit, Minks isn't really that bad. Not that I'm dying to call her tomorrow so we can go shopping for leather together. But she seemed OK, and she didn't seem to be after my boyfriend. At least, I don't think so.

I am so frustrated! I want to do the movie more than anything. But I love Sam! Why can't he let me follow my dreams? I know I was a jerk last time I tried to be a star, but I know I can keep myself from going overboard this time. All I'm asking for is a chance.

Oh, it's hard to be excited about it now,

but the requests (and checks) are pouring into Letters R Us. I may have a screwed-up love life, but at least I'll be rich.

Tuesday night, later
Every time I think of Sam sitting in that booth with Minks, I tense up. No, he's not leaving me for her. But he could! And he will, if he learns about Charles's movie.

I keep telling myself Sam loves me too much to dump me like that. But then I remember how serious and steel-cold his voice sounded at Secca Lake. "If you get hooked up with another Hollywood acting gig," he warned me, "then you'd better find another boyfriend." It was way harsh, but he meant every word.

So I've made a decision, Diary. I can't risk losing Sam. I love him too much for that. I don't want to tell him the truth, but I hate lying to him. So there's only one thing I can do. I'm stopping this whole movie thing from going any further. I won't call Charles, ever again!

Thank goodness I told him never to call me at home. The last thing I need is Elizabeth poking her big-sisterly nose into my business. This is a situation I need to deal with as a singleton. (Isn't that a great word, Diary? It means a person who isn't a *twin. Bet you didn't even know there was a word for that.)*

Friday

Letters R Us received a note today from someone we know! Of course, we're still anonymous letter writers with a post office box, so she doesn't know that we know her.

I was hot for gossip when I saw Shelley Novak's name on the return address. Shelly's more a friend of Elizabeth's than mine. She's a total beanpole, which makes her a great basketball player. But it's hard to be popular when you're three feet taller than most of the guys at school. Still, she dates Jim Roberts. And until today, I thought they were happy together.

Then I read Shelley's letter. You're not going to believe what she wants us to write. And who she wants us to write it to. . . .

"I'm a junior at Sweet Valley High," I read aloud from Shelley's letter. "And lately I've developed an enormous crush on the boyfriend of one of my friends—"

This was primo gossip. Not even Amy had this story yet, I knew. Even Caroline Pearce was still out of the loop! It reeked that I couldn't spread it around without risking the secrecy of Letters R Us. I read on, wondering who's boyfriend the beanpole was hot on.

"He's tall, with brown hair and eyes, and he's the star forward of the boys' basketball team."

Oops. Shelley was in love with Elizabeth's boyfriend. And she wanted Elizabeth to write Todd a letter, divulging Shelley's deepest feelings for him.

"Oh, no!" I gasped, tossing the letter onto my bed. Elizabeth did not deserve this.

Oh, Diary. I do not deserve this either. Now I have to figure out what to do about it. Do I help Shelley steal my sister's boyfriend? Do I pass her letter on to Elizabeth, so my twin can write the boyfriend-stealing letter herself? Should I send back Shelley's money and tell her to forget the whole thing?

If it were Sam that Shelley wanted, I know exactly what I'd do. I'd rush right over and slam-dunk her tall, skinny face!

Saturday
I rewrote Shelley's note to us, leaving out any details that would let Liz in on which gorgeous guy she was talking about. I pretended that she went to a different school. I needed a name besides "Shelley" to sign the note with. I couldn't get Checkered Houses out of my mind, so I called her "Blythe."

Then I showed Elizabeth my new and improved version, instead of Shelly's original, and I let her write a reply to that one. Unfortunately, Elizabeth thought "Blythe's" feelings for this boy were sweet. She wrote a romantic letter for "Blythe," actually expressing Shelley's love for Todd. I kept begging her to tone it down, but she wouldn't. Of course, Liz has no idea she's helping another woman steal her own boyfriend! Then I changed the names and sent off the letter.

I know, Diary. I'm overreacting. Steven thinks so too. (Well, I had to get advice from someone, right?) Todd will be flattered by Shelley's letter. But it's Elizabeth he loves. He'll let Shelley down easy, and Shelley will go back to Jim. I hope.

Am I doing the right thing? Maybe I should have dumped the whole thing in Elizabeth's lap and let her handle it.

Friday

Between school and our booming letter-writing business and trying to see Sam whenever I can, I've been swamped! That's why I haven't written lately, Diary. Liz and I are making a ton of money, but we're thinking of quitting the business when we've reached our financial goals, which should be in a couple more weeks.

Elizabeth has seen Todd even less than I've seen Sam. Boy, is Todd getting cranky about that! I tried to tell her she's neglecting him. I even suggested that she break down and reveal what we're so busy with. But she insists on keeping Letters R Us a secret. She wants Todd's new warm-up jacket to be a surprise.

Speaking of warming things up, I've decided red walls are too intense for a bedroom. Amy says a lot of red produces feelings of anxiety. She reads too many psychology magazines at Project Youth. But maybe she has a point. Now I'm thinking of painting the ceiling midnight blue, with stars. I could do the walls in sky blue, with fluffy white clouds. Wouldn't that be spiffy?

Thursday

I messed up again, Diary. I've screwed up Elizabeth's relationship with Todd. . . .

On Wednesday, our post office box contained a note in Todd's handwriting, raving about an incredible love letter he received from a girl he'd only thought of as a friend. "A couple of weeks ago I would have just brushed this off," Todd's letter said. "I've been going steady with my girlfriend for a very long time, and I thought we were very much in love. But lately, she's always tied up with something she's very secretive about—she tells me it's some sort of writing project."

If he only knew, I thought.

Todd went on to say he was afraid the romance was gone from his relationship with his girlfriend. So now he found himself intrigued by this letter from a friend. "I think I should at least give this other girl a chance," he said, "if only to shake my girlfriend up."

That would shake Elizabeth up, all right, I thought. And it would shake up all of them if they had any idea of the convoluted plot we had going here. Todd wanted Letters R Us—in other words, his own girlfriend, though he didn't know it—to write two letters for him. The first letter would be a "Dear Jane" to his girlfriend; in other words, Todd was asking Elizabeth to break up with herself for him. The second letter would be to Shelley, asking her out.

> *This was way harsh. So I stepped in, with the best of intentions—and made things even worse. I don't know what else I could have done, though. I couldn't pretend the letter hadn't arrived. Elizabeth knew how many had come; she was already asking where the last one was.*

So I came up with a plan. I decided to do almost the same thing as before. I'd write a new version of

Todd's letter—changing the names to protect the guilty. Elizabeth would write two letters in response to my "edited" version. But I couldn't risk Elizabeth deciding again that Todd and Shelley's predicament was something out of a romance novel. So I'd write my own letters, convincing everyone to go back to dating the original loves of their lives. And at the last minute, I'd replace Elizabeth's letters with mine. Everything would be hunky-dory, and we'd all live happily ever after.

I didn't count on Shining Steel. Yes, I'm talking about Bill Lacey's band. Sam called me at the last minute and said he'd finagled tickets to the sold-out show. This group is the hottest thing around. And with my connections, I figured we could get backstage. So I was out until late Wednesday night. Unfortunately, that left me with no time to replace Elizabeth's letters with new ones. So Elizabeth's letters got mailed! Without knowing it, she'd just broken up with herself and asked another girl to go out with her boyfriend.

> *Friday*
> *What an unbelievable mess! I was only trying to help. But I'll be blamed for destroying my sister's life. I'm joining a convent. No, I'm moving to Bolivia. No, I'm painting my room purple and locking myself inside it forever. And I will never even look at another letter as long as I live.*

Oh, I forgot to mention that I decided on the color scheme for my bedroom. Purple has always been my favorite color, so it only makes sense. I'm doing the walls and ceiling in purple. I'll spend some of this letter-writing money on a new purple bedspread and a chrome daybed. And I'll throw around some purple pillows, along with black ones and shiny silver ones, as accent colors.

What do you think, Diary? Do I have a career in interior design ahead of me like my mom? Sigh. . . . I've once again blown my chance to be Hollywood's Next Big Star. I have to find SOMETHING to do with myself for the next sixty or seventy years! It's a sure bet that I'm not scoring any points as a matchmaker.

Or a mailbox burglar. . . .

I had to stop Elizabeth's "Dear Jane" letter from reaching Todd. OK, that wasn't a well-thought-out goal, but it was the only thing I could think to do. I knew that as soon as Todd received the letter from Letters R Us, he'd turn around and mail it to Elizabeth. Then she'd figure out the whole, sordid story, including the fact that I was in the middle of everything.

I had to do something to fix things. So I decided to get the letter back from the U.S. Postal

Service before it got delivered. I lurked in front of Todd's house on Friday morning—dressed from the Junior Boring department, so I could pretend to be Elizabeth. And I waited for the mail carrier.

"Mr. Ramsey!" I called, intercepting him as he reached the Wilkins's front path. Luckily, it was the same guy who delivers our mail.

He assumed I was Elizabeth, and I didn't tell him otherwise. I made up a story about how I'd broken up with my boyfriend in a letter, but had changed my mind, and wanted Mr. Ramsey to give me the letter back. No go.

"I'm sorry, Elizabeth," Mr. Ramsey said. "I'm quite surprised, actually, that you would ask me to do such a thing. Tampering with the mail is against the law."

"But I wrote the letter! Isn't it my property?"

"Not once you put a stamp on it and send it."

I considered tackling the mail carrier, grabbing the letter, and running. But he was bigger than me. Elizabeth wouldn't make a scene, and I was supposed to be Elizabeth, right down to my conservative pale-pink cotton sweater and boring old jeans. So I accepted defeat and trudged away, praying that Todd would change his mind and decide not to mail either letter.

Saturday afternoon
Sam Woodruff is the most wonderful
guy in the world! I told him all about the

letters. And he was totally supportive. He advised me to tell Elizabeth the whole truth. And he's right. I will, Diary, I promise. As soon as I find the right time.

Now I just wish I had the guts to tell SAM the whole truth. Because the truth, Diary, is that I've stopped by the phone a hundred times in the last couple weeks, my heart beating as hard as the drum track on Shining Steel's newest album. I've imagined picking up the phone and calling Charles Sampson, telling him I still want to be Blythe—the Checkered Houses Blythe, not the letter-writing Blythe—more than anything in the world.

I know I promised I wouldn't call him, Diary. And I haven't. And I won't. Sam means too much to me. So why can't I stop thinking about Charles and his movie?

Monday evening

I blew it, Diary. Gosh, I'm saying that a lot lately. Maybe I'll have it inscribed on my gravestone: "Here Lies Jessica Wakefield. She Blew It."

This time, I blew it with both Sam and Elizabeth. As expected, my sister received the Dear Jane letter she wrote to herself. And man, was she stunned! Even more, she was out for my blood. I knew I should have *told her sooner. Once she got the letter, there was no point in trying to hide the rest. So I confessed to her the whole, muddled, pathetic story.*

Liz is heartbroken about Shelley and Todd! But I'm having trouble believing that it's over between my twin and the Toddster. Mashed potatoes and meat loaf, remember? They'll find their way back to each other eventually. They always do.

I'm more worried about Sam and me. Last night I couldn't help myself. I called Charles. I know I said I wouldn't. So arrest me. I couldn't get that movie role out of my head! Charles was great. He said he couldn't get ME out of his head, and that he'd been hoping I would change my mind. The part of Blythe is still mine if I want it. And I do.

Tonight I'm meeting Charles in Malibu, at his famous sister's beach house. There'll be lots of movie-industry types there, including finance people. Charles thinks it'll help if I'm there to talk up the movie with him and let everyone see Blythe in person. . . .

Elizabeth was in her room writing something for the newspaper on Monday night. And my parents were downstairs watching a movie. I made a big show of yawning and telling everyone I was going to bed early.

Charles had said the party was casual. But I doubted he meant tank tops and blue jeans. So I pulled on a long, fuzzy sweater—loose, but low-cut enough to be sexy—in pure white, but with subtle gold threads running through the weave. I paired it with tight white leggings. I stood in front of the mirror, admiring the effect.

It wasn't my usual style, Diary. In fact, I "borrowed" the sweater from my mother's room. My mother! (Don't you dare tell a soul!) But something about the fuzzy white sweater just felt like Blythe. At the beginning of the movie, she's timid and innocent. She's only just starting to realize her power over men. She'd never dream of wearing a stretchy black miniskirt to a Shining Steel concert like I did last week.

By the end of the movie, Blythe is no stranger to spandex and spangles. That part would be especially fun to film. But for this party, I wanted to be the unjaded Blythe.

Besides, I was gorgeous, if I do say so myself! The outfit made me look like a real movie star—a classy, understated actress, like you'd expect to see starring in an award-winning independent film.

It was late for me to be leaving the house at night. My parents would've freaked if they'd glanced out the window and seen me, shining white like a ghost against my black Jeep, as I fiddled with the key in the door lock. I guess they stayed away from the windows, 'cause nobody stopped me. I started up the Jeep, and I drove to Malibu. . . .

This party was more relaxed than the ones I'd been to with Brandon Hunter. Grace Sampson's beach house was way cool, but it wasn't fancy. It had lots of red cedar paneling and comfortable furniture, with almost no decorations except huge picture windows with breathtaking views of the ocean. As magical as the waves looked by moonlight, I could hardly pull my eyes off of the people who were there for the party that night. The place had more stars in it than the Milky Way!

Jackson Croft, the movie director, was there. I spotted him right away because I'd met him before. His daughter, Susan Stewart, was a junior at Sweet Valley High. Elena Borova, a classy-looking actress with dark, sultry eyes, stood in the corner with a woman I recognized as a Hollywood producer, though I couldn't remember her name.

Charles's sister Grace was urging canapes on two dark-suited middle-aged men who I guessed were finance people. Without her movie makeup, Grace didn't look much older than me. But her high cheekbones and cinnamon hair were even more striking in person than on the big screen.

But most incredibly of all, a six-foot-five blond man with hypnotic blue eyes was strolling toward me, his hand outstretched. It was Gordon Edvalson, star of *Space Outpost Delta*, the hottest science-fiction show on television. On his show, he looks like a twenty-second-century Greek god. In person, he was so gorgeous I nearly fainted.

"You're Jessica Wakefield, aren't you?" he asked. He reached for my hand as if *I* were the one who was a major celebrity. I nearly melted under the gaze of those indigo eyes.

"Yes, this is Jessica, my choice for the lead role in *Checkered Houses*," Charles said while I searched for my voice. I'd almost forgotten he was standing at my elbow. Of course, with Gordon Edvalson in front of me, I'd almost forgotten my own name. "Jessica, this is Gordon Edvalson," Charles added unnecessarily.

"Mr. Edvalson, I'm so happy to meet you!" I said, in control again. "I love your work on *Space Outpost Delta*." *That was good,* I told myself. *Admiring, but professional—one actor to another.*

"Call me Gordon," he insisted. He wore a loose-cut gray suit with a sparkling white shirt and no tie.

"Of course," I replied smoothly, but inside I was dancing a jig of glee. "And you *must* call me Jessica."

"I've been wanting to meet you ever since I saw

you on *The Young and the Beautiful*," Gordon continued in his sexy Scandinavian accent. "I've never seen such a promising debut. A lot of young actresses are pretty. But you're both beautiful and talented."

My head buzzed with an adrenaline rush. This was even better than hot-wiring Bruce's Porsche! "Thank you," I said calmly. "It was a very educational experience."

He laughed. "I believe Brandon Hunter was the one who got educated." I blushed furiously. "Don't get me wrong, Jessica," Gordon continued quickly. "It was an education Brandon sorely needed!" He winked at me, and I smiled knowingly. Then he was swallowed up by the crowd, and Charles steered me toward another cluster of people.

Meeting these people was amazing, Diary! I was thrilled every time someone recognized me from the soap opera, though I'm sure Charles must have filled them in ahead of time.

I know, a few months ago I was raving about the parties Brandon took me to. But this one was different. It wasn't a publicity stunt. There were no reporters or photographers. The actors weren't sequined to the max and trying to impress each other. They weren't dropping names or bragging about openings they'd been invited to. They were talking about making movies and television shows. About acting and producing. And I felt like a part of it all. Me, Jessica Wakefield!

Of course, I'm not really part of it yet. But I can be! That's the most awesome part of it. I really can be! All I have to do is tell Charles I'm in. And then be the best Blythe Carson anyone could be.

Sam's right that I got carried away last time. I don't think I'm going off the deep end now. But I can't turn my back on this movie project.

> *Tuesday afternoon*
> *I think I made a mistake today. OK, I know I did. I lied to Sam. . . .*

Sam was already at the Dairi Burger waiting for me when I arrived there after school on Tuesday.

"Where were you last night?" he asked before he'd even said hi.

"Hello to you too," I replied.

"I mean it, Jess," he said. "You said you'd be home, and you weren't."

"Nobody told me you called," I said, stalling for time while I concocted a better story than *I went to a party in Malibu with a cute director who wants to star me in a movie.*

"I didn't call. I stopped by after midnight and

threw pebbles at your window like I always do. At first I thought you were asleep, but the Jeep was gone!"

"What were you doing outside my house in the middle of the night?"

Sam shrugged. "I just wanted to kiss you good-night, that's all. The house was dark, and I didn't want to wake your parents."

"Oh, Sam! That's so romantic!" I said, gazing into his pretty gray eyes.

"It would have been!"

"I spent the night at Lila's," I said, glad to know she was safely at the mall with Amy, and wouldn't be walking in the door any minute to contradict my story.

"I talked to you only a few hours earlier, and you didn't mention going to Lila's."

"I know," I said with a shrug. "She called me right after we hung up. She was having a bad-hair crisis like you wouldn't believe. She begged me to drive over and help her through it."

Sam laughed and shook his head. "If it were anyone but your friends, Jess, that would be the most idiotic story—"

"What can I say? If the Holy Grail really exists, it's filled with styling mousse."

I feel rotten about lying to him, Diary.
You're right. Lying never bothered me
before. But I don't like lying to Sam! When

197

I can't avoid it, I prefer to mislead him slightly, or to leave out parts of the truth. But this is just plain lying. And it's about something I'm doing that I specifically promised him I wouldn't do.

The worst thing about lying is the possibility of getting caught. Sooner or later, Sam will find out about this movie. What will he do when he realizes I've been keeping it from him all this time?

Thursday night, late

I saw Charles Sampson this afternoon after cheerleading practice. We read through the script together, each playing half the roles. It was a blast! And the more I get to know Charles, the more I like him. Even scarier is that I'm more convinced than ever about doing this movie. But I don't want to turn my back on Sam either.

It's not fair! Why do I have to choose?

Monday night

At least one problem in my life is solved. I'm officially off the hook for screwing up Elizabeth's love life. Shelley wasn't really a threat to her. Shelley and Todd went out Friday night and decided they liked each other only as friends. I spilled the whole story to Todd the next *day, and he spilled his guts to Liz in a letter.*

Now Elizabeth and Todd are together; Shelley and Jim are back together. Best of all, Elizabeth and I are through with the letter-writing business. From now on, the only letters I plan to write are to you, Diary.

But right now, I have a bedroom to paint!

Part 3

Tuesday afternoon

Dear Diary,

This is Jessica Wakefield, your teen-on-the-scene in Sweet Valley, California. It's been a week since my last report. My gloriously purple room is fantastic, even if Liz says it looks like a six-hundred-pound grape exploded. And I've seen Charles twice in the last few days to talk about the movie!

In the "So what else is new?" category, we have another chapter in the Never-Ending Chronicles of Saint Elizabeth. My overachieving sister's latest overachievement: She's the acting editor in chief of The Oracle for the next two weeks. Penny, another disgusting overachiever, is in Washington, D.C., following a senator *around. No, she hasn't decided on a career as a stalker. She was picked for some dweebed-out program for teen journalists who want to be political reporters.*

To nobody's surprise—except maybe Olivia Davidson's—Penny and Mr. Collins chose Liz to fill in as editor while Penny's away. Olivia seemed bummed out when she congratulated Liz. I think Olivia wanted the job herself. But she's too good a friend of Elizabeth's to admit it.

All I heard at school all day is how talented a writer Elizabeth is, how responsible Elizabeth is, how dedicated and hardworking Elizabeth is. This is getting old. Fast.

Listening to everyone admire the Perfect Twin makes me even more determined to go through with Charles's movie. Elizabeth isn't the only talented twin in the family! And what Sam doesn't know won't hurt him.

Wednesday
Charles took me to meet some potential investors this afternoon. And he actually introduced me as his partner. His partner! This is so exciting! I wish I could blab it all to Liz or Lila. Keeping secrets is the pits!

I was late meeting Sam at the Dairi Burger because of the thing with Charles, but Sam was only a tiny bit annoyed.

Thursday night

A little virus can be a wondrous thing. The flu is going around. And around. And around. . . . You wouldn't believe how many kids were absent from school today! The best part is that viruses infect teachers too! Mr. Frankel was out sick today, so my math test was canceled. I was so happy I could kiss someone! Preferably someone who doesn't have the flu.

There aren't that many of us left. Luckily, Lila is among the healthy. Her biggest complaint is that she doesn't know what to do with her hair. We're planning a major shopping trip on Saturday. Maybe some new CDs will take her mind off her mousse. I think Rhomboid has a new album out.

Friday night, late

The latest flu casualties are Enid Rollins, Bruce Patman, and Mr. Collins. All three went home early today. The latest romantic casualty was my date with Sam tonight. He's beginning to suspect that I'm hiding something. . . .

I called Sam on Friday afternoon to cancel out on his bike race Saturday. "I can't believe this!" I wailed into the phone. "I was really looking forward to the race tomorrow, but now my mother's making me go shopping with her."

Sam laughed. "I've never heard you complain about going shopping before."

"This is different. She wants me to help her pick out a special anniversary present for my grandparents."

It was almost true. My parents really were going shopping for that anniversary present. And I was going shopping too. I just left out the part in which I go with Lila instead of with my folks.

The truth is simple: Watching sweaty guys race filthy bikes is one of the worst ways in the world to spend a Saturday. It's boring, it's dirty, and it smells. But it would hurt Sam's feelings if I told him I'd rather spend the day at the mall. I knew he'd be happier thinking I love watching his races but was prevented by parental decree.

It wasn't the first time I'd lied to Sam that week. When I was late meeting him at the Dairi Burger Wednesday, I claimed cheerleading practice ran overtime. On Thursday night, I told him my phone had been busy for two hours because I was counseling Lila through more hair-related trauma. The phone call was actually to Charles, who wanted my advice on some script changes on *Checkered Houses*.

Sam and I had a date planned for Friday night. So a few hours after my little white lie about the grandparent present, we were dancing to the Droids at the Beach Disco. I looked smashing in a bare little minidress—hot pink, with spaghetti straps and polka dots.

Dana Larson, a classmate of mine and the Droids's lead singer, was onstage in leopard-print spandex and a press-on nose stud. But at this particular moment, she was sliding through the lyrics of a slow, romantic song, a cover of Jamie Peters's newest ballad, "In My Arms." She has the most wonderful, fluid alto voice, the kind that gives you chills. Sam and I were listening to her as we leaned against each other on the open-air dance floor, swaying gently under the twinkling lights.

Suddenly, Sam started pulling me off the dance floor, toward the beach.

"Where are we going?" I asked.

"Somewhere where we can be alone," he replied. Like every other couple that hangs out at the Beach Disco, we occasionally slipped away from the crowd to find a dark, private spot for kissing on the beach. But this time, the look in Sam's eyes seemed more intense than passionate.

When we were well away from the lights of the disco, I turned to Sam, put my hands on his shoulders, and kissed him. He kissed me back, but only for a moment. Then he gently pulled away.

"I love you, Jessica," he told me.

I took a deep breath of the salt-tinted breeze. One blond curl was hanging in his eyes, gilt-edged in the moonlight. I reached up and brushed it aside. "I know you do, Sam."

He stared at me hard. "Jess, is there anything you want to tell me?"

"I love you too," I said.

"Isn't there something else?"

"What do you mean?"

He shook his head. "I'm not sure, Jess. But I know you're hiding something. I can always tell."

"What makes you say that?" I asked carefully.

"You've been showing up late for things, disappearing without any explanation—"

I forced a laugh. "Is that all? Sam Woodruff, you know I never wear a watch. If I started being on time, you'd have a stroke! And I'm sorry I haven't always told you where I was. It's only because I've been busy."

"Busy with what?" he asked, looking me in the face.

"Nothing top secret!" I said. "For a while, that letter-writing business took a lot of time. Since then, I've been swamped with school and cheerleading. . . ." My voice trailed off.

"And Lila's bad hair days," he said.

I nodded. "She's been obsessing."

"Lila's hair looks the same as it always looks— long, brown, and wavy! Are you sure her hair isn't an excuse for not spending time with me?"

I laughed. "Lila's hair does look the same as always. That's the problem. She wants to do something different to it," I told him truthfully.

"I still think there's something you're not telling me."

I felt a tightness in my chest. What if someone had spotted me with Charles and had told Sam I was seeing an older man? What if he'd heard some show-biz gossip about *Checkered Houses* and its tentative star? What if Sam knew everything and was now giving me a chance to tell the truth before he confronted me with it?

I dismissed the idea. That wasn't Sam. If he knew something, he would come right out and say so. Sam had always been honest and open with me. And I felt like the world's biggest liar—and worst girlfriend.

"There's nothing, Sam," I told him. "I'm just busy, like I told you."

"Jessica, if you're mad at me for something—"

"I'm not mad at you," I assured him, wrapping my arms around his waist. "I love you! And I'm not hiding anything. You're being paranoid."

He nodded. "OK. But if you think of anything you want to get off your chest, you know where to find me."

We had fun the rest of the night, Diary. But I felt uncertain after that. It was like my lies had built an invisible force field between us.

I have to stop this! But how? If I'd been honest with Sam from the start, maybe I could have found a way to do this movie without losing him. But everything has gotten out of hand. He might have forgiven me just for pursuing this acting job. He'll never forgive me for hiding it from him.

Saturday

For a change, somebody besides me did something outrageously dumb! No, not Liz (though I can dream). My perfect sister is spending the weekend working on her first Oracle *edition as supreme dictator, which will no doubt be as perfect as she is.*

The person who did a dumb thing is Lila, who has now proven that money can't buy you brains. You'll never believe this— she had her hair dyed and straightened! But she didn't go blond, like any normal, sensible brunette would do. She streaked it with a nightmare shade of plum!

Yes, I'm into purple. But Lila's hair looked like something out of Night of the Living Dead. *I didn't want to hurt my best friend's feelings. So I kept my mouth shut.*

Other people weren't as considerate. When Lila found out that they were laughing at her, she blamed ME for not telling her she looked like a freak show! Now she's fixed her hair back to the way it was. But she's totally ticked at me, as if the whole fiasco was MY fault.

Sunday morning

It's all over. Last night I had a date with Sam. And all I could think about—again— was how I'm deceiving him. I had to take action. So I called Charles as soon as I got

home and asked to see him. Then I did one
of the hardest things I've ever had to do. . . .

I met Charles at Jackson's Bluff, which was probably my first mistake. But I needed a place where nobody I knew was likely to see us together, and I didn't have time to drive far. Jackson's Bluff is a beautiful spot, even when it's drizzling rain, as it was that Saturday night. It's a high ridge overlooking one of the best surfing beaches in southern California. Couples go there to be alone. But not my friends. The Sweet Valley High crowd prefers Miller's Point. Jackson's Bluff is strictly for Big Mesa kids.

Charles was already there when I arrived. I parked my Jeep in the darkest corner of the overlook, near the trees, and scurried through the drizzle to Charles's vintage Mustang. But once I climbed into the front seat, I just sat there like a loser. I stared at the raindrops on the windshield and couldn't say what needed to be said.

"What is it, Jessica?" Charles asked after a few minutes of listening to the sizzle of rain and the distant drumming of the surf. "What did you want to tell me?"

"Oh, Charles, you're going to be so furious with me. . . ." I blinked hard to push back the tears that were stinging my eyelids.

Charles put a hand on my shoulder. "Whatever it is, Jessica, it's all right. I won't be mad at you!"

"You will when you hear what I have to tell

you." I bit my lip. "I wish I didn't have to tell you."

"Tell me what?"

"You know I want to be in *Checkered Houses!*" I cried. "You know how much I want to play Blythe!"

His hand rubbed my shoulder soothingly, radiating warmth. "Of course."

"Well, I can't! I can't do the movie!" I blurted out.

His shoulders slumped a little, so I knew he was disappointed. But all I saw on his sweet, handsome face was concern for me. "Why, Jessica? What's wrong? Is it something I've done?"

"No, Charles—"

He slid closer to me on the seat. "I've been asking you for a lot of creative input, and even for help on the business end," he said, his deep voice gaining intensity. "Is it too much, Jessica? Would you be more comfortable sticking to the acting?"

"It's not that!" I assured him. "Oh, Charles, you've been wonderful. I've loved being involved in the whole film, not just one role. But I'm neglecting the rest of my life, and I've lied to people who care about me—" I pressed my lips together and tried not to cry.

He gently lifted my chin with his finger. "It's all right, Jessica. I'm not mad at you." He smiled, and I couldn't believe how adorable he looked. "This is my fault," he said, his eyes as deep and rich as melted chocolate. "You were worried about the time commitment from the start, and I kept pushing you. I'm sorry."

I laughed weakly. "You can't be sorry! I'm the one who's sorry. I'm the one who's walking out on you—"

Before I realized what was happening, Charles leaned forward and kissed me. As his lips touched mine, his warm, strong hand slid over my shoulder and around to my back. I was wearing a tank top, so his fingers brushed my bare skin, and heat shot through my body.

I pushed him away.

I opened my mouth to speak, but no words came out. I shook my head helplessly. Then I opened the door, climbed out of the Mustang, and stumbled back to the Jeep, ignoring the cold rain that spattered my shoulders. When I sped away a minute later, Charles was sitting in his car, staring out at sky and ocean while moonbeams danced with raindrops on the hood.

I can't get that kiss out of my mind, Diary. I'm breathless just thinking about it. I didn't kiss him back. But I still feel totally, horribly guilty! Sam would be destroyed if he knew! I'll just have to make sure he never finds out.

Tuesday evening
Get ready, world! If I can't be a famous actress, I'm going to be a famous writer. At least for this week. . . .

Elizabeth had been rushing around for two days in a total panic about the newspaper. Almost her entire staff was out sick. The last straw was when Jennifer Mitchell turned six shades of green on Tuesday and had to go home without handing in the article she owed my sister. Even an overachiever like Elizabeth couldn't write an entire newspaper herself before Wednesday. So she bummed stories from the most unlikely people imaginable.

Rod Sullivan, who as far as I know had never written anything in his life that wasn't required by a teacher, volunteered to submit an article. He was Olivia Davidson's boyfriend. But I'd seen him making goo-goo eyes at Elizabeth, who was too totally blind to notice.

The next unlikely article writer was Whizzer Wilkins himself. Todd's a good student, but he hates writing! Still, his girlfriend was in a jam. He knew what was good for him—if he ever wanted another evening at Miller's Point. So he was whipping up a "Name the Flu Bug" contest for that week's *Oracle*.

Of course, Elizabeth's most brilliant idea was to ask me to write. First she related her plight in all its tragic detail. You'd have thought the entire country was infected with bubonic plague, and the only hope for printing the next day's *New York Times*—containing the recipe for the *cure*—was for Elizabeth Wakefield, Girl Journalist, to take charge. With Jessica Wakefield, Loyal Sister, helping out.

And people say *I'm* the manipulative twin.

I could tell she was expecting me to argue. "Well?" she asked, her voice desperate. "What do you think?"

I nodded. I love being unpredictable. "Sure. I'll do it right after dinner."

Elizabeth's lower jaw hit the floor. "You will? You'll write a piece by tomorrow?"

"Yeah. I don't have any homework because half my teachers are out, and Sam's got a date with his spark plugs tonight. So I have nothing else to do."

Well, it'll be more interesting than sitting in my room, pining over the Movie Career That Never Was.

I know exactly what I'm going to write, Diary. It's an editorial on something I've been thinking a lot about in the last few weeks: honesty. I plan to call it, "To Tell the Truth." But I better make it anonymous if I want anyone to take it seriously. I don't exactly have George Washington's reputation (or Elizabeth's) for never telling a lie.

Friday

My article made a huge splash! Everyone's talking about it. I was going to keep my identity a secret, but I did tell a few people. Only because Lila guessed it, though. She asked me outright, so of course I told her the truth. After all, honesty is the best policy!

Monday afternoon
To make up for all my lies, I've decided to be nothing but totally honest from this day forward.

Wednesday night
Poor Lizzie! She's been accused of plagiarism!

Rod Sullivan was helping her out with a paper she had to write for English class. I know, it sounds bizarre that Elizabeth Wakefield, Writing Machine, would need help. But the assignment was to compare a particular piece of literature to some painting. And my sister knows even less about art than I do. Rod, on the other hand, is an artist.

The Oracle had sucked up so much time that Elizabeth had to rush through her English paper. She handed it to Mr. Collins and resigned herself to getting a lousy grade. Like a B.

When I came home from cheering at the track meet Wednesday, Elizabeth was lying across her bed. Her eyes were all red and puffy. At first I thought she was coming down with the flu. Then I realized she'd been crying. She told me why. Collins had accused her of copying parts of her English paper straight out of an art magazine!

"I don't believe this!" I yelled, pacing. "How could anyone accuse *you* of plagiarism? I've never heard anything so ridiculous in my entire life!"

I was livid, Diary! I was ready to stalk out of the house, drag Mr. Collins from whatever dingy little cave he was hiding in, and brand his forehead with the entire, HONEST truth about what a dirtbag he is! How can he accuse Lizzie of such a thing?

In my prehonesty days, I might have done something like copying out of a book—if I knew I wouldn't get caught. But Elizabeth? No way! My twin is so clean she squeaks when she walks.

Elizabeth could probably get used to seeing that F at the top of her paper. But she's heartbroken that Mr. Collins doesn't trust her anymore. As if that's not bad enough, he even suspended her from The Oracle!

"You can't blame Mr. Collins," Elizabeth said loyally. "What else could he believe? He saw the evidence with his own eyes. And anyway, it's true. I did use someone else's ideas."

I sat down beside her on the bed. "But you didn't do it purposely!" I pointed out. "I think you should have told Mr. Collins the truth. Maybe you did repeat everything Rod told you, and maybe that's wrong. But it's still not the same as deliberately stealing ideas from a published work. Rod should take some of the blame for this. He's the one who started it. He knew he was giving you this other guy's ideas!"

"I couldn't do that," Elizabeth protested. "I can't just turn Rod in."

Elizabeth was mystified about why Rod would do such a thing. So I enlightened her with a blinding flash of the obvious.

"You really are too much, you know that?" I said. "Why do you *think* he did it? Obviously, he wanted to impress you."

Elizabeth blinked, as if I'd startled her. "I'm not sure," she said after a minute.

"Wake up, Liz! Rod has a crush on you. He didn't tell you all that stuff to get you in trouble," I told her, referring to the information Rod had given her out of that art magazine. "He told you all that stuff because he wanted you to like him!"

"Do you really think so?"

I rolled my eyes. "Of course I do. It couldn't be more obvious if he announced it on television."

"But this is even worse!" Elizabeth wailed, sitting up straight and pounding a desperate fist into her pillow. "It means that not only am I guilty of plagiarism, I'm also guilty of encouraging Olivia's boyfriend!"

"He didn't need much encouragement, if you ask me. I've seen the way he looks at you, Liz. And if anybody looked at me like that, Sam would run him over with his dirt bike."

Suddenly, without meaning to, I recalled every detail of Charles's face leaning close to mine, just before he kissed me that drizzly night at Jackson's

215

Bluff. I shoved it out of mind and concentrated instead on my sister's problem.

Elizabeth threw herself back down on the bed and buried her face in the pillow. "What am I going to do?" she cried. "This is the most awful mess I've ever been in!"

"Tell Olivia exactly what happened," I advised, secure in my newfound doctrine of total honesty. "I guarantee she'll thank you for telling her the truth."

Thursday night
Elizabeth received a letter from Prince Arthur today. That's Prince ARTHUR Castillo, the eldest son of King Armand and Queen Stephanie of the kingdom of Santa Dora—as opposed to Prince ALBERT, the golden retriever of Wakefield in the kingdom of Calico Drive.

Elizabeth and Arthur have been pen pals forever. Well, at least they have been since he was an exchange student here in the sixth grade. Santa Dora is a tiny little kingdom on the Mediterranean somewhere. As soon as I saw the postmark on the envelope, I hoped his letter would cheer Elizabeth up. But as rotten as she feels right now, the envelope could contain the crown jewels of Santa Dora, and I doubt she'd crack a smile.

Friday
I'm getting mixed reactions to my total-honesty policy. . . .

Amy had a fit when I told her people laugh at the way she runs when she plays softball. Jennifer Mitchell stopped speaking to me because I told her John Pfeifer was about to break up with her. And Bruce got on my case when Mr. Jaworski asked my opinion of Bruce's oral report in history class, and I gave it. Why shouldn't I say he was superficial and monotonous? It was the truth! Besides, Bruce is *always* superficial and monotonous.

On the other hand, lots of people were coming up to me to ask things like, "What did so-and-so really say about me?" now that they knew I'd tell it like it is.

I love being honest! I don't know why I never tried it before. You don't have to remember exactly which fake excuses you gave to which people. You don't have to make up nice, vague things to say when someone asks how you like her tacky new halter top. I feel clean and pure and virtuous. Kind of like Elizabeth must feel, when she's not being called a plagiarizer. (Plagiarist? Plagiarer? Whatever.)

Somebody-or-other once said, "The truth will set you free." I finally understand what that means!

Saturday night

Things are great with Sam and me. But Elizabeth's life stinks! She talked to Rod and to Olivia. Rod denied doing anything wrong. Olivia can't believe Rod would lie about it, but deep down she's got to suspect! Now Olivia's mad at Elizabeth for saying bad things about her beloved boyfriend, even though he's a sleazy little piece of bottom-dwelling slime. (Honestly.)

All Rod has to do is admit he made a mistake! That would be enough to get Elizabeth back in Mr. Collins's good graces.

Todd wants to be his usual boring-but-loyal-boyfriend self. But he can't right now. It's his turn to be in bed with the Mother of All Flu Bugs. That leaves Enid and me for moral support. I stormed into Olivia's house today and demanded that she talk to Rod and clear my sister's name. As far as I know, it did no good at all. Some people like to hide from the truth.

Anyhow, with all this going on—and with lots of trips to Miller's Point with Sam—I don't miss Charles and Checkered Houses at all. Really, I don't.

Monday night

Today was a "special" holiday at Sweet Valley High. A holiday orchestrated by my

alleged best friend. She called it Total
Honesty for Jessica Day. And everybody
knew about it ahead of time—except me.

Maria Santelli told me I had a pimple on my
chin. April Dawson said I looked fat. Some guy I
never even met came up to me in the cafeteria to
tell me I was eating too fast!

The last straw was when Annie Whitman stopped
beside my lunch table and started to report what A. J.
Morgan—my ex-boyfriend—had said about me.

"That's enough!" I yelled. A wave of giggles rippled around the table. "This is all your idea, isn't it,
Lila Fowler?" I accused. "You put everybody up to
this, didn't you?"

"Who, me?" Lila asked, the picture of innocence.
But she finally admitted that she was the mastermind
behind the student body's unified attempt to give me
what they called a dose of my own medicine.

Just then, Elizabeth dropped by to say she wanted
a word with me about going to Olivia's house behind
her back. I slapped my hands over my ears.

"No more!" I begged. "I don't want to hear it. I
promise I'll never tell the truth again, no matter
how hard people try to drag it out of me!"

Elizabeth wrinkled her forehead. "What are
you talking about? I wanted to thank you for being
so honest and direct. You practically saved my life."

"You're not mad at me for telling the truth?"

"Of course I'm not!" Elizabeth said, giving me a

hug. "I'm completely and totally grateful."

After my little talk with Olivia that weekend, Olivia had looked into my story. And she realized Rod also plagiarized the article he wrote for *The Oracle!* Everyone had been amazed that the boy could write so well. He couldn't. He was channeling *Thomas Jefferson!*

Olivia reported all this to Penny, who had just returned to town. They both stormed Mr. Collins's office Monday morning, the way Lila and I storm a half-price sale at Lisette's. Rod got chewed out. Elizabeth got cleared of plagiarism. She also got a second chance to write her paper. Most important, she got back her old job on *The Oracle.*

And now she was thanking me for being straight with Olivia.

"Well, I'm glad *someone* here can appreciate the value of honesty," I said, glancing at Lila.

But Lila never could last more than five minutes in a conversation that wasn't about herself. She was no longer paying the slightest attention to us. I followed her gaze. It led straight to John Pfeifer.

Everyone thinks John is a great guy. He's kind of cute too. But he's not Lila's usual type. Meaning he's not rich. He's also more intense and serious than the guys she usually dates. Believe me, she's dated plenty. Still, the plum-colored streaks in her hair proved that my friend wants to boldly go where no Fowler has gone before. Everyone needs a change now and then.

Ever since John and Jennifer broke up, Lila has stalked her prey like a panther prowling around after . . . I don't know, whatever it is that panthers like. Anyhow, I sense she's about to move in for the kill.

As for Elizabeth, well, I just thought of something wild. For a few days, I was Saint Jessica the Truthful, while Elizabeth the Perfect became the plagiarism poster child! Wow!

Still, I've had enough total honesty to last a good, long time, thanks to the evil Ms. Fowler. If one more person tells me about this pimple on my chin, I will personally take my leftover cans of purple bedroom paint and color Lila's hair in lovely, grapey streaks!

And that, Dear Diary, is the truth, the whole truth, and nothing but the truth.

Wednesday night

Dear Diary,

Today's mail contained another letter with a Santa Dora postmark. I'm beginning to wonder if Prince Arthur is developing a crush on Elizabeth. Why else would a pen pal write so often? A prince! Some people have all the luck.

Speaking of handsome princes, I've no-
ticed John Pfeifer and Lila sneaking
glances at each other ever since he dumped
Jennifer. I'll keep you informed.

My own prince is as charming as ever—
even if he rides a motorbike instead of a
white steed. And even if he absolutely refuses
to have us dress as Cinderella and her hand-
some prince for the big costume party Lila's
throwing next week. Sam also nixed Romeo
and Juliet. He says real men don't wear
tights. I should be mad at him for not liking
any of my costume ideas, but he was so
adorable this afternoon. And so irresistible!

In fact, I'm worried about Sam and me,
Diary. We like each other a little too much,
if you catch my drift. . . .

Sam had just stopped his car in front of my house
to drop me off. We were arguing about the costume
party, but we were kissing at the same time.

"I'm not running around in public in a pair of
your pantyhose, and that's all there is to it," Sam
declared.

I ruffled his curly blond hair, and gave him the
tiniest of kisses. "You're sure?"

When he kissed me back, an electric pulse
darted through my body. "I'm very sure," he
replied in a husky voice.

I grabbed him by the collar and pressed my lips

against his, long and hard this time. "Positive?"

"Positive," Sam whispered, wrapping his arms around me. His mouth was so close to mine that my lips felt the brush of his voice before my ears heard it. "Absolutely certain."

Our kisses grew longer and more urgent. Every bone in my body melted into honey in his embrace. It was dusk outside, and I knew Elizabeth could see us from inside the house, if she was near a window. Next door, Mrs. Beckwith was out in her yard, finishing up mowing her lawn. But I didn't care. I could hardly hear the buzzing of her lawn mower anymore. My own heartbeat was drowning it out. All I knew was that I was sitting in Sam's car with Sam's arms around me, kissing Sam's lips and touching Sam's back and never wanting to let him go. Every inch of my skin was screaming for his fingers. I felt like we were levitating into the sky, where we would explode in a burst of fireworks.

Sam pulled back at the same time as I did. His eyes were dilated, and he was breathing hard. For a minute we just stared at each other. Then he fell back against the headrest. It took him a minute to catch his breath. "You know what I think we should go to Lila's party as?" he asked finally.

"What?"

"A nuclear bomb."

I knew exactly what he meant. Every time we kissed, it caused a chain reaction that was getting harder and harder to stop. "This is serious, Sam," I

223

said quietly. "I'm really getting worried about this. What if I lose control?"

Sam draped his arm around my shoulder, and it felt comforting there—safe. "What are you talking about, if *you* lose control? You're not the police force here, Jess. We're both involved. Nothing's going to happen if we don't want it to, and we don't. Just because we like kissing doesn't mean we're going to go too far. We've discussed that already."

I snuggled against him. "I know that, but I can't help feeling that's it up to me. I mean, I'm the girl," I said, as if he needed reminding. "If I can't keep myself, you know, more in check, how can I expect you to?"

"Jessica Wakefield," he said seriously, "I may be a boy, but I'm not some sort of wild beast, you know. It's not like you kiss me and I go brain dead right away. I'm a person too. I have as much responsibility for what happens between us as you do." This time, he kissed the top of my head. And even that soft little peck melted something inside of me. "I care about you, Jess. You know I would never hurt you."

I smiled back at him. "Does this mean you'll wear the tights?"

No luck on the tights, Diary. I'll have to keep working on him. Anyhow, after Sam left, I went in the house and flopped down on the foot of Elizabeth's bed. And I asked my sister for advice. . . .

"How do you and Todd stay so close and not . . . *you know?*" I asked. "The other night Sam and I were kissing so hard that we fell out of the car."

Elizabeth laughed and wanted to know how we managed that. *How should I know how we managed it?* I wasn't taking notes.

"This isn't funny!" I said finally. "Once I start kissing Sam, I practically forget what planet I'm on."

"And you think Todd and I don't?" my sister asked. "You think Todd and I just shake hands and give each other a peck on the cheek?"

That blew me away, Diary. I mean, Liz and Todd? Sure, they're as tight as peanut butter and jelly. But they're also just as wholesome! And as boring. It's hard to imagine them getting passionate. My sister says they do, but they set themselves limits and force themselves to stop.

So far, Sam and I have been able to do that. But I'm not sure I trust myself to always remember those limits when things get . . . intense. Or to care.

Thursday night, late
It happened again. Or it almost did. Sam came over to help me with my math homework. Who can keep track of all those numbers and symbols anyway? As long as you can count money and figure out your

225

dress size, what's the use? Unfortunately,
Mr. Frankel (also known as the sadistic Dr.
Frankelstein, math teacher and torturer of
innocent teens) doesn't agree.

Sam was leaning over my shoulder at the
kitchen table, pointing to something nonsensical in
my math book and muttering mysterious incanta-
tions about something called polynomials.

Even if you have half a clue to what polynomials are—and even if you *care*—it's impossible to
concentrate on a foreign language when the cutest
boy in California has his cheek next to yours. And
if he's wearing that woodsy, pine-smelling after-
shave, well, you might as well be studying history,
because that's what your homework is.

Sam was so close that I just had to kiss him.
Naturally, he kissed me back. Goodbye, polynomials!
When we came up for air, it was two hours later, and
Mom and Dad were pulling into the driveway.

"I knew Sam was fast on a dirt bike," Elizabeth
said when I confided in her after he left. "But this
is ridiculous!"

"Tell me about it," I said. "This really isn't
funny anymore, Liz. I'm just as bad as Sam is.
Every time I'm near him I want to kiss him. I'm
like a moth to a flame."

Elizabeth was trying hard not to laugh. "It seems
to me that the problem isn't that you *want* to kiss
him," she said. "The problem is that you *do*."

"We're going to have to have a guard," I said glumly.

"Oh sure. Maybe Grandma could come out to be your chaperon. I'm sure she'd love going to dirt-bike meets and dances."

"Well, something drastic has to be done! We can't go on like this."

Elizabeth suddenly looked serious. "Jessica, promise me one thing. Promise me you won't go overboard like you usually do. This isn't the megacrisis you think it is."

"Overboard?" I repeated. "When have I ever gone overboard?"

"Jessica, we don't have five hours for me to stand here and list all the times you've gone overboard. All I'm trying to say is that this is no big deal. Todd and I have gone through exactly the same thing. Every couple does."

I can accept that Liz and Todd kiss. I can even accept that they kiss seriously. But let's face it. Todd is about as exciting as a plate of cold mashed potatoes. And Elizabeth has less passion than gravy. There's no way that she really understands what I'm talking about here.

So I came to my own decision. Sam and I are not going to be alone. We'll go everywhere in groups. When we kiss goodnight, it will be under the porch light. As long as we're never alone, it'll be fine.

I told this to Elizabeth, and she only made fun of me. "It's going to be pretty crowded in Sam's car with half of Sweet Valley High in the backseat," she said. She thinks I'm overreacting, that all I need is a little self-discipline.

How do you like that? Here I am, happy-go-lucky Jessica, trying hard for once to do the responsible thing. I mean, I'm seriously afraid of my own hormones! And my twin just laughs.

Is it possible to be too much in love with a boy?

Liz got a letter from Prince Arthur yesterday. And believe it or not, she got yet another one today! I bet he's running up his country's budget deficit, printing all that fancy cream-colored stationery embossed with the Castillo family crest!

I'm going out with Sam tonight, and I fully intend to enforce my new motto of "zero temptation." If he's driving the car, I'll sit in the backseat. It's the only way to be safe.

But I'm not the only one with plans for tonight. Lila and John are going out! I haven't seen her so excited about a first date in months. Elizabeth says John is excited too. He told her at The Oracle office this week that he can't believe a girl like Lila is interested in him. I really hope they have a fantastic time!

Tuesday night

Something's been wrong with Lila since the weekend. She has dark circles under her eyes, and she came to school in baggy sweats today. How un-Lila can you get? She looks like she's about to burst into tears every minute. Amy and I figured she'd be bubbling over with news about her date with John. But she's hardly said a word about that or anything else. Not even to me, her closest friend.

She even mentioned today that she's thinking of canceling her costume party this Saturday! Lila's never canceled a party in her life. I'm worried about her.

Saturday night, late

Something terrible has happened! I'm sorry about the teardrops on this page. I can't stop myself. I feel so awful for Lila. Now I know why she's been so upset. Everybody knows.

At first, I was relieved that she decided to go ahead with her costume party. Nothing cheers up Lila more than hosting a bash the whole town will talk about for weeks. They'll talk about this one, all right. . . .

Sam and I finally decided to dress as Han Solo and Princess Leia from *Star Wars*. And we looked sharper than your average space cadets, if I do say so myself. Elizabeth and Todd came as the sun and the moon. Dana Larson, the Droids's lead singer, was a punked-out Statue of Liberty, with a lava lamp for a torch. In fact, Fowler Crest was an explosion of popular culture, filled with clowns and storybook characters and Klingons. The music rocked, the conversation rolled, and the guacamole flowed freely. All in all, it was a pretty blistering fiesta.

Even Lila was getting psyched. She dressed as Peter Pan, and I noticed she was wearing makeup for the first time in a week. It wasn't as sexy or glamorous an outfit as she usually puts together for these parties. But she looked cute. And I actually saw her smile.

Then the pirate walked in. He looked familiar from the instant he entered the room. But he wore an eye patch, a fake beard, and a mustache, so it was hard to pinpoint his identity. With him was a fuzzy blue bunny I vaguely recognized as a cute little sophomore named Julie something.

Lila was watching the pirate curiously. I could tell from her face that she recognized him at the same moment that I did. It was John. But what I saw in her face was horror. Without even thinking about it, I began pushing my way through the crowd toward my best friend, dragging Sam behind me. I kept my eyes on Lila's face as Peter Pan and Captain Hook exchanged tense words at the punch table. Lila's hands were shaking.

John smiled triumphantly. Then he turned his back on Lila and walked away. And Lila's expression turned to one I knew well: pure rage.

"Why don't we get out of here now, Julie?" John said to his date in a voice meant to be overheard. He slipped his arm around the bunny's waist. "This party is boring. Let's go somewhere where we can be alone."

"No!" Lila screamed, stepping toward them. "Don't go with him!"

By now, I was beside her. "Lila," I whispered, trying to take her hand. Voices hushed. Everyone in the room turned to watch her. Lila shook me off and strode right up to John's date. Julie's confused gaze shifted from Lila to John and back again.

"I mean it," Lila told her in a grim voice. "You'll be sorry if you leave with him. Take it from me."

"I don't know what you mean," the girl faltered. "John?"

"Don't listen to her," John said coolly.

Elizabeth and Todd were beside Sam and me now, just a few steps behind Lila. I started to walk toward my friend, but Sam gently pushed me aside. Something serious was happening here, and one thing was clear: Lila was not only angry with John; she was terrified of him. Sam and Todd stepped forward, one on each side of her. But Lila didn't seem to notice.

"Tell her!" she screamed at John. "Tell her why she shouldn't go with you. *Tell her how you tried to rape me last Saturday night!*"

231

Somebody turned off the CD player.

Sam moved closer, his arm touching Lila's.

"Tell her!" Lila screamed again. Tears streamed down her face as her body shook with sobs. "Tell her what going someplace alone with you is like!"

John was as calm as a snake watching its supper scamper near. "I don't know what you're talking about, Lila," he said with a smug smile. "We both know what happened last Saturday, and it wasn't rape. In fact, it was anything but." He raised his eyebrows suggestively, and only Elizabeth's restraining arm kept me from leaping forward and scratching his eyes out.

Lila opened her mouth to reply, but nothing came out.

I was so proud of Sam then. He stepped in front of her protectively. "I think you'd better get out of here, John," he said in a cold, even voice. "If you know what's good for you."

John smirked. "You mean if *you* know what's good for *her.*"

Elizabeth had to hold me back again.

Lila fled upstairs. I pounded on her door for the next two hours, long after everyone went home. But she wouldn't open it, no matter how hard I begged her to let me in.

Sunday evening
Men can be such pigs! Who could have dreamed of such a terrible thing? John always seemed normal. He's a friend of my

sister's, for heaven's sake! What could be safer than a friend of Elizabeth's?

I keep thinking about the article Liz wrote on sexual harassment. She said women who've been victims are afraid to speak up. They're afraid nobody will believe them. Or they're afraid that what happened was their own fault.

Lila finally talked to me today, and that's exactly what she said. She thought she was to blame because it was her idea to go to Miller's Point. And she'd liked kissing John. She'd liked it a lot! But when she asked him to stop, he wouldn't. He accused Lila of leading him on. He banged her head against the door frame. He grabbed her by her hair. She only got away by stabbing him in the neck with his keys.

Lila trusted John! The whole school trusted John! I guess nobody will anymore.

Tuesday evening

I was wrong. Teenagers are the lowest creatures on the planet. Almost everyone believes John. They're blaming Lila for what happened! Lila is so depressed she can barely speak. I think she's beginning to see why so many women don't report sexual assaults. It's like being in the middle of a nightmare that won't end. . . .

I was crouching at my locker Monday morning, digging for my gym shoes, when I discovered Lila's ordeal was just beginning.

"Did you hear what happened at Lila Fowler's party Saturday night?" asked a girl's voice on the other side of my open locker door.

"You mean with John Pfeifer?" asked a second girl.

"That's right," said the first girl. "Can you believe it? I mean, I don't know John personally, but he's always seemed like such a nice guy. You know, steady and serious."

The other girl banged her locker shut. "Yeah, but we've only heard her side of the story." She laughed. "After all, you do have to consider the source. You know the sort of reputation she has as well as I do."

I was on my feet in an instant. "Just what are you trying to say?" I demanded. "Are you suggesting Lila's lying?"

The stunned girls stared at me. "Look," the second one said calmly, after she'd recovered from her surprise, "I know Lila's your best friend and everything, Jessica. But you have to face the facts. Lila's a flirt. Everybody knows that. She does everything she can to attract boys, so what does she expect?"

"She expects a little more understanding from other girls, that's what she expects!" I shot back.

Things only got worse as the day wore on. Everywhere Lila went, boys laughed and made snide remarks. Girls stared and pointed and whispered.

"Look at how people are staring at me," Lila whispered as we crossed the cafeteria at lunchtime. "I feel like I should be wearing a sign that says, She Got What She Deserved. Amy and Caroline and I ate lunch with her, and we all tried to be as supportive as we could. Amy urged her to call Project Youth for counseling. Caroline promised to broadcast the truth about John Pfeifer on all her usual gossip channels. And I did my best to keep Lila's spirits up. But it wasn't easy.

By Tuesday morning, Lila was seriously thinking of transferring to a school where nobody's ever heard of her.

Lila wishes she'd kept her mouth shut about John. I can't let her think like that. I know she was right to speak out!

You know, people would be acting exactly the same way if this had happened to ME. They might take the word of a girl like Elizabeth or Penny. A girl who's considered mature and responsible. A girl who's not a flirt. But if you're like Lila and me—if you try to look great and dress stylishly and have fun—you're toast! Forget the fact that Lila has no reason to lie about it. Do people think she likes being treated like dirt? Why would she go through this on purpose?

Elizabeth says it's a complicated issue. Even she and Todd and some their closest friends can't agree. These aren't mentally challenged airheads. They're reasonable people. They were there Saturday night and saw the horror on Lila's face. They believe her. But even Elizabeth says she can't condemn John without proof. What kind of proof are people waiting for?

I'm sorry, but Lila didn't have her video camera along that night.

Among the guys, even a lot of those who believe Lila's story still insist she deserved what happened. Why is it that when a pretty girl is involved, we don't hold men responsible for their actions? I know people can control their hormones if they try! Sam can. Even I've been able to, despite all my worrying about it. So why doesn't our society expect men to? It makes me sick.

I disagree with Liz. I don't think the issue is complicated at all. The issue is respect. Women have the right to be respected. And no matter how a woman is dressed or how many other guys she's gone out with before, she has the right to say no.

Why is that so hard to understand?

Wednesday night, late

I knew something was up this morning when I arrived at school early and caught Lila slipping a note into John's locker. She pulled me aside and said she wanted him to meet her at the Dairi Burger tonight. She told

236

me her plan and asked me to be there. . . .

When Lila walked into the Dairi Burger Wednesday night, the place was packed. I was sitting in a corner booth with Elizabeth, Sam, and Todd.

Lila met my eyes and Elizabeth's, and she nodded. I knew she was relieved to see us. Lila was with a girl I barely knew, a stunning sophomore named Susan Wyler. The two of them snagged a table and fiddled with their menus while they waited for John to arrive.

John showed up a few minutes later, accompanied by most of the boys' volleyball team, their hair still wet from the showers after that night's game. They sat at a big table in the middle of the restaurant, and I cringed. Whatever Lila said to him, everyone in the room would hear it. I prayed that her plan would go off the way she hoped.

As soon as Lila appeared at John's table, the volleyball players started smirking and nudging John with their elbows.

"Well, if it isn't the princess herself," John said in a loud voice. The room hushed when everyone saw Lila standing at John's side. He grinned. "Don't tell me you've finally decided to apologize to me for defaming my good name."

The other boys whistled and leered. But Lila kept her poise. She asked to speak with John privately, but he refused.

Lila stood up straighter. "All right, Mr. I-Have-Nothing-to-Hide," she said. "I just wanted to tell you that I discovered something last night that I think you should know about."

"What?" John asked, pretending to be scared. "That you've changed your mind again?"

I slid from my booth and walked across the restaurant until I was standing behind Lila, next to Susan. Elizabeth, Sam, and Todd were right behind me, just in case Lila needed us. But I don't think Lila noticed. She was talking over the boys' snickers.

"No, that I have something in common with Susan Wyler," she said. At the sound of the sophomore's name, a flicker of worry lighted John's green eyes. For the first time, he looked uncertain, as Lila continued in her sweetest voice, "You remember Susan Wyler, John. Susan Wyler is the other girl who had the misfortune of going out with you recently."

John looked around at his friends. "I don't know what she's talking about!"

Susan stepped out from behind Lila. "Oh, yes, you do, John," she said in a nervous voice. "You know exactly what we're talking about."

The boys at John's table suddenly looked confused and uncomfortable. One of them, a senior I knew only as Dean, nudged him. "What's going on here, Pfeifer? Susan's my kid sister's best friend, you know. She's practically part of my family."

"Nothing's going on. The two of them think they're funny, that's all."

"Oh, sure, John," Susan said with growing confidence. "We think *you're* real funny too. First you try to attack me, and then you try to attack Lila! Can't you see you have a problem, John? Can't you see that you should be trying to get help, not trying to act like nothing happened?"

"Susan and I are very worried about you, John," Lila added. "We think that you should get some professional help." She turned to John's friends, who seemed to be backing away from John. "Don't you think that someone who can't go on a date without trying to attack a girl should seek professional help?"

Dean stood up, staring at John as if he'd never seen him before. "Yeah! Yeah. I do think he should."

"Oh, come on, Dean. You don't believe—"

"Susan Wyler doesn't lie! And neither does Lila Fowler, from what I can see." He shoved his chair so roughly the table jerked. "Which leaves *you*, doesn't it, John?"

Without another word he strode from the restaurant.

John appealed to the rest of the volleyball players, but now they were staring at him, shaking their heads. Within minutes, they'd drifted away. And John was left alone at the table with a dazed look on his face.

What a night! Three cheers for Lila Fowler—and for women everywhere.

John doesn't realize it, but he's lucky. Lila could have pressed assault charges. Now, I think he really will get counseling. And I know Lila will.

Susan apologized for not speaking up sooner, but she was afraid people would blame her—exactly the way they blamed Lila. She only came forward when she heard what happened at Lila's costume party. If she'd stood up for herself earlier, maybe Lila wouldn't have had to go through this.

Something still bothers me, Diary. What if Susan hadn't come forward? Why does John have to attack TWO women before anyone pays attention? He tried to rape my best friend! That should have been enough, but it wasn't. Nobody cared. Why is it OK for him to do what he wants, as long as there's only one victim?

I'm beginning to see why Elizabeth is a feminist.

Saturday morning

So much was happening with Lila that I forgot to mention some other important news. Arthur Castillo explained to Elizabeth why he's been writing so many letters lately. He's coming to Sweet Valley in two weeks! Real royalty! Right here! How romantic.

Elizabeth insists the two of them are just friends. That is so lame. Why would anyone in her right mind choose Todd, the slam-dunking Boy Scout, when she could have a real, live prince? It's obvious that Prince Arthur has a thing for my sister. But she's not interested.

I wonder. . . . I look just like Liz. Could Arthur fall in love with me just as easily? Dating a prince would be even more glamorous than starring in a movie.

What am I saying? I'M IN LOVE WITH SAM! He may not be a prince, but he adores me. Even more since I realized that my Never-Be-Alone-Together philosophy was dumb. And I adore him!

So why am I daydreaming about Prince Arthur of Santa Dora? Why can't I ever be happy with what's in front of my face?

It's a good thing I have this diary for auditioning my boneheaded ideas before I unleash them into my real life!

Three weeks later

It's very late on a Saturday night, and I haven't written in ages. I guess I've been too depressed. And too busy screwing up my life. I'd never admit this to anyone but you, Diary. But sometimes I think I should wear a permanent dunce cap. Or maybe I'll buy Elizabeth or Sam one of those shirts that says "I'm With Stupid." Well, Elizabeth anyway. Sam will probably never speak to me again.

Yes, once again I've upset Sam and made myself look like a jerk. I've developed a real talent for that. At least I wasn't the only one. . . .

From the minute we heard that Arthur Castillo was stopping in Sweet Valley during his world tour, almost every girl at school totally lost her mind.

For one thing, Arthur was a sixteen-year-old prince who would someday be king of a whole country—even if it is a little bitty country. Arthur lived in a castle, traveled in limos and yachts, and hung out with Princess Diana when he was in London.

As if that wasn't enough, Arthur was a hunk! One of the best-looking boys any of us had ever seen in our entire lives. He was tall, dark, and handsome—the perfect fairy-tale prince. Almost too perfect to be real. Maybe they put something special in Santa Dora's water supply.

Lila decided immediately that she was the perfect girl for him. After all, she's the closest thing to royalty we've got. I begged to differ. I reasoned that money was irrelevant to someone as rich as a prince. I thought he'd be more captivated by a sparkling personality. Nobody sparkles like I do. Of course, every other girl had her own reasons why she was the one who'd catch the eye of the handsome prince. Our boyfriends were not happy campers.

Only two girls in school were unaffected: Elizabeth and Dana. From the tone of Arthur's letter-writing blitz, it was clear to me—and even to Enid, who's clueless about men—that the prince's feelings for my sister had matured somewhat since sixth grade. In other words, he was crazy about her! But Elizabeth, being Elizabeth, still had eyes only for Todd.

Dana's eyes were focused strictly on her sheet music. It's not as if she were dating someone. She just had zero interest in Arthur. In fact, she had some serious attitude about him. Dana is tall and funky and strikingly pretty. And she dresses in nutty, outrageous styles. I like that in a person. But Dana can be a real dweeb-head. For instance, she had this weird theory about monarchy being an outdated system. She said royalty was obsolete—that princes lived extravagant lifestyles at the expense of their people. Blah blah blah.

Yes, I thought as she explained this in English class when Arthur was visiting. *And your point is?* I mean, *get real.* What's the good of being a prince if you can't take advantage of the perks?

So Mr. Collins set up a debate between the two of them. Dana made some OK arguments. But Arthur won, and she fled from the room in disgrace.

Anyhow, unlike Dana, I had no problems with royalty. If I couldn't be a movie star, a princess sure sounded like a good alternative.

The focal point of my efforts to make Arthur fall in love with me was a Saturday night party with an all-American theme. I worked like crazy on this party. The Droids were singing; Dana didn't want to, because she disapproved of Arthur, but the rest of the band voted her down. There's that democracy she's so hot on!

People were playing water volleyball in the pool. We ate hot dogs and hamburgers and apple pie. My decorations were totally red, white, and blue. Even my new bikini had stars and stripes!

Everyone raved about what a terrific party it was.

So why am I having such a rotten time? I wondered. But I knew exactly why. It was because Arthur had danced with practically every other girl there. But not with me. I decided to bribe him with apple pie.

"Hey, you read my mind," called a familiar male voice as I carved two wedges of pie. "I'm in the mood for dessert."

Sam!

"Although I'm not sure which is sweeter," he murmured, slipping an arm around my waist and nuzzling my neck. "You or the pie!" As usual, at Sam's touch, my insides began to melt—despite his corny language. In fact, I nearly dropped the plates I was holding.

But Sam was not royalty.

"Um, actually," I said, wriggling away from him, "this is for Arthur."

Sam rolled his eyes. "Right, I keep forgetting. There's a prince in the neighborhood. The rest of us guys might as well be invisible."

"Sam," I reminded him, "Arthur is my guest of honor! I'm just trying to be a good hostess."

"What about being a good girlfriend?"

"Wait a minute!" I demanded. "Since when am I not living up to your definition of a good girlfriend? Just because I'm not hanging all over you, you take that as a rejection?"

"That's not it, and you know it," Sam objected. "I don't expect you to hang all over me, but I also don't expect to have to watch you hang all over some other guy."

"It doesn't mean anything!" I swore, though I wished it did. "Arthur would be offended if I didn't cater to his every wish." That wasn't true either. In person, Arthur is a down-to-earth guy, not at all bossy or pretentious. But I had to tell Sam *something*. "He's a crown prince, and crown princes expect—"

"I don't care who he is!" Sam snapped at me. "Look, Jessica, I've been cutting you slack all night, but I've had as much as I can take. I don't know why you even invited me, since you obviously don't want me around!"

A minute later, Sam was storming across the patio—and maybe out of my life!

> It wasn't just tonight, Diary. If that had been all, Sam would have chalked it up to me stressing about playing hostess. I've been obsessing about Arthur since the day we heard he was coming to town. I knew it was wrong, but I couldn't help myself. My only consolation is that Lila has been acting even more possessed than me.
>
> Stressed, obsessed, possessed. That's Lila and me both.
>
> You wanna know what the crowning insult is (if I can use the word crown in this particular context)? Arthur isn't the least bit interested in either Lila or me!
>
> In other words, I acted like a total ditz in

front of everyone, bragging about how this party would make him go postal for me. I spent eons of time and tons of money to make it the best party of my life. I drove away poor Sam, who wanted nothing more than a little attention and respect. And in the end, Prince Charming plucked me from the crowd to ask me that soul-stirring question: "Would you please ask Dana to dance the next song with me?"

That's right, Diary. Prince Arthur danced the night away with Dana Larson—even though she had dissed him in front of everyone about being a parasitic tyrant. He said he likes her independent spirit and quick mind.

Gag. I'd have had more fun if I'd spent the night with Prince Albert! And he's a dog.

Thursday afternoon

Life has improved. My sweet, long-suffering boyfriend has forgiven me for treating him like a doormat. Sam is just too good to me, Diary! I don't deserve him.

We're not the only two people around who are totally in love. The newest, most surprising couple in town: Arthur and Dana.

That's right, it's The Prince and the Punker. A man who will rule a country, and a woman who breaks all the rules. Arthur, his gold sash covered with medals, and Dana, with her paint-on tattoos.

They've ridden all over town in his chauffeur-driven stretch limousine. They've been sight-seeing, sailing, and even bowling. And I never would have believed it, but they've fallen in love in just a few days.

I'm cool with that. My prince-chasing days are over. But Lila is livid! And she's freaking, in a very un-Lila-like way that's giving me an overwhelming sense of ickiness. I don't understand why she's so ballistic about Arthur. After what happened with John, I'd have thought the last thing Lila would do was chase after a guy.

And chasing is exactly what she's doing. Her plan begins with sucking up to Arthur's cute bodyguard, Paolo, to squeeze information out of him about Arthur's schedule. She's sneaking around in her lime-green Triumph (now that's a discreet car to tail someone in), following the prince's limo when Arthur and Dana go on dates! She spies on him at the hotel gym where he works out.

I'm sorry to say that I went along with Lila on some of this stuff. But no more! Arthur is with Dana now. Get over it, Lila.

Tuesday night

Man, oh man, oh man. This is just too unbelievable. But the headline was on the

front page of the Sweet Valley News *today*
and even made the national tabloids. It was
all anyone could talk about at school. . . .

I brushed aside a stray copy of the *Sweet Valley News* as Lila and I staked out a table in the cafeteria. I wasn't fast enough. Lila whisked the paper out of my hand.

"*Santa Dora Prince May Wed Local Teen,*" screamed the headline. We'd both seen it a dozen times. But that didn't make it any easier to swallow. Especially for Lila.

"I can't believe it!" she declared for the hundredth time that day. "I just can't believe it!"

Supposedly, Arthur had asked Dana to marry him the preceding Friday night, on a moonlit beach. She hadn't given him an answer yet. But she already had the diamond ring. Right now they were sitting at a table on the opposite side of the cafeteria, surrounded by curious kids. We had no desire to join the throng.

Lila is still scheming for a way to break
up the happy couple so she can steal Arthur
for herself. She's planning to research Santa
Dora customs and history, as if that'll do any
good. Lila in a library! Now there's a weird
image! I don't know what she expects to find.
I told her to count me out.

She doesn't have much time. Everyone's

*expecting a formal engagement announcement
at a party this Saturday. Ironically, the party is
at Lila's house. Her father set it up when we first
heard the prince was coming to Sweet Valley.*

         *Late Saturday night
Lila the One-Woman Demolition Derby
has done it this time. She managed to break
up Arthur and Dana. And it didn't do her a
bit of good. . . .*

Lila hit pay dirt. Her research turned up a
weirded-out Santa Dora custom that's kept pretty
much hush-hush outside the kingdom, though it goes
back to around the Age of the Dinosaurs. When the
next king reaches the age of seventeen, he is formally
named the crown prince, kind of a king-in-waiting. But
he spends the year before it preparing for that day.

We already knew Arthur's around-the-world trip
was traditional for a sixteen-year-old Santa Doran
prince. What we didn't know was the real reason behind it. It was basically one big, expensive shopping
trip. And what Arthur was shopping for was a *wife!*

By his seventeenth birthday, Arthur had to be engaged. On that day, if he hadn't found a fiancée on his
own, he was stuck with anyone his parents picked. In
Arthur's case, that meant Lady Tracy Windsor, a notoriously obnoxious relative of the queen of England.
The press had nicknamed her the British Brat.

Arthur didn't have to get *married* at seventeen. He

was expected to have a long engagement while he finished his education. But Arthur's birthday was a month away, and Sweet Valley was the last stop on his world tour. If he didn't find a girl here, it was *Hello, Tracy.*

Suddenly, Lila thought she understood why the prince had chosen Dana instead of her. Or me. She was available, and they got along fine. Dana wasn't the British Brat. Besides that, Arthur didn't have time to be choosy.

After some careful checking, Lila decided that Dana didn't know about Santa Dora's engagement rule for crown princes. Dana thought Arthur wanted to marry her because he loved her.

Nobody else seemed to know about the engagement rule either. So Lila leaked it to the Sweet Valley Times and waited for the fireworks. Dana was sure to be pissed off at Arthur for not telling her the whole story. After she dumped him, Lila could take her rightful place as the future queen of Santa Dora.

> *Gosh, Diary. It all seems so devious. Even to me, and I'm the Queen of Devious. But it's more than that. It's just too weird. I don't understand what's going on in my best friend's head at all. I just don't know who Lila is anymore.*

Lila's plan worked. As soon as Dana learned that Arthur had a short deadline for choosing a bride, she reacted just as Lila knew she would. She jumped to the conclusion that he'd never loved her at all but was only using her to avoid Lady Tracy. Dana stormed into Arthur's hotel suite, flung the diamond ring at him, and shouted that she never wanted to see him again.

The fairy tale was over.

Sunday night
So much has happened in the last twenty-four hours. Where should I begin?

Arthur tried and tried to talk to Dana, but she refused to see him. Finally, he gave up. Lila practically threw herself at him at the party at her house Saturday night. But Arthur barely noticed her. Heartbroken, he decided to cut short his trip and return to Santa Dora the very next day.

I was still mystified about Lila's odd behavior. But Elizabeth helped put it in perspective for me as I ate breakfast Sunday.

"I have a feeling that for Lila, getting Arthur to like her meant a lot more than just snagging a rich boyfriend," Elizabeth said thoughtfully. "I still think what she did to Dana was pretty horrible. But I do think I'm beginning to understand her motives."

"I think I see what you're saying," I said slowly. "There were times during Arthur's visit when I thought Lila was losing her mind. All those crazy excursions—" I stopped, realizing Elizabeth knew nothing about Lila and me tailing the prince's limo in the lime green Triumph.

"What crazy excursions?"

"Never mind the details," I advised. "The point is that she was getting really out of hand, even for Lila. It was like she'd do *anything* to make Arthur notice her."

"I think," Elizabeth began, "that for Lila, Arthur represented a boy totally different from John Pfeifer. John seemed like a nice guy, but he wasn't what he appeared to be. Lila probably thought there was less of a risk that Arthur, brought up to be polite and respectful, would turn out to be a creep."

"And he didn't," I pointed out.

"I'm not saying he did. What I'm saying is that to Lila, Arthur's not showing any real interest in her was more than just your average rejection."

"Poor Lila!" I said. "Arthur was probably the only guy in Sweet Valley who didn't know about what happened with John Pfeifer."

Elizabeth sipped her coffee. "I'm just glad that Lila is still in counseling at Project Youth. It's going to take a while for her life to get back to normal."

As for Dana, I'm not sure if her life is back to normal either. Elizabeth took a last stab at talking to her Sunday morning, trying to convince her that Arthur really did love her and deserved to be heard out. Dana rushed to Arthur's hotel and managed to catch him in the lobby as he prepared to leave for the airport.

Dana apologized for getting mad at him and not giving him a chance to explain. Arthur apologized for assuming she knew about the engagement deadline and not realizing how it might offend her. He assured her that he'd want to marry her, deadline or not. As they spoke, their anger and hurt melted away.

"It was all my fault," Arthur concluded. "But one good thing did come from all this."

"What's that?"

"Late last night, I made a decision," Arthur said. "It's time for me to stand up against this unfair, outdated tradition. I'm not going to announce my betrothal before my seventeenth birthday, and I'm also not going to marry anyone I don't want to."

Dana gasped. "But what will your parents say about that?"

"I don't know. I'll talk it over with them as soon as I get back to Santa Dora. Either they will agree with me that it's time to abandon this particular custom, or they will make my younger brother crown prince in my place."

"I'm proud of you," Dana said, her eyes glowing.

I've heard that story a million times around S.V.H.—everybody's talking about it. Arthur and Dana still love each other, but they didn't make a commitment before Arthur left for Santa Dora. Maybe they'll give things another try in a few years.

It would have been nice to have a princess-in-waiting in our class. Now we'll have to go back to the usual routines around here. Dull with a capital D.

At times like this, I miss Checkered Houses the most. I wish I could have at least helped Charles get his financing. He has a wonderful vision. He deserves to see it on the screen—even with another actress playing Blythe. But our letter-writing service didn't exactly put us on the New York Stock Exchange. And I never got chummy enough with Prince Arthur to pawn the crown jewels! But that's OK. Being a princess wasn't my dream. It was just a diversion.

As for my other dream, I can't say I have no regrets. But I chose to follow my heart instead of my star. Sam really does love me, Diary. No matter what other amazing things I see and do, nothing will ever be as amazing as that.

Wherever Charles is right now, Diary, I hope he's working at making his dream a reality. And I hope he knows I'm pulling for him.

Part 4

Dear Diary,

There's a weird new girl at school. She's always staring at me. It gives me the creeps. I know her name is Paula. And that's all I want to know about this girl.

Luckily, there's much more exciting news to report. I've found a way to jump-start my acting career—without making Sam go ballistic. Listen to this: David Goodman is staging a production of Macbeth at Sweet Valley High! Mr. Goodman is a big-time theater director. But every year he picks one high school for a special project. Because he's so famous, it gets lots of publicity. Even the big newspapers will run reviews. This is my chance to

*get noticed! And Sam won't mind if I star
in a school play.*

*I do mean star. I plan to play Lady
Macbeth. I've been practicing for the audition for days, Diary. And I know I can do
it better than anyone. Even Lila. We were
all talking about it at lunch today. . . .*

Amy, Lila, and I were eating at our usual cafeteria table, and Annie pulled out a chair to join us.
"I'm thinking of trying out for the play," she said.

"I don't want to discourage you, Annie," I told
her, "but you ought to be more realistic. You don't
have a chance at playing Lady Macbeth. Not with
me trying out."

"And me," Lila added.

Annie's certainly pretty enough to be an actress.
She's small and graceful, with dark hair. In fact, she
looks like her mother, who's a professional model. But
when it came to playing royalty, she'd be no match
for Lila or me. Besides, Annie was only a sophomore.

Annie giggled. "Oh, I'd never dream of trying
out for Lady Macbeth. Besides, you've got that in
the bag, Jess."

I smiled modestly at Annie and cast a triumphant glare at Lila.

Annie explained that she was bored stiff lately.
She'd broken up with Tony Esteban. And her
mother was in New York for the next month on a
big assignment. So Annie said she'd only be sitting

at home alone every night. The play would give her something to do with herself.

"Bill Chase is sure to get the part of Macbeth," Amy said. "He's the best actor at school."

She smiled wickedly at me, and she and Lila launched into a discussion of how badly I treated poor Bill when we starred together in the school production of *Splendor in the Grass*. But I couldn't help it if he had a crush on me.

Elizabeth and Todd breezed by to tell us some more news. My sister was asked to be student publicity director for the play. Now this was totally cool.

"Liz, this is fantastic!" I told her. "You can make sure my picture is on all the posters!"

Todd rolled his eyes, but Elizabeth laughed. "Thanks for your selfless support," she said, bopping me on the head with her French book.

As I dodged her, I noticed the thin, mousy girl who sat at a nearby table, staring at my friends and me.

"There's that girl we saw in the hall yesterday!" I whispered. "And yesterday afternoon she was outside school when Sam picked me up. Every time I turn around, she's there."

Everybody turned to see, and the mousy kid looked away. Lila, eyebrows raised, scrutinized the girl's tacky blouse, which was at least five years out of style. Then she turned away, rolling her eyes.

"I've seen her too," Elizabeth said, ignoring Lila's disdain. "I think she's a transfer sophomore."

Annie nodded. "That's right. She just started here

257

a few weeks ago. Her name's Paula Perrine. She's in my English class, but she mostly keeps to herself."

"It's getting weird," I remarked. "Not only did I see her twice yesterday, but last week she was hanging around outside the gym after cheerleading practice. I think she must be following me."

"Aren't you being a little paranoid, Jessica?" Todd asked.

"I'm sure it's just a coincidence," Annie said quickly.

"Yeah," I agreed. "It's probably just a coincidence." When nobody was looking, I glanced over at Paula again. This time, she didn't look away.

> *Wednesday evening*
> *Our next-door neighbors, the Beckwiths, are moving to Washington, D.C., at the end of the month. I wonder who will buy their house. I hope it's somebody with a cute teenage son!*
>
> *(Yes, I'm still in love with Sam. But I can look, can't I?)*

> *Friday night*
> *I did it! I, Jessica Wakefield, will be playing the part of Lady Macbeth in the biggest dramatic production S.V.H. has ever staged! This almost makes up for not being able to do Charles's movie.*
>
> *Bill Chase, as expected, is my husband.*

Jennifer Morris is my understudy—not that she'll ever need to worry about that! Winston is Banquo, which ought to be good for a laugh. But the funniest casting of all is the witches: Annie, Rosa, and Lila. Yes, the beautiful, rich, snobby Lila Fowler is playing a witch. She had a fit, of course. But Winston and Amy convinced her that the witch's parts are the most difficult, and she was chosen because she has such "range" as an actress. It worked. As always, the best way to get Lila to do something is to tell her how wonderful she is.

I won't have time to write much in the next few weeks. I'm giving up everything—except Sam—so I can devote every moment to rehearsing. I am going to be the best Lady Macbeth anyone has ever seen!

Oh, I was wrong about Paula. She was only watching me all the time because she admires me and wants to be my friend. But she was too shy to say. I met her earlier this week, after the second round of auditions. . . .

I pushed open the heavy side door of the auditorium and stepped out into the sunlight. Just outside the door was Paula Perrine, wearing a faded plaid skirt and a clashing sweater. She startled me, and I felt a sudden wave of irrational fear. I recovered my composure and stared coldly at her. "I've seen you watching me."

259

"Oh, yes!" Paula admitted fervently. "I have been watching you. Who wouldn't? I think you're just great!"

The girl was a little whacked-out, I decided, but she wasn't all bad.

"I know you'll get the part!" Paula said. "I love the theater, and I can tell you're meant to be a star."

"Well, thanks," I said, a little uncomfortable. Was this girl for real? I began walking across the parking lot toward the Jeep, and she fell in step with me. "It's Paula Perrine, right?"

Paula gasped. "Oh, wow! I don't believe Jessica Wakefield actually knows my name!" She stopped, blushing. "I'm sorry. I didn't mean to embarrass you. It's just that you and your friends are so beautiful and so popular, I never dreamed you would notice someone like me."

"Hey, it's OK. We may be popular, but we're not stuck-up." I stopped, thinking of Lila. "At least, some of us aren't. Well, this is my Jeep. I've gotta go. It was, uh, nice to meet you."

"Oh, the thrill is mine, I swear!" Paula said. "And Jessica, if there's anything I can do for you— anything—just let me know!"

As it's turned out, there's been plenty for her to do. When I started preparing for auditions, Elizabeth helped me translate Shakespeare's funky, old-fashioned language into real English, so I'd know what I was saying. But now my twin didn't have time to run through my lines with me. As publicity director, she was too busy writing press releases and running a contest for the best poster.

So Paula offered to help me rehearse. She is turning out to be an awesome friend! She's happy to serve my every whim, which makes her exactly the kind of person I get along with best! She loves the theater, though she says she's too shy to ever go on-stage herself. My other friends were skeptical at first, because she's so shy and dresses like a dweeb. But they're warming up to her. I've decided I'm going to help Paula come out of her shell.

She was over tonight, running lines with me. And she talked to Elizabeth for a while when I was on the phone with Sam. I didn't know anything about it until a couple hours later, when I was in my room alone and Elizabeth walked in. . . .

I said I didn't have time for a chat. I had a monologue to work on. But Elizabeth took my script from my hands and set it aside.

"It's Paula that I want to talk to you about—and it can't wait," she said. She moved a stack of papers from my desk chair and sat down. "Has she told you much about her family?"

"Why would we want to talk about her family? I

told you, rehearsals start Monday. We have to concentrate on the play!"

"Jessica, did you know that her mother died last year?"

I sat down on the bed. "Gee, Liz, she never told me. Poor kid. Hey, but why would she tell that to *you*? *I'm* her friend."

"I don't know, Jessica," Elizabeth said. "But she really admires you. Maybe she was embarrassed to have you know about her family problems."

"What's so embarrassing about her mother dying?"

"Jess, it gets worse. Her father is an alcoholic. He used to drink and get abusive toward Paula and her older brother. She said that as long as her brother was there to protect her, it wasn't too bad."

This was too horrible for words. "So what happened to her brother?"

"He ran away from home a couple of months ago," Elizabeth said quietly. "Paula couldn't handle her father by herself, so she left too. She came here to Sweet Valley to live with some friends of her mother."

"Oh, Liz! How awful! I had no idea she'd been through all that. She never said a word!"

"I know," said Elizabeth. "Actually, I wasn't sure I should tell you. I know the other kids are beginning to like her too, but you're still closer to her than anyone. You may be able to help her. Besides, I got the feeling that she wanted me to tell you."

Tuesday night

The play is going along wonderfully. Mr. Goodman acted impressed about how well prepared I was. Before rehearsals even started, I already knew most of my lines. And I'm so glad Bill is playing Macbeth. He's terrific.

Lila is being such a brat. Tracy Gilbert, who's in charge of costumes, designed the witches a dark gray, shapeless dress thing. I mean, they're witches, right? I thought it was way witchy looking. But Lila wants to be a pretty, sexy witch. Today she asked Tracy to design her something in lavender with glitter. Tracy reminded her that she was a witch, not the Sugarplum Fairy. Lila went postal.

I'm getting a little weirded out about Paula. She's dressing more stylishly, which I guess is my expert influence. And I encouraged her to try out for one of the smaller parts in the play, the gentlewoman who will be my lady-in-waiting. It's only one scene and just a few lines. Paula got the part!

After her audition, I could've sworn I saw her flirting with Mr. Goodman's gorgeous assistant, Frank. It sure didn't take her long to come out of her shell! I guess I'm a better role model than I thought. But she still acts shy and uncertain around me. Elizabeth says she's probably working hard to act sophisticated

*with other people, and feels she can only be
herself around me.*

*Then there was that incident during re-
hearsal. . . .*

I was onstage with Bill, finishing up a scene.
"Only look up clear. To alter favor ever is to fear."
As I said my line, I was remembering what Liz had
told me about the words. To look up clear meant to
look innocent. If Macbeth had a guilty expression
on his face, people would be suspicious and think
he had something to do with killing the king.

Bill, looking frightened but determined as
Macbeth, nodded in agreement. Then he exited,
leaving me alone. I looked offstage in the direction
Bill had gone, and I prepared to say my last line.
Then I froze.

Paula was standing in the wings, laughing with
Frank and a group of cast members. Lila, Annie,
and Winston were all there. But Paula was the center of attention. She was saying something that the
others seemed to find hysterically funny.

Paula caught my eye and stopped abruptly.

That two-faced traitor was laughing at me!

I wrenched my attention back to the king's
murder and pronounced my last line: "Leave all
the rest to me," but I was seething.

*I don't understand what's happening,
Diary. Is Paula deceiving me? Or am I being a*

total, reality-impaired brat? I'm afraid it's me.

I blew up at her after rehearsal today. I yelled at her to stop telling me how wonderful I am and how pathetic she is. I screamed at her to stop apologizing all the time. I was possessed.

"You're absolutely right, Jessica," Paula replied tearfully. Her voice was so soft I could barely hear it. "You keep telling me I should have confidence in myself. *I try so hard!*" She paused, sobbing. "And sometimes I think I'm making progress. But then I hear my father's voice inside my head, *telling me I'll never be good at anything!*"

I was aghast. How could I be so cruel, after everything Paula had been through? "I'm the one who should be sorry!" I cried. "I can't believe I said something so awful to you when you've been so nice to me. Can you ever forgive me for being such a jerk?"

"Of course I forgive you, Jessica," Paula said, smiling through her tears. "You're the best friend I ever had."

Saturday night
Here's a Winston Egbert joke: "What did Lady Macbeth say when she put out the dog?" Give up, Diary? "Out, out, damn Spot!"

Tuesday afternoon
Elizabeth had the Jeep this afternoon,

265

*so Annie Whitman gave me a lift home
from rehearsal in her mother's silver Ford
Escort. Before she dropped me off, she told
me something that gave me this awful, pan-
icky feeling. But I don't know what to do
about it. There's not a thing I can do.*

*At first, we were having a perfectly nor-
mal conversation. . . .*

"I love driving down your street," Annie said
wistfully. "Mom and I have been in that little apartment only since the divorce, but it seems like forever. It's nice to remind myself of what a real
neighborhood looks like." She paused. "But where
was Paula today? I know she would have been
happy to give you a ride—even to the moon, if you
asked her."

"Paula doesn't have a car," I said. "She only bor-
rows one sometimes from the people she lives
with. This afternoon she said she had to take the
bus downtown to run a lot of errands. She didn't
even have time to rehearse with me tonight."

"You know, Jess, I've really gotten to like Paula.
She seemed so shy at first, but she's got a terrific
sense of humor. It's great that she was picked to replace Jennifer as your understudy. I know how
much it means to her."

"She was picked for what?"

"You know, to understudy Lady Macbeth." We were
at a stop sign, so Annie turned to look at me, confusion

in her deep green eyes. "You mean you didn't know?"

I'd known that Jennifer was sick and had to drop out of the play. But I didn't know her replacement had already been chosen. And I had no idea Paula would even be in the running.

"When did this happen?" I asked.

"Thursday," Annie said. "Oh, that explains it. Weren't you in a costume fitting?"

"But we rehearsed together all weekend and she never even mentioned it!"

Annie pulled the car to a stop in front of my house. "I guess she assumed you already knew."

Thursday

I've been so busy with the play that I hardly see any of my friends anymore. They don't seem to mind. They say I'm a prima donna who bosses everyone around. I admit I'm a perfectionist about this play. But I'm not asking anything of them that I'm not asking of myself! I just want this to be right. There's no reason why Rosa can't memorize her lines like the rest of us. And there is no room in Shakespeare for Lila's childish complaints about the "gross" witch's dialogue!

It seems that my friends like being with Paula more than they like being with me. Lately, it's Paula who goes to the mall with Amy and Lila. Last weekend, everyone had

267

a bash at Secca Lake. Paula was there, but I wasn't even invited! Am I being unfair? How can I be mad at the girl for having friends? But it feels bigger than that. If feels like Paula is taking over my life.

Elizabeth's right. I am obsessing about this. I tried to explain it to her, but she thinks I'm jealous. Or delusional. The truth is that Paula scares me, and I don't know why.

I wish I could put my finger on one rotten thing Paula has definitely done. But I can't. I just know that something's not right.

Friday night
My instincts about Paula were on target! The girl should have been cast as a witch in the play. She sure fits the part!

Paula had heard me say I wouldn't be at the Dairi Burger with the gang Friday night. Steven was home from college for a few days and was depressed because Cara hadn't written lately. I was tired and decided to keep him company at home, since he still wasn't dating anyone. Paula had told me that she wasn't going to the Dairi Burger either.

At the last minute, I decided I needed to get out of the house. I needed to have fun with my friends again. Steven was content to be a couch potato, so I left him home and drove to the Dairi Burger. I stepped inside, into the usual Friday night din of talking, laughing, and music. I was psyched for a good, old-fashioned night of fun with my friends. I could already taste the onion rings.

Suddenly my mouth went dry. Across the room in a corner booth sat Paula—with Sam.

Paula looked anything but shy now. Her makeup was perfect. Her formerly dull brown hair shimmered with highlights. She was wearing a sexy, stylish dress—a bright green floral print that left her shoulders bare. But the scariest thing was the way she was acting. As I watched from the door, Paula leaned across the table provocatively. She whispered something in Sam's ear and then laughed. Sam laughed too. They were both having a great time.

"Jessica!" called Lila's voice from another part of the room. "Over here!"

I wanted to turn around, drive home, and spend the rest of the evening in front of the television with my brother. But I forced myself to join Lila and the others. As I sat down, I realized they couldn't see Paula and Sam's table from where they were sitting. It was clear from the way they greeted me that they had no idea another girl was stealing my boyfriend only a few yards away.

Sam and Paula showed up at our table a few minutes later. But now Paula was hanging back, acting shy. I wasn't sure exactly what was going on, but I wasn't about to blow my cool in front of everyone. No matter what I suspected about Paula, nobody would believe me anyway. I still had no proof.

"Jessica!" Sam cried, holding out his arms. I stood up and let him hug me.

"Thanks for talking me into coming tonight, Jessica," Paula said. "I never would have if it hadn't been for you."

"Great," I mumbled. Paula was right. I had urged her to go to the Dairi Burger tonight. She'd declined. But now I tried to remember if that had been before or after I told her I wasn't going to be here. "It's nice to see you both. But I've got to get home. Steven's waiting for me."

I turned and bolted from the restaurant.

Sam followed me out, and we had a major fight in the parking lot.

"I didn't expect to get here and find you flirting with Paula behind my back!"

"Flirting? Is that what you think? We were only talking, Jessica. She's interested in dirt-bike racing and had some questions for me. What's gotten into you?"

"Dirt-bike racing?" I cried. "How did she know you were into dirt-bike racing?"

Sam shrugged. "I don't know. You probably mentioned it to her once."

"No, Sam. I never did. I'm sure I didn't."

"So what's the big deal? Lila or Amy probably said something about it. She was sitting with them when I came in. She could have heard it from anyone. It's not exactly a deep, dark secret. What does it matter where she heard it? I told you, we were only talking!"

I stared into the darkness at the other end of

the parking lot. "You never look at me that way when we're only talking."

"Jessica, I don't know what's wrong with you lately. You know you're the only girl I care about. But you seem to go off the deep end whenever Paula's involved. She's a perfectly nice girl, she's got a great sense of humor, and she has nothing but good things to say about you! Its not like you to be so paranoid."

"Sam," I began, trying to keep my voice from shaking, "I am not paranoid. Paula is trying to sabotage me somehow. You've got to believe me!"

"Sabotage, Jess? Aren't you being a little melodramatic? How is Paula trying to sabotage you?"

"I don't know!" I screamed. "I just know she is!" I continued in a quieter voice. "It's bad enough that my sister and all my friends are on Paula's side. Now you're on her side too."

"This isn't about taking sides, Jess."

"Then why is sticking up for her more important to you than I am?"

"Jessica, you're making me angry now. And I see what's going on. Your little protégée is ready to make her own friends, and you can't handle that." He stalked away. But halfway across the parking lot he turned around and yelled back at me. "What do you want, Jess? To control Paula? She's not your puppet, you know!"

No, she's not, Diary. But I may be hers.
Steven says Macbeth is a cursed play.
I'm beginning to think he's right.

Thursday evening
Tomorrow is opening night. I'm so excited I won't be able to sleep a wink! Things are still a little awkward with Sam. But he'll be there in the auditorium to cheer me on tomorrow, sitting with my parents, Elizabeth, and Todd.

Dress rehearsal went great, which is supposed to be a sign of a disastrous opening night, if you believe theater superstitions. I don't. We are going to be awesome!

Saturday morning
Finally, Diary, the world knows I was right about Paula. She's not just creepy, she's evil. And possibly insane. . . .

Friday afternoon I arrived home to an empty house—empty except for Prince Albert, and his tail wagged happily when I came in. I wished I could feel so carefree. Instead, I was a total nervous wreck. I wished Elizabeth was home, but she had stayed at school late to put together press kits for the reviewers we were expecting for our opening-night performance. Todd was dropping her off. After Elizabeth changed her clothes, she and I would drive back to school together.

"What if I get bad reviews?" I asked my dog. "How will I ever face everyone again?"

Prince Albert only cocked his head.

"Panicking won't do any good," I told myself aloud, though I knew I was on the verge of it. I laughed nervously. "Neither will talking to a dog. Practicing my lines—that's what would help."

Except I couldn't remember them. Not a single one. At least, not for a few minutes. Finally some dialogue popped into my head and I ran with it. I jumped when the phone rang.

It was Paula, and she was crying. I'd noticed that she hadn't been in school that day, but nobody knew why. Now, there was no mistaking the terror in her voice.

"Paula, you sound far away. Stop crying and tell me where you are and what's wrong."

"I'm sorry to be such a baby, but I'm so scared, Jessica!"

"What happened? Where are you?"

"I'm at a gas station in Cold Springs, calling from a pay phone. Jessica, it's my father!" She began sobbing again.

Through the phone I heard thunder at the same time it crashed outside my window. Outside, it was beginning to pour. It hardly ever rains in Sweet Valley. I wondered vaguely if this was part of Steven's *Macbeth* curse.

One thing I knew for sure was that my fears about Paula were trivial compared to her problems with her abusive father. She explained haltingly that her father's poker buddy had called her the night before. He said Paula's father was in the hospital. As afraid as she was of him, he was still her father. So Paula had taken a bus to Cold Springs to see him. But the story was a lie.

"He wasn't in the hospital at all," Paula sobbed. "He was perfectly fine—just drunk. He wanted money, and he said I'd have to stay and live with him from now on! I sneaked away this afternoon, but he took all the money I'd brought with me for the return bus trip." She paused. "Jessica, I'm stranded here. I know the first performance is tonight, but what if my father comes looking for me? What if he finds me and drags me back with him? I need your help! Will you come get me?"

Of course I said yes, Diary. She was in trouble. I calculated that I had just enough time to drive to Cold Springs, pick up Paula, and bring us both to school by curtain time—if I ignored speed limits, which I tend to do anyway. My first entrance wasn't until scene five, so I'd still have time to get into costume.

That wasn't exactly the way it happened. . . .

Paula's directions were bogus. I drove around Cold Springs in the pouring rain, searching for a street that didn't exist. Finally, I admitted that I'd been duped. To make matters worse, I'd forgotten to leave a note at home for Elizabeth. So nobody knew where I was. The clock in the Jeep said six-thirty. Curtain was at seven. I stopped at a pay phone and called the school.

"Mr. Goodman!" I yelled into the phone. "It's Jessica Wakefield. There's been a problem—sort of an emergency."

"Ms. Wakefield!" the director said coldly. "I had expected to see you here by now."

"I'm sorry, Mr. Goodman. It's a long story. I'll explain later. But I'll be there in less than an hour. I'm not in the first few scenes anyway. You'll need to hold the curtain for only fifteen minutes or so. Can you do that?"

"I'm afraid the show must go on as scheduled, Ms. Wakefield. But don't worry. Just get here as soon as you can. Your understudy has saved the day. Paula is already in costume and ready to go on."

She was brilliant, Diary—as cold, cruel, and calculating as any Lady Macbeth could be. Onstage and off.

By the time I slipped into the dark auditorium, Elizabeth, Sam, and Todd had figured out the whole thing. Paula lied to everyone from the start! Her mother and brother are alive and well and living in Sweet Valley. Her father died years ago. There was no abuse. The only thing Paula had been honest about was her love of the theater. But her ambition to be a star was way out of my league.

The cast party afterward was at Fowler Crest in the formal ballroom with its crystal chandeliers. I slipped in through a side door and stood behind a potted palm, watching. Sam followed me in, his hand on my arm.

Everyone was raving about the play. Bill got his share of compliments, but Paula—the understudy who'd stepped in and wowed the audience—was clearly the center of attention. She was promenading around on Frank's arm, wearing a strapless, full-skirted white gown. Her silky hair was drawn into a sleek French twist, and she carried an armful of long-stemmed roses.

"I always knew I'd make a great Lady Macbeth!" Paula boasted to everyone. "I've been practicing the role all my life. It's been my dream since I was a little girl!"

That's when I made my move. "I know it was," I said in a firm, loud voice. The crowd parted as I strode toward my understudy. I was wearing jeans and a rain-spattered sweatshirt. But I felt Lady Macbeth's power filling me. "And you'd do anything to make that dream come true."

Paula smiled triumphantly, and her eyes looked like gray ice. Smudges of eyeliner, left over from her stage makeup, made her look older and very dramatic.

"Oh, yes, you'd do *anything* to achieve your dream," I repeated, gliding to a stop in front of her. "You'd pretend to be too shy to step onstage—and then become my understudy behind my back. And then you'd lie about being in trouble to get me out of the way for tonight."

Paula laughed. "You're just jealous! You've been jealous of me since the moment I moved here."

"That's what you wanted everyone to think. It was all part of your plan. And you convinced them, all right. That innocent act of yours was a better performance than anything we've seen tonight."

Sam had stepped forward to stand behind me. Now, I noticed out of the corner of my eye, Elizabeth and Todd had joined him. Around us, the room was utterly silent, as if people were watching Paula and me perform a scene in a play.

"You knew how much I wanted to play that role," I said. "But you also knew that I'd never be the Lady Macbeth you are offstage. You knew that when it came down to it, I'd risk my ambition to help a friend in trouble—something you would never do. So you called me, crying. You said you'd been stranded by your abusive father. Your father who died ten years ago!"

"Jessica Wakefield, you're as paranoid as ever," Paula replied, shaking her head.

Several cast members had been clustered around Paula. Now, Lila, Amy, and Annie stared at her in disgust and pointedly walked over to me.

"Your plan worked beautifully," I continued, not taking my eyes off Paula's face. "You played Lady Macbeth in the opening-night performance.

You won, Paula. People like you always win."

"That's the first sensible thing you've said this evening!" Paula retorted. "Think about it tomorrow morning when you're reading my name in all the reviews!"

Paula and I stared at each other silently for more than a minute. She looked away first. When she flounced out of the mansion, accompanied by Frank and a few other people, the entire room exploded in applause. And this time, it was for me.

> *Sunday morning*
>
> *Everything's great. My friends never stopped loving me; they just felt left out because I didn't have time for them. Best of all, I played Lady Macbeth last night, and I was truly awesome!*
>
> *Paula didn't show up for the performance. So Elizabeth played the gentlewoman. She's been around the rehearsals so much that she already knew the lines. The makeup people worked on her face so we didn't look identical, and she wore a red wig. We may have looked different, but I never felt so close to Elizabeth. It was great, being onstage together, performing a scene! I'm loving every minute of being with Liz and my friends this weekend.*
>
> *There's only one thing, Diary. Playing Lady Macbeth has made me even more determined*

*to be an actress. My fingers are itching to grab
the telephone and call Charles Sampson about*
Checkered Houses. *But I can't. I won't. Not
after that kiss he laid on me. It wouldn't be
right.*

> Sunday
>   *It's been a while since my last entry.
> Two weeks, I guess. You know how it is.
> But I've got news! No, I didn't call Charles.
> I'm still determined not to. This news is en-
> tirely different: Sweet Valley is finally mov-
> ing into the modern world. We're going to
> have a real, live interracial couple living in
> the house next door!*

I saw the realtor take the For Sale sign off the
house on Sunday. I realized that our soon-to-be
new neighbors were visiting their house. Still hoping for a handsome teenage boy, I scampered over
to introduce myself. Elizabeth followed.

"Hello!" I called into the open doorway.
"Anybody here? We're the people next door."
Footsteps echoed in the empty entryway, and then
Annie Whitman, of all people, appeared at the
door. "Annie?" I asked, confused. "What are you
doing here? I was looking for our new neighbors."

Annie grinned. "We *are* your new neighbors!"

"What are you talking about?"

"My mom just bought this house," Annie said.

"Why? This is a pretty big place for just the two of you."

"But it'll be about right for the four of us!"

Then she told me some cool news. Her mother just got engaged to a photographer in New York City. He has a daughter named Cheryl who's the same age as Annie—she's only a sophomore, but she just turned sixteen. The really wild thing is that Annie's new stepfather is a celebrity! She didn't even realize how famous he is.

"*The* Walter Thomas?" I asked.

"Yes," Annie said, her green eyes wide. "You know him?"

"Well, sure! He's one of the greatest fashion photographers of all time! He did a great layout on leather jackets in *Ingenue* a couple of months ago." I turned to Elizabeth. "You've seen him too," I told her. "*Style* did an article on photographers a little while ago, and they had an interview with him and pictures of him and his daughter in their loft in New York City."

Elizabeth shook her head. "I don't really remember seeing it."

"I'm sure you did," I reminded her. "I showed it to you because I liked Cheryl's bedroom." She still didn't seem to recall it, so I tried prodding her memory further. "She's the black girl with the room that's done in a really contemporary style. Remember?"

"Yes, now I remember."

I turned back to Annie. "I can't believe that Cheryl Thomas is going to be your sister! She's so beautiful and sophisticated. The outfits she wore for the pictures were fantastic! And the article said she studies piano and she's good enough to play professionally!"

Annie seemed a little worried about adding a new sister and stepfather to her family. I guess I don't blame her. That's a lot to get used to all at once.

She might also be worried about the racial thing. I mean, I don't think Annie's the least bit prejudiced. Tony Esteban is Latino. She dated him for a long time—and they're still in love, if you ask me. But she may be worried about how other people are going to accept Cheryl.

It's no secret that there aren't a lot of African Americans at school. But I think most of the kids are pretty open-minded about race. They'll be more worried about whether she likes the right music and wears cool clothes.

Of course, there was some racial tension a while back. Andy Jenkins was beaten just because he's black. I was totally shocked. I never thought it could happen in Sweet Valley. I know there are still some bigots around, like Suzanne Hanlon, Charlie Cashman, and even Jim Sturbridge. But not many.

I guess the rest of us will just have to do our best to show Cheryl she's welcome here! I already want to invite her to join PBA. It's the most exclusive sorority at school. Once she's in, she'll be guaranteed acceptance by all the people who count!

Saturday evening

Elizabeth and I helped Annie and her family (future family?) move in today. Cheryl is great! I loved hearing about New York. I couldn't believe how different it all is. Cheryl's sixteen, but she doesn't know how to drive! Have you ever heard of such a thing? In New York, she says, even a lot of grown-ups don't own cars. And she's never seen a football game. Her old school didn't even have football!

Despite that, Cheryl is pretty cool. She even knows the rock group Rhomboid! Personally, I mean. Her father is shooting the cover for their next album, and he got the band to play at her going-away party in New York.

Annie seemed uncomfortable around Cheryl. I'm sure they'll be the best of friends, once she gets used to having a sister. Elizabeth told her that having a sister your own age is the greatest thing in the world. It felt so good to hear her say that, I wanted to hug her on the spot. That's one issue we agree on completely!

Except when we're mad at each other.

Sunday night
*Annie had a party this evening to wel-
come Cheryl to Sweet Valley. It was fun.
But it was weird. . . .*

Annie was afraid Cheryl would feel out of place.
So she invited every minority kid she could think of,
even though she didn't know a lot of them that well.
One person she could have invited but didn't was
Tony Esteban, I noticed. He'd been trying, big time,
to get back together with Annie. They had broken
up in the first place because he was seeing someone
else behind her back. Now he knew it was Annie he
loved. But she was afraid to trust him again.

Another odd thing about the party was that
Annie didn't tell most people ahead of time that
Cheryl and her dad are black! I don't know why
she left out that part. I guess she was afraid of
making a big deal out of it. She'd mentioned it to
Robin Wilson. And Liz and I knew it, because of
the magazine spread. But everyone else had this
second surprise when Annie introduced Cheryl.

The double takes didn't mean anything. Most of
the kids have no problem with her race. But they
weren't expecting Cheryl to be black. And their
surprise showed. It must have been uncomfortable
for Cheryl. I think a lot of the evening was.

"It seems like almost everyone I've met tonight
is into sports in some way," I overheard Cheryl say
when she met Amy and Barry.

283

I was nearby with Sam, and he was bragging about his bike. So I guess my mind was wandering around the room, searching for a subject more exciting than motor oil.

Cheryl was right. Sports are a major activity at Sweet Valley High. Since she didn't seem at all interested in them, I figured she must feel left out.

Amy smiled. "I guess most of the people here are involved in sports in some way," she said with a glance around the room. "That's probably because Annie's a cheerleader—we usually hang out mostly with athletes. Some kids are more obsessed with sports than others, though. Barry and I aren't so bad—we also volunteer at Project Youth, a teen hot line. How about you? What sports do you play?"

"I'm not much of a sports person," Cheryl said with a friendly smile. "But Project Youth sounds interesting. What do you—"

Annie did what she'd been doing all night. She tried too hard to help Cheryl fit in. In the process, I think she embarrassed her. "Cheryl's not a sports person yet," she interrupted, speaking too quickly. "But then she's just moved here from New York. Did you know that her father's Walter Thomas, the famous photographer? And that she knows Rhomboid?"

"Uh, no," Amy said.

"It's true!" Annie rushed on. "They played at her going-away party. Cheryl's a great musician too. She plays piano. And a magazine article about her said she's good enough to play professionally!"

Cheryl, Amy, and Barry all looked embarrassed. I felt bad for Cheryl, but also for Annie. I knew exactly what she was trying to do. She wanted to show Cheryl and all our friends that her soon-to-be-sister could fit in here. But she was being too pushy about it.

Amy and Barry went to get sodas. As soon as they were gone, Cheryl turned to Annie and took a deep breath. "Annie, I don't think it's really necessary to tell them everything about me. I'm perfectly capable of carrying on a conversation by myself."

Annie reeled as if she'd been slapped. I don't think she'd had any idea how she was coming across.

"And there's something else I wanted to ask you about," Cheryl went on, sounding uncomfortable. "What gives with all these black, Asian, and Hispanic kids here?"

Cheryl had noticed right away that the white kids at the party tended to be Annie's close friends, and that a lot of the others were people she barely knew. She pointed it out to Annie, who was too flustered to say anything coherent.

A minute later, Annie was in the kitchen crying.

The party wasn't a disaster by any means. Almost everyone had fun. Cheryl met a lot of people she liked. She hung out with Guy Chesney for a long time. He's the keyboard player for the Droids, so I guess they were talking piano. And Patty Gilbert asked Cheryl if she'll be the accompanist for a solo dance piece Patty's choreographing.

Unfortunately, Annie's now feeling like a dweeb. She knows she embarrassed Cheryl, and she's afraid she really offended her. But she doesn't know how to bring up the topic.

You know, Diary, it's strange how uncomfortable the subject of race and racism makes people. I just don't see what difference it makes. Cheryl has a sense of humor, she's stunningly gorgeous, and she dresses great. She even has a famous father and knows major rock stars! Only a very superficial person would say she's not worth getting to know just because she's black. The color of a person's skin shouldn't mean anything more than the color of her eyes.

During that awful period at school when Andy got beaten up, Mr. Jacobi did an experiment in social studies class. Those of us with blue or gray eyes were second-class citizens. The dark-eyed people could treat us any way they wanted to. We weren't even allowed to talk!

Cara decided she wanted Amy's seat. Maria Santelli threw her own books to the floor and made me pick them up. Mr. Jacobi called me a liar when I said I hadn't knocked them off the desk. "All you Light Eyes are liars!" he said.

I knew it was only a school activity to

prove a point. But I almost cried. I couldn't believe how horrible it felt to be singled out and abused because of the color of my eyes. It wasn't fair! I was angry and humiliated. I don't ever want to feel so horrible again. I hope Cheryl doesn't have to either.

Thinking about that experiment makes me even more determined to get her into PBA. Once she's in our sorority, nobody will dare discriminate against her! Annie seems glad that I thought of it. I'm just worried that Suzanne Hanlon might try to keep her out. Suzanne is a total snob who can't stand anyone who's the least bit different. Heck, she makes even Lila look like Mother Teresa!

Saturday night
Cheryl went to her first football game today. Of course, Annie and I couldn't watch it with her. We had to cheer. She sat with Elizabeth, Todd, and Steven. A few minutes into the first quarter, she was bored stiff and actually pulled out a book and started reading! Right in the middle of a Sweet Valley offensive assault!

Steven came to the rescue. He spent the rest of the first half explaining the game to her. And she had a great time! Tomorrow he's going to start teaching her how to drive a car, so she can be a real Californian.

Tuesday night, late
You won't believe what I've gotten my-
self into now. I didn't call Charles. I swear
I didn't!
But he called me....

I was sitting on my bed Tuesday, studying and listening to music. Well, sort of. I did have a copy of Faust open in front of me, but it made even less sense than Shakespeare. So I was paying more attention to the Jamie Peters song that was playing on my stereo. The phone rang, and I nearly stopped breathing when I heard Charles Sampson's voice.

"Jessica, this is Charles. Can you talk?"

"Charles?" I cried. I suddenly could feel the memory of his lips against mine as we sat in the front seat of his Mustang on that rainy Saturday night. I shook my head firmly. "You weren't supposed to call me at home!"

"I know. I'm sorry. I planned to hang up if anyone but you answered," he said. "Is this a bad time? Are you alone?"

"Um, it's OK, I guess," I said. I shoved Faust aside. "I'm alone in my room. I was just, uh, studying."

"Jessica, if you'd rather not talk to me, I'll understand. I'll hang up right now with no hard feelings. But I need a huge favor from you. It's important."

I was mystified. And curious. "I'm listening," I said cautiously.

"Have you heard of Martin Pederson, the film producer?"

"Of course," I said. "Everyone's heard of Pederson Productions. He doesn't make blockbusters, but his films win a lot of awards." Then I gasped, thinking I knew what he was leading up to. If I was right, it was the most fantastic news I'd heard in ages. "Are you telling me Martin Pederson will help finance your movie? Oh, Charles, that's wonderful!"

"Whoa, Jessica!" Charles said, laughing. "He hasn't agreed to anything yet. But he's considering it."

"I know he will!" I exclaimed. "All he has to do is read the script for *Checkered Houses* and hear you describe your vision for it. You'll sell him on it, Charles! I know you can!"

"Maybe," he said. "But I'm afraid this might be my last chance, Jessica. If Pederson turns me down, there's nobody else to ask."

"He won't turn you down," I said confidently. "Nobody can describe this film the way you can!"

"I can't do it alone, Jessica. I need your help."

"What can *I* do to help?" I asked. "I told you I can't be in the film, Charles, as much as I want to."

"Martin Pederson and some of his associates will be in Santa Barbara this weekend. They want me to do a read-through of the script for them. Jessica, this is my big chance to get the rest of my funding. But I haven't found a Blythe yet."

I gulped. "You want me to read Blythe this weekend for Martin Pederson?"

"If you don't mind," he said. "Jessica, I know you didn't plan to have anything more to do with this film. I tried to get my sister. But Grace is filming in New York this weekend. I'm not asking you for any other commitment to this film. Just Saturday in Santa Barbara."

"Won't Pederson expect the actress who's really playing Blythe?"

"Not necessarily," Charles said. "It's typical for a film not to be cast at this stage. Of course, I could just hire an actress for the read-through. But nobody understands this part the way you do! You're my best bet for getting Pederson to produce my film. Will you do it, Jessica? Please?"

"Yes!" I cried instantly. "You can count on me."

"Thanks, Jessica. I owe you one!" he said gratefully.

I said it without thinking. I couldn't help myself, Diary. But I don't think I regret it. Checkered Houses *is a terrific project. If I can help Charles get the funding, it's worth a day trip to Santa Barbara.*

It's not that big a deal, is it? I'm not agreeing to make the movie. It's only a reading. It's one day, and I don't even have plans with Sam, so I won't have to break a date. I'll just have to be careful to keep my emotional distance from Charles. Why does he have to be so darn cute?

I know, I promised myself I was through with Charles and his film. But he needs me. How can I say no?

Wednesday midnight
I called Charles this evening and asked him to meet me, late, at the Box Tree Café. I wasn't sure if I was doing the right thing by calling him. But I was stressing about Saturday. Before spending hours alone with him on the way up the coast, I wanted to make sure he didn't have the wrong idea about us. After all, we never had talked about that kiss. But it still haunts me every time I look at Sam.

"I think I know what you wanted to talk to me about," Charles said as he sat down across from me at the Box Tree Café. "We never got a chance to talk about what happened the last time I saw you. That night in the rain. I want you to know—"

"Charles, I have a boyfriend!" I blurted out. "I like you a lot, but I *love* Sam. I was interested only in the movie, not in . . ."

"I know that," he assured me. "And I want *you* to know that I never planned what happened that day. My interest in you as an actress was—and still is—completely sincere."

I smiled. "Thank you for telling me that."

"I was out of line that day, and I'm truly sorry.

291

You're beautiful, Jessica. And you're warm and funny and bright. I guess I've been attracted to you all along. But I should have handled my feelings better. I had no business—"

"It's all right!" I said. "I was upset, but I got over it." If I'd still been on my total-honesty kick, I'd have had to tell him more—that one of the reasons I was upset when he kissed me was because I liked it.

"I suppose you're worried about going to Santa Barbara with me this weekend," he said.

"No, Charles, I'm not—"

He held up a hand. "Of course you are. And I don't blame you a bit. But I swear to you, Jessica, you have nothing to worry about. From now on, it's all business between us."

"*All* business?" I asked. "I was hoping we could keep on being . . . you know, *friends?*"

Charles grinned. "I'd like that."

You heard it here, Diary. Charles swears that from here on we're nothing to each other but business associates and friends. I had to make sure that was clear before we go off on this crazy trip Saturday. I had to know he wasn't hoping for more than that. It's the only way I can feel right about this trip. I just hope he keeps his word.

Because the scariest part about that night in the rain was the part where I really wanted to kiss him back.

First, the facts. Cheryl Thomas is not joining the PBAs. Elizabeth said she seemed unsure about it all along. But she never came right out and told Annie not to nominate her. And she came to the sorority party at Suzanne Hanlon's house—the party where the members would have the chance to talk to Cheryl and the other nominee before we voted on whether to accept them.

The pool party was on the Hanlons' back patio, but Annie made all the food. That seemed weird at the time. But I wasn't complaining. The food was awesome! There were these miniature tacos—vegetarian, since Cheryl doesn't eat meat. And rice salad, and empanadas, which are like little pillows of bread dough with stuffing inside. Some PBA events are members only. But not this one. So Todd and Sam came with Liz and me.

Tony Esteban was there too! And he and Annie actually had a talk that night and decided to start dating again. I'm glad. I always thought they were a good couple.

For a long time, everyone ate and talked and danced a little. Then it was time for the two nominees to say a few words. Stacie Cabot went first. She gave exactly the kind of speech you'd expect. She thanked Suzanne for the party, and she said how much she wanted to be a PBA.

Then it was Cheryl's turn. First she made sure to thank Annie for making all the food, since Suzanne had let everyone think that she herself was responsible. We all cheered for Annie. As I said, it was a primo spread. Then, Cheryl stunned everyone.

"It was nice to have had the chance to speak with all the members of Pi Beta Alpha, but I've decided that I'm going to withdraw my name. I just found out that I have the chance to work on a couple of very challenging music projects, and so I don't think I'll be able to devote enough time to Pi Beta Alpha. Thank you."

Whew! That was really something. I mean, nobody turns down membership in PBA.

OK, so Rosa Jameson did. She'd wanted so hard to fit in when she moved here that she pretended her family background was English, not Mexican. We tried to make her a member. But then she decided she was proud of her heritage, so she told everyone her family name started as Jimenez. Most of the PBAs didn't mind that she was Mexican. She didn't want to hide it anymore, so she didn't join.

Personally, I think that was a mistake. Rosa's a nice girl. But since then, she's always been on the fringes socially. As a group, the PBAs will never forgive her.

And now, Cheryl goes and does the same thing! I don't blame Annie for being furious.

Cheryl embarrassed her big time! And after Annie (with my help) tried so hard to get Suzanne and her snobby friends to go along with Cheryl's nomination, I'd be furious too!

Annie confronted Cheryl about her little speech as soon as the conversation around us resumed.

"I was trying to do you a favor!" Annie hissed. "I wanted to help you fit in! So I went up in front of all the Pi Betas and told them I thought you'd be a great member. And I even gave in to Suzanne's blackmail and made all that food—and paid for it all myself too—just so she'd be sure to vote for you."

That explained the refreshments. Suzanne Hanlon is scum.

Cheryl's dark, pretty eyes opened wider. "You let Suzanne talk you into all that work just so she wouldn't vote against me?"

"Yes, I did!" Annie exclaimed. I was afraid she was about to cry. "And look what you do to me in return!"

Cheryl's tone was cold. "Maybe you should have asked me if I really wanted to join," she suggested. "I went along with being nominated and coming to this stupid party just so you wouldn't feel bad. But I didn't know I owed you anything."

"You aren't grateful at all for everything I've done for you!" Annie cried, her voice rising. "I took you around with me everywhere for the last two weeks and nominated you here. And it was all for your benefit! I certainly didn't want to do all those things!"

"Oh, that's it!" Cheryl said, sounding so angry I was afraid she'd hit somebody. Obviously, she was mad about a lot more than this one party. "I'm supposed to be grateful to you, am I? That's the way it always is—black people are supposed to be grateful to white people for trying to turn them into white people too." She put her hands on her hips and faced Annie defiantly. "Well, I've got news for you, Annie. I'm black. I don't want to be a typical, white, California sorority cheerleader like you. And if you don't like it, too bad!"

As I said before, *Whew!*

It looks to me like the problem here isn't racism, but communication. Annie never asked Cheryl what she wanted. She just assumed that a new student would want to fit in, so all along she's been trying to get Cheryl involved in the things Annie thought would make her feel like "one of the pack." But Cheryl's more a "lone wolf" type. In her mind, fitting in doesn't mean being like everyone else. It means finding her own, special niche.

This isn't all Annie's fault. Cheryl made assumptions too. She assumed Annie was being racist when Annie wasn't. And she let Annie think she wanted to do the things Annie was introducing her to—like joining PBA. Then she got mad because Annie hadn't figured out that she didn't.

I know better than anyone what it's like to have a sister. A lot of the time, it's awesome.

*But sometimes it reeks! Annie and Cheryl are
a lot like Liz and me. In some ways they have
a lot in common with each other. In other
ways they're from separate galaxies! Elizabeth
and I get along the best when we talk about
things. When we don't, well, keep us away
from the kitchen knives. And we have the advantage of being identical twins. Sometimes
we really can read each other's minds.*

*People who can't read each other's minds
shouldn't assume things. They have to talk.
When Annie and Cheryl have had more practice being sisters, they'll understand that.*

If they're ever on speaking terms again.

*But there's more, Diary. As you can see, it's
been a busy evening. Annie and Cheryl's problems are minor compared to what I'm facing.
Tomorrow is the big day! Charles and I are
sneaking off to Santa Barbara.*

*Sam drove me home from Suzanne's party
tonight. And lying to him about this weekend
nearly broke my heart. . . .*

Once again, Sam and I were in one of our favorite places, doing one of our favorite activities.
We were making out in the front seat of his car.

First he said goodnight and kissed me. Then,
instead of jumping out of the car and running up
the front walk to my house, I said goodnight again,
and kissed him again. Then we talked for a few

minutes more, so we had to say goodnight again. And that meant more kissing. We were both breathing heavily, as though we'd just run a 10K. And my temperature was rising so fast I thought I'd spontaneously combust.

I gently pushed him away, and Sam nodded. In the light of a street lamp that reflected off the windshield, I could see that his face was flushed. I giggled and reached up to wipe a smudge of crimson from his cheek.

"Lipstick," I explained, still panting a little.

Sam smiled. "I had a great time with you tonight, Jess," he said, "despite the fireworks between Annie and Cheryl."

I ran my hand down the side of his face. "I'm much more interested in the fireworks between you and me."

"Let's spend all day together tomorrow," he said impulsively. "Let's go to the beach!"

"Oh, Sam, I'd love to," I began, biting my lip as I thought of Charles. "But I can't."

"Come on, Jess. It's Saturday! What else do you have planned? Helping Lila dye her hair orange? You'll have more fun with me."

"I know I'll have fun with you, but I just can't. Why don't we have breakfast on Sunday—"

"That's two days away!" he objected. "I can't wait that long. Besides, I have a bike race Sunday. I have to see you tomorrow morning!"

"You have to?" I teased. "Get over it, Sam! You

know for a fact that you will not die if you have to wait two days to see me again."

"I might!" he insisted. "Why don't you want to go to the beach with me?"

"I do want to," I said. "But I told you, I can't. I promised Elizabeth I'd go shopping with her."

"Shopping again?" Sam asked. "You can go shopping anytime. And Liz isn't a power shopper, like you and Li. She won't mind if you cancel."

"She will this time," I said, making this up as I went along. "She needs my help picking out a new outfit."

"Since when does Elizabeth ask you for fashion advice?" Sam asked. "You like totally different clothes!"

"Yes, but she's nervous about this outfit. It's, uh, for a special date with Todd."

Sam stared at me for a moment, his forehead wrinkled up. Finally he said, "OK, we'll go to the beach another time. I'll call you on Sunday." He leaned over and pecked me on the cheek. "Goodnight, Jessica."

"Goodnight," I said, reaching for the door handle. I turned back to look once more at his sad face. And on an impulse, I threw my arms around him and held him close. I was surprised to feel tears in my eyes. "I love you so much, Sam!" I whispered.

"I love you too," he said, surprised.

I held his warm, strong body against me, and I

299

had this horrible sense of dread. It felt like we were saying good-bye forever.

Sunday afternoon
Wow, Diary. So much has happened. Where to begin?

Early Saturday morning, I told Mom I was going to Lila's for the day and that I would be back late. Luckily, she didn't see me leaving the house in a silk dress. Charles picked me up at the corner of Calico Drive, and we were off for Santa Barbara. . . .

It was a great day for driving up the coast. The sun was flashing off the hood of Charles's Mustang. And the convertible top was down, so my hair blew behind me in the breeze. It was awesome.

Things were fine between Charles and me. We talked mostly about *Checkered Houses* and the scene we would read together. For today, Charles would be reading the part of Eddie, the older man who tells Blythe he loves her and eventually pulls her into his seedy life of crime.

But the closer we got to Santa Barbara, the more distracted Charles became.

When we arrived at Martin Pederson's mansion outside of Santa Barbara, I could hardly believe two hours had flown by. We'd stopped at a diner a few minutes earlier so I could fix my windblown hair while Charles put the convertible's top up. So I was confident about my appearance as we climbed out of the car. I wished I felt as confident about my task. This was the big league. If I screwed up this reading, Charles wouldn't get his financing. And *Checkered Houses* might never be made.

Pederson's mansion sprawled along a low bluff, surrounded by palm trees. It was a Spanish-style villa with white adobe walls and a red tile roof. Expanses of glass along one side offered a commanding view of the Pacific Ocean.

"Jessica," Charles began as we stood by the Mustang, gazing at the view, "once we're inside, Pederson or his cronies are sure to ask if I've signed you to play Blythe. I know this is awkward, but is it OK if . . . I mean, would you mind if I implied . . . ?"

I laughed. "You want to imply that I'm still considering taking the role?" I asked, amused. "Sure! If it helps you get the money, imply away!"

"Thanks, Jess," he said. He took a deep breath, and I realized that Charles was jumpier than I'd ever seen him. "As I said before, I owe you," he continued, but I could tell his mind wasn't on our conversation. "Just rest assured that I'm not trying to pressure you into changing your mind. I respect your decision to put other parts of your life first right now." Then he looked straight at me, and his brown eyes twinkled. "But it might make my life easier if Pederson doesn't know about that decision!"

"Just don't tell him I'm definitely doing it!" I added quickly. *That was all I needed,* I thought.

301

Some production company bigwig spills to an entertainment reporter, and the whole world reads that soap opera starlet Jessica Wakefield has been cast in her first movie. The whole world, including Sam.

"Never!" Charles assured me as we walked up the long path to the door. "That kind of little white lie can get a director in a lot of trouble down the road, if the funds come through just because Pederson likes *you!*"

Charles was talking too fast, and his voice was shaking. I decided it was up to me to calm him down.

"No chance! The funds will come through, but only because of a great script and a great director."

Charles grinned, but he was still nervous. "I bet you're an ace cheerleader," he said. "Nobody outside of my own family has ever believed in me the way you do."

He rang the bell, and we were ushered into a large room with a magnificent view of the ocean.

Martin Pederson was a big, tall man of around fifty, with ebony skin, a shaved head, and a goatee. Charisma and power surrounded him like a halo. I was petrified. He greeted Charles heartily. They'd never met, but he knew Charles's father well.

"And this is the young actress?" he asked. He reached out to shake my hand. "Welcome, Ms.—"

Charles opened his mouth to introduce us, but I saw no need. The poor guy was having enough trouble controlling his nerves.

"I'm Jessica Wakefield," I said in my bravest

voice, firmly shaking the big man's hand. "And I'm so thrilled to meet you, Mr. Pederson. I just loved your film, *In the Night Café*."

"Call me Martin, please!" he urged, beaming.

Charles's eyes were so full of gratitude I was afraid he'd kiss me again, right there in front of everyone! *Hey, what can I say?* I thought at him. *When necessary, I can brownnose with the best.*

I'd actually never seen one of Pederson's films until that week. His production company made a variety of movies, but the stuff Pederson directed himself was tons more eggheaded than the kinds of movies I usually went for. To prepare myself for Santa Barbara, I'd rented *In the Night Café* on Thursday. I had planned to watch it with Elizabeth and take mental notes on every intelligent-sounding comment she made. But when she unexpectedly invited Olivia over for the evening, I knew that the universe was my friend. Olivia is not only a writer, but an artist as well! And a brain.

"I'm pleased to hear you liked the film," Martin exclaimed. "The critics raved, but I'm afraid it was too subtle for much of the viewing audience. I'm surprised to find a fan in a girl your age."

"I thought it was brilliant, the way the camera work reflected the themes and amplified them," I said, parroting my smart sister and not having the slightest idea what I was talking about.

"You didn't find the lighting effects obtrusive?" he asked, as if the fate of the cosmos depended on my answer.

"Not at all!" I gushed, remembering a remark of Olivia's. "I thought the fluctuations from light to dark underscored the shifting relationship between hope and despair."

"Exactly!" he exclaimed, steering me toward a cluster of expensively dressed people and motioning for Charles to accompany us. "That was precisely my intent."

So I hit it off with Martin right away. I even managed to keep the conversation going after we moved on to subjects Elizabeth and Olivia hadn't discussed on Thursday! Sure, he was intimidating. But I swallowed my fear and forged ahead, being bubbly and outgoing. Charles kept grinning at me as if he couldn't believe his luck.

Of course, Martin didn't have time to hang around gabbing with a teenager all day. I talked to several of his associates, who were every bit as awe-inspiring. The faces were mostly unfamiliar, but I recognized a lot of the names!

The acquisitions director for Pederson Productions was Kathryn Twotrees, a young woman with a pale complexion and stark black hair. George Lacoste was Martin's partner, the one who handled finances while Martin oversaw the artistic end. He was only as tall as me, but round as a bowling ball. His eyes glittered sharply under thick, bushy eyebrows. I'd heard that his tongue was even sharper— that he ate independent filmmakers for breakfast, on toast. I prayed he would like our reading.

Shelly Harald, the president of a new cable movie network, was tall and thin, with a face that looked as if she'd been sucking on limes. Martin wanted her perspective on commercial appeal. Several others were there, as well. All were high-powered, confident, and intimidating.

Before I knew it, it was time for our reading. Charles and I were doing a scene toward the end of the movie. Blythe is disillusioned with the city and wants to return home. Eddie wants her to stay, at least long enough to help him with one more scam.

I really got into it this time, Diary. Even without costumes and sets, even with a script in my hand, I was acting. And nothing in the world compares with the thrill of putting on a whole new person like you'd put on a dress. Of being that person, for a time, convincingly enough so an audience roots for you. I'd felt it during Macbeth. I'd even felt it on The Young and the Beautiful. When your character takes hold of your body and speaks through you, it doesn't matter if the audience is a bunch of wimpy school kids or a bevy of powerful movie producers. All that matters is the role.

The role. Blythe. Me.

As soon as we finished the reading, a crash of applause nearly catapulted me across the room. That applause cinched it. I knew I

305

had to play this part. I had to play it in the real, actual movie.

When I first agreed to go to Santa Barbara, I'd realized I was flirting with disaster. I just didn't know what kind. Now I knew for sure that the biggest threat to my relationship with Sam isn't Charles. It's Blythe.

And now that threat is real, Diary! Before we left Martin's house early Saturday evening, he gave us the news: He's going to back the movie! In part, he said it was my brilliant portrayal of Blythe that swung the decision. He knew I wasn't signed yet. But he said he hoped I would be. And once again, I wanted it more than anything.

Charles and I acted cool as he and Martin arranged a business meeting at Pederson Productions to discuss the details. We continued to act cool as we said our good-byes and walked casually through the house to the entrance foyer. We strolled coolly down the walkway to the drive where Charles's Mustang waited.

Then we went totally and completely bonkers! I'd avoided catching Charles's eye while we were still inside. I was afraid I'd lose it completely and start jumping for joy. But now we were alone.

"Yippee!" I yelled, and flung my arms around him. "This is totally awesome!"

Charles hugged me back, for a minute, tightly.

Then we both pulled away, looking anywhere but at each other.

That hug was awkward, Diary. I mean, it felt so natural at first. We were both so incredibly happy and excited and relieved! But then we realized we were doing it, and we both felt a definite "error" message.

Sam's face swam into my mind, and it filled me with a beautiful, sad, overwhelming rush of love and guilt. Sure, I felt guilty about hugging Charles. But I knew it wasn't that big a deal. What I felt for Charles was friendship—and, I admit, infatuation. But that was all. Sam had nothing to worry about.

The thing I really felt guilty about was all my lying and secrecy. For such a long time, I'd been hiding the truth from him. Suddenly, what I wanted more than anything was to be back in Sweet Valley with Sam. I wanted to look into his eyes, hold his hand, and tell him the truth. I loved him too much to deceive him any longer. I was going to be Blythe in Checkered Houses. There was no longer any way I could NOT play the part. I would tell Sam the whole story. And the next move would be his.

"Charles, I know I've changed my mind a million times," I said as soon as we jumped into the

Mustang. "But if you'll still have me, I want to be in your film."

"*If* I'll still have you?" he asked. "Jessica, there's nobody I'd rather have. But are you sure? What about your other commitments?"

I shook my head. "I know, I know. And I'm probably crazy. But the reading today convinced me. I have to play that part, Charles. I want to be Blythe!"

"I'll let you in on a secret," he said with a smile. "I was hoping the day would end this way!"

"So I've got the part?" I asked, hardly daring to believe I'd been cast in an actual, professional movie that was really going to be made. "For real?"

"For real."

Despite what Charles had said, the day didn't end that way. Neither one of us predicted what happened next. On the way back from Santa Barbara, Charles took a different route, one that led along back roads, through the woods.

And as the last light of day was streaking across the sky, the old Mustang died. It just died. . . .

Charles leaned over, peering beneath the open hood.

"What's wrong with it?" I asked from the front seat.

He shrugged. "Beats me. My sister's the one who's good at cars."

"Mine too," I said glumly. "Elizabeth's in charge of changing the oil. I'm in charge of changing stations on the car radio."

"I wish all we needed was an oil change," Charles said.

"Can you even make a guess about what's wrong?" I ventured. I'd always been told guys had this genetic thing about engines, the way I do about eyeliner.

"Oh, I don't have to guess. I know exactly what's wrong," he replied. *"The car won't go."*

"Brilliant, Sherlock." I opened the glove compartment with a sigh. "OK, where's your cell phone?"

"Jessica, um, I don't have one."

The hors d'oeuvres I'd eaten at Martin's house suddenly lurched in my stomach. "What do you mean, you don't have one?"

He shrugged. "My car isn't an office. I don't like being interrupted by business calls when I'm driving."

"What? Are you crazy?" I yelled. "This is southern California! And you're in the movie business! You're supposed to have a telephone in your car. It's the law! Everybody knows that."

"Calm down, Jessica," he said, opening the driver's door and parking himself in the seat. "We'll think of something. Maybe we can flag down a passing motorist."

"What passing motorist?" I ranted. "I haven't

even seen another car since we turned onto this road! We're in the middle of the woods, there are no buildings anywhere nearby, and it's nearly dark."

"I guess I should have stuck to the main highway," he said. "This is a pretty isolated spot. We might not see another car until morning."

"*Morning?*" I shrieked. My parents would murder me. Unless Sam murdered me first.

"Don't worry," he said. "There has to be a way to call a tow truck from here."

I tapped my collarbone and paused as if to listen. "Rats. I left my communicator pin on my other uniform," I joked.

"If this were *Star Trek*," Charles pointed out, "we could beam ourselves back to Sweet Valley."

I pointed to a squirrel. "Carrier squirrel," I suggested. "We tie a message to its tail and hope it scurries by a service station."

Charles smiled weakly before slumping back in the seat. "I'm sorry about this, Jessica. I don't know what to do."

"I'm sorry too," I said with a deep sigh. "I shouldn't have freaked out on you. Let me take a look at the engine." I jumped out of the car and began poking around under the hood while Charles looked on. I don't know what I expected. Maybe a little arrow with a sign that said, *"This widget is the dead one."* But I didn't even recognize most of the widgets I saw. Of course, this car was a zillion years old. "It doesn't look anything like my Jeep!"

"I know," Charles said. "Obviously, we can't fix it by ourselves."

"No, we can't," I agreed.

"That leaves us with two choices. Either we stay here, or we walk.

"Walk where?" I asked. "I don't even remember passing a house in the last ten miles. And we're at least twenty miles from Sweet Valley."

"I guess we just made our choice. We stay here—at least until a car comes by."

In other words, we suddenly found ourselves on an unplanned camping trip. We had no tent or sleeping bags. But we still had most of the snacks I'd brought along in case we got hungry on the way to Santa Barbara, including a couple bottles of mineral water. Charles had a book of matches, so we could build a fire. Luckily, the weather was warm. But there was also a blanket in the trunk.

Charles had an emergency overnight bag there too. He unzipped it and tossed me a big flannel shirt. "You might as well put this on over that silk dress," he said. "That doesn't look like it was designed for the woods."

He was right, so I did. We found a spot just off the road, not far from the Mustang. We built a little campfire and broke out the peanut butter crackers. And we settled in for what was probably going to be the entire night.

311

I was not a happy camper. In fact, I despise camping! Why would somebody intentionally spend the night somewhere with no television, hot showers, hair dryers, or clean sheets? This is fun?

It could have been worse. At least Charles had toothpaste and soap in his overnight kit. I had to make do with my finger as a toothbrush, but at least I didn't have to go to bed with my teeth all furry. Gross.

Charles had given me the blanket, and I wrapped it tighter around myself as I lay on the hard, bumpy ground, staring into the fire. It wasn't cold, but I shivered. The woods were full of weird little chirps and flutters and shufflings. I'd been trying to sleep for at least an hour, but it just wasn't happening. I rolled over abruptly, trying to get comfortable. And I pressed my head into the blanket to muffle the sounds of the forest creatures.

Charles's voice rose softly from a few feet away. "Lions and tigers and bears, oh my!"

I giggled. "You read my mind," I said. "I know it's more like chipmunks and crickets and birds and . . . I don't know, whatever lives out here, miles from the nearest Coke machine. But I still don't like hearing those creepy noises they make."

"Don't worry, Jessica," he said, sitting up and wielding an imaginary sword. "I'll protect you."

I sat up too, and tossed another stick on the

312

dying fire. It tumbled halfway out of the flames, smoldering. So I picked up another stick to use like a fireplace poker, to shove it back in.

"You're doing it all wrong," Charles said, scooting himself closer so he was sitting directly behind me. He reached around my shoulder and took the stick from my hand. And I was suddenly very aware of the warmth of his face nearly touching mine.

He was aware of it too. He flung the stick into the flames and turned me to face him. For what seemed like an eternity, he gazed at me. Reflections of firelight glowed in his eyes. "Jessica, I've been trying to ignore these feelings. But I—"

"Charles," I interrupted. "Please don't—"

"I have to tell you what I'm feeling," Charles said. "I know it's wrong. You're too young, and we're only supposed to be working together. Jessica, I love you."

I inhaled sharply. "Charles!"

"I've been trying to deny it, but it's the truth," he said helplessly.

"Oh, Charles," I said, wishing he hadn't said it. "I like you a lot, and I respect you. But—"

"It's all right," he said. "I know you don't love me."

"Maybe I had . . . I don't know, a little bit of a crush on you. But no, I don't love you."

"That's OK," he said softly. "And I still want you in *Checkered Houses*! You're the best person for the role. And I won't let you throw away your big chance, just because I—"

"I don't see how I can still do the movie, Charles. Not with the way you feel—"

"*I'm* in love with *you*. But that's my problem, not yours," he insisted. "I'll have to find a way to live with it."

I rose to my feet and paced across our makeshift campsite, mostly to put some physical distance between us. "I already know a way," I said in a quiet, resolute voice. "Being together so much, to make the film. It would cause too many problems for us both. We'd be uncomfortable, distracted. Neither of us would be giving our best work."

"Jessica, you're still the best actress for—" he began again.

I shook my head. "No, I'm not! Not anymore. I might be able to convince my boyfriend to put up with the acting. But Sam will never go for close encounters with a guy who's in love with me."

"He doesn't have to know what's in my mind," Charles said.

"I can't lie to him again, Charles."

"Jessica, I'm not telling you to lie," Charles said, rising slowly to his feet. "There's nothing to hide except one kiss. You're not being unfaithful to him, just because *I* can't get you out of my mind. You haven't done anything wrong!"

"Yes, I have. I lied to him, and I hid the truth. I've been doing it for months! When I decided today to go ahead with *Checkered Houses*, I also decided to tell Sam the whole story."

"I guess I can't fault you for being honest," Charles said, looking away. After a few seconds, he turned back to me and took a step closer. "So this is definite? You won't be my Blythe?"

"It's definite," I said as a few disobedient tears began rolling down my face. "I won't be in the movie."

For an instant, Charles rested his hand on my shoulder. "You must love him very much."

I knew Charles was trustworthy. But I didn't want to tell Sam—or feel guilty for NOT telling Sam—that I spent the night sleeping near Charles by the fire. So I dragged the blanket over to the Mustang and curled up in the backseat.

A car came along at dawn, and we flagged it down for a ride to Sweet Valley.

I lucked out, Diary! Mom and Dad were asleep when I sneaked into the house. I slipped into a warm pair of pajamas and then into my own soft, deliciously comfortable bed. Nothing ever felt so awesome. . . .

After a few hours of sleep—blissfully free of weird little chipmunk noises—I took a long, hot, soapy shower. Then I pulled on a clean pair of white shorts and a low-cut turquoise T-shirt. Totally spiffy.

I breezed into the kitchen at noon. My parents and brother and sister were sitting around the table, making sandwiches from a big platter of cold cuts, cheese, and vegetables.

"Good morning, family dear!" I sang out. I was pretty sure nobody knew exactly how late I'd been out the night before. But if my parents were suspicious, it was better to act as if I had nothing to hide.

"I think you mean afternoon," Elizabeth said.

I shrugged and stole a pickle off her plate. "Whatever."

"You're awfully chipper, Clone Number Two," Steven said.

I stuck out my tongue at him. He knows I hate that nickname.

"Especially for someone who was out past curfew last night," my mother added pointedly. "You were told to be home by eleven."

"It wasn't *that* much after eleven, was it?" I asked, wondering exactly how much they knew. "I, uh, didn't look at the time."

Mom and Dad glanced at each other.

"How late would you guess you were, Jessica?" my father asked. He and my mother were looking at me curiously, like they really didn't know the answer. Steven had lost interest and was reading the sports section. Elizabeth gave me a sidelong glance and then focused on her sandwich.

I swallowed. "Maybe a half hour late?" I paused. "No, I admit it. I was a lot later than that. Maybe forty-five minutes past curfew. It might have even been midnight. I'm sorry! Lila and I got busy, and we lost track."

My mother chuckled. I could have kissed her for it. "Your father and I both fell asleep a little after eleven and didn't hear you come in," she admitted.

I can't believe I didn't even get grounded! My parents decided to cut me some slack. But I have strict orders not to do it again, or else.

I'm sure Elizabeth knows what time I really got in. But that's OK. She won't rat on me. Normally, I'd just tell her the truth, now that I won't get in trouble. But this is different. This one's between Sam and me. I still haven't decided how much to tell him. But I know I won't lie to him. As for Elizabeth, if she asks, I'll make up something to explain why I was out until six o'clock this morning. She probably won't believe me. But she'll give me my space. Lizzie never pushes when I'm not ready to talk about something important.

This is it, Diary. Sam just called. He's coming over in a few minutes, and he sounded serious. . . .

Sunday night, late
Nothing is ever simple, is it? This morning I thought I was in the clear. I was wrong. . . .

317

When Sam came to the door Sunday afternoon, we walked out to the pool, where we could have some privacy.

I had no idea what I was going to say to him. I didn't want to lie. But I didn't think he really wanted the truth, the whole truth, and nothing but the truth. As I learned on Lila's infamous Total Honesty for Jessica Day, the whole truth can hurt! And the last thing I wanted to do was hurt Sam.

I wasn't doing the movie. I hadn't done anything with Charles. So telling him everything wouldn't serve any purpose. Would it? I'd been going around in circles all day.

He kissed me on the forehead as we settled ourselves on the edge of the pool, our feet dangling in the water. And I knew I had no choice. If he had questions for me, I would answer them truthfully. I wouldn't tell him everything about Charles and the movie if I didn't have to. But if he asked, I wasn't going to lie. If that meant he would be mad at me, then I would have to live with that. If that meant he didn't want to see me anymore, I would have to live with that too. But I didn't know how I could.

We sat so close that my shorts brushed against his. But Sam was staring at the shimmering water, not at me. Obviously, he had something on his mind. *He knows,* I thought.

"What is it, Sam?" I asked finally. "What's wrong?"

Sam looked at me, and reflections of the

shimmering pool water turned his gray eyes almost blue. His eyes were sad. He reached for my hand and held it tightly. I watched as he took a deep breath. "Jess, you know I was disappointed that you wouldn't go to the beach with me yesterday," he began in an even, controlled voice. "But I still wanted to see you. So I decided to surprise you."

"What kind of surprise?"

"Breakfast," he said with a quick smile. "I tried to drop by here early Saturday morning with coffee and donuts."

My heart stopped beating. "And?" I choked out.

"Just down the block, I saw you climbing into a white Mustang with some guy I've never seen."

This was it. Sam was wrong about why I had deceived him. But he knew that I had. And now he was breaking up with me. It was tearing my heart in two. But I knew I didn't deserve him. And he deserved the truth. I dipped my cupped hand into the pool at my knees, and let the cool, clear water slip through my fingers.

I took a deep breath. "Sam, the truth is—"

"No, Jessica," he stopped me, gently squeezing my hand. "I don't want you to tell me. I don't want to know what happened, or why."

I stared at the clear, rippled surface of the pool.

"There's only one thing I want to know," Sam continued. "Just one thing."

"Anything," I said, meaning it absolutely.

We gazed into each other's sad, scared eyes. "Jessica, do you still love me?"

I opened my mouth, but nothing came out.

"Jessica, if you still love me and want to be with me, then that's all that counts," Sam rushed on. "I'll give you the benefit of the doubt. I'll trust you enough to assume you had a good reason for lying to me about yesterday. Jess, do you love me?"

I still couldn't talk. I was so surprised and so touched and so grateful. And so much in love. I nodded as tears began streaming from my eyes. And I threw my arms around him. "I love you, Sam Woodruff!" I whispered finally. "You're the world's greatest boyfriend. And I love you with all my heart!"

And then, Diary, we did just what you'd expect. We kissed. And kissed. And kissed. In fact, we kissed so long and so hard that in the end we toppled right into the swimming pool!

Sam will never know just what I gave up for him—a starring role in a movie! No other guy in the world is special enough to make me sacrifice so much for him. I always thought I wanted to be an actress more than anything. Now I know there's one thing I want more. Need a hint? It has curly blond hair and rides a dirt bike!

Hollywood is on hold. But I've got Sam. I guess love really does conquer all!

Monday night

Annie and Cheryl made up! I was in Santa Barbara on Saturday and missed it all. Steven had a long talk with Cheryl that afternoon and helped her understand where Annie was coming from. Annie's mother ended up in the hospital for an emergency appendectomy. And Cheryl was there for Annie when she needed a friend. A sister.

In the end, they started talking. It'll take a lot of time for them to get used to their new family, but I think they'll be OK.

One thing's for sure: They couldn't ask for better neighbors!

late Saturday

Guess what, Diary? Steven and Cheryl are an item! He's teaching her to drive. They go out for coffee all the time. They hang out at our pool together. I'd noticed all that over the last few weeks. But I never connected the dots. Until tonight at the Dairi Burger, when the proof was unmistakable: They were snarfing food off each other's plates!

I, for one, plan to support their relationship a hundred percent. This is the first time Steven has been in love since Cara moved away. And Cheryl is one of the coolest kids around, and one of the best-looking. They're great together! Let's hope everyone else in Sweet Valley is as open-minded as I am.

Friday evening

I was right to worry about closed-minded weenies giving Steven and Cheryl a hard time. Why can't these jerks deal with a white boy dating an African American girl? Why do they care anyway?

It's not just the people you'd expect. Even kids at school who are OK with friends and teachers of other races have this huge mental block when it comes to romance. Lila likes Cheryl as a friend. But she wrinkled up her nose and said it was "kind of odd" for Steven to be attracted to Cheryl. A lot of other people have been much meaner.

Steven and Cheryl will show everyone! As you know, Diary, I've become a great believer in love triumphing over all.

Saturday, three weeks later

Three things happened today. First, Annie's mom married Cheryl's dad! It was in their backyard, and it was gorgeous. I cried like crazy. I couldn't help thinking about what my own wedding will be like—mine and Sam's.

(Don't worry! We're not running off to Nevada anytime soon. It'll probably be, like, ten years from now.)

The second thing that happened is that Steven and Cheryl broke up! They realized they were together only to prove a point to the bigoted twerps. The two of them still like each other, but as friends.

The other thing that happened was even more unexpected. It happened after I went home. The wedding was over. Sam had just left. And the rest of my family was still next door, helping to clean up. I stepped outside to bring in the mail. And there was a package addressed to me. . . .

I was still wearing the awesome minidress I bought for the wedding—peacock blue, with big black buttons down the front. Sam couldn't take his eyes off me all day!

Now there was no one to see if my outfit was complete. And my feet were sending letter bombs to my brain. So I kicked off my high-heeled strappy sandals, and I plopped down on the couch, exhausted.

I grabbed the package from the coffee table and wondered what in the world was in it. The return address was too blurry to read. I shook the box, but it didn't make a noise. So I tore it open and dug through a mound of those foam popcorn thingees.

Underneath them was a little statue. A gleaming gold statue. I pulled it out, and popcorn showered the carpeting around me.

"Oh, my gosh!" I breathed. The statue was a miniature Oscar.

I pawed through the popcorn in the box until I found a note.

"*Dear Jessica,*" I read aloud. "*Thanks for all your help. My sister, Grace, is playing Blythe, but not like you would have. I know you'll make it to Hollywood when you're ready. When you do, I bet one of these statues will be waiting with your name on it. Affectionately, Charles.*"

I held that statue tightly. I had tears in my eyes but a smile on my lips. I thought about being a star. I still wanted it. Badly. But I knew I could wait. I had all the time in the world.

Then I noticed some writing on the back of the note. "*P.S.,*" I read, "*Sam is a very lucky guy.*"

And you know what, Diary? He's right!

Epilogue

When I closed my secret diary, tears were streaming down my face. I loved Sam! I loved him so much that it hurt. I may fall in love with other people. I may become a famous movie star. But nothing that happens to me will ever compare with that special way I felt when Sam held me in his arms. Sam's gone now. But I'll never forget him . . . or what it feels like to be truly, deeply, madly in love.

"Face it, Jess," Lila had told me. *"You're just too superficial to ever really fall in love."*

Lila was wrong.

It's true that I didn't want a special relationship with Michael Lewis. But that doesn't mean I'm after nothing but shallow flings. I know more than Lila does about falling in love. I know what true love feels like! So I can't pretend my feelings for a simple, nice guy are more than they really are.

Oh, I can pretend to my friends for a few days, maybe. I've done it lots of times. But I can't pretend to myself.

I guess I'm waiting for another Sam. As if there could be somebody else like him. Sam was so sweet, so funny, so generous. He understood me the way nobody else in my life—except Elizabeth—ever has. And he loved me.

I set my diary on the pillow, as gently as a bird's nest full of eggs. Then I stepped across the room to the window. I parted the curtains and gazed out at the night. The moon had risen, almost full. It shone like a pearl in the black satin sky. I thought of the way Sam's hair had always glimmered in moonlight, gold outlined with silver threads.

"Goodnight, Sam," I whispered.

Then I took a deep breath and headed downstairs. Now I was ready to watch Charles's movie. And to remember what I did—or in this case, didn't do—for love.

After you read Volume III of Elizabeth's and Jessica's Secret Diaries, you'll definitely want to check out **A Night to Remember,** *a stunning SVH Magna Edition. It's the most shocking and*

*devastating Sam Woodruff story in SVH history!
Don't miss it!*

*And next month, journey with Jessica and
Elizabeth to Château d'Amour Inconnu, a French
castle by the sea, for a summer of royalty and romance. Don't miss Sweet Valley High #133,* **To
Catch a Thief,** *the second book in an enchanting
three-part miniseries. It's a fairy tale come true!*

Bantam Books in the Sweet Valley High series
Ask your bookseller for the books you have missed

Win a Beach Vacation!

Enter our *Hot Summer Fun* Sweepstakes!

RETURN COMPLETED ENTRY TO:

Hot Summer Fun Sweepstakes
Bantam Doubleday Dell, Series Marketing
1540 Broadway, 20th Floor
New York, NY 10036

Name _____

Address _____

City _____

State _____ Zip _____

Date of Birth _____ / _____ / _____
              Month   Day   Year

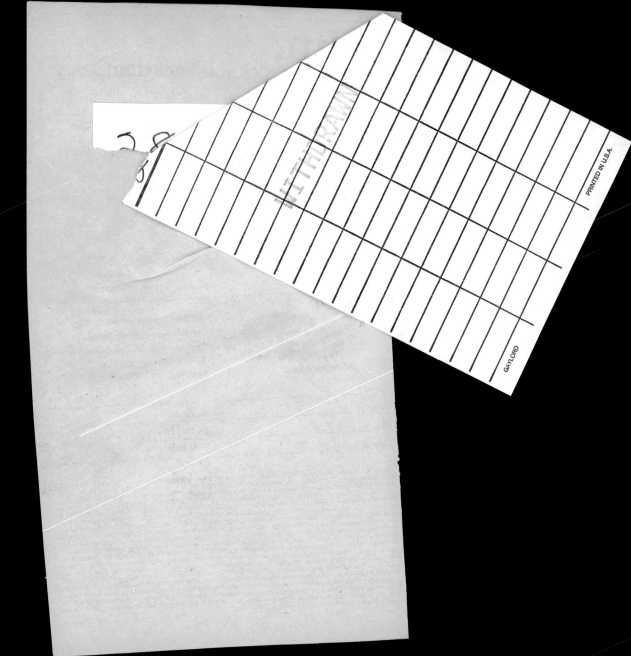